More Critical Pra

for *Gam*

"*Narnia* for the Social Media Generation." —*Wall Street Journal*

"Drawn from both video gaming culture and the rich tapestry of Jamaican myth and folklore, blending pointed social satire and mystical philosophy, this exuberant, original hero's journey is a real trip . . . Exhilarating, thought-provoking and one of a kind." —*Kirkus Reviews*

"Farley's middle-grade debut draws from Jamaican mythology and beliefs, as well as from other cultures, to weave a fast-paced, whimsical mixture of magic and action . . . The setting lends itself well to memorable imagery and a fun experience." —*Publishers Weekly*

"Farley blends video gaming and Jamaican folklore in this intense, fast-paced middle-grade fantasy that is sure to quickly grab readers." —*Booklist*

"Here (finally!) is a middle-grade action novel that showcases West Indian mythology and features protagonists of color." —*School Library Journal*

"*Game World* is unique in that its fantasy world, as its name suggests, is built upon characters and stories from actual Jamaican folklore." —*Philadelphia Review of Books*

for *Before the Legend: The Rise of Bob Marley*

"[This book] has taken me to places that I've never heard of, and things that I've never read before . . . It brought tears to my eyes because it's exactly how Bob was." —Rita Marley

"Christopher J. Farley has respect for the root of black music and art . . . Trust me, Mr. Farley clearly makes one *feel* the importance of a culture." —Chuck D of Public Enemy

"Want to know how Bob Marley made it from nothing to become the strongest presence in music worldwide? Read Christopher John Farley's book!" —Perry Henzell, director of *The Harder They Come*

"An informative portrait of Marley prior to superstardom." —*Washington Post Book World*

"[A] great biographer and critic." —Martin Scorsese

for *Kingston by Starlight*

"*Kingston by Starlight* is an extraordinary achievement. Filled with heart-racing voyages, exploits, and adventures—not to mention extraordinarily vivid and elegant prose—it surprises and amazes you at every turn. I could not put it down."
—Edwidge Danticat, author of *The Dew Breaker*

"What makes this different from all other novels I've read recently is the writing—superbly poetic. There are sentences and passages that make you want to stop and read them again and again. There are Caribbean colors that will swim through your head long after you've put the book down."
—Frank McCourt, author of *Angela's Ashes*

"A wonderfully swashbuckling tale of life on the high seas . . . Wonderful descriptions of seafaring recall passages from the likes of *Moby-Dick* and *Treasure Island* . . . An engrossing and exciting story."
—*Library Journal*

"Perfect for: A weekend afternoon. Get a cool glass of lemonade and journey to the eighteenth century with Farley's powerful and poetic writing."
—*Essence*

for *My Favorite War*

"Finally a young brother with a powerful voice, not afraid to say it loud and proud. I welcome him!"
—Terry McMillan

"Read it and laugh. Read it and sigh. *My Favorite War* provides a provocative, irreverent, and ultimately challenging portrait of the screwed-up shambles of a world we have allowed our rulers to create for our children."
—Derrick Bell, author of *Faces at the Bottom of the Well*

"*My Favorite War* is a work of comic brilliance. Farley plays the nineties American Zeitgeist like a violin. But don't let the laughs deceive you. He hits some literary home runs about a whole bunch of issues: politics, race, and sex." —Ishmael Reed

"*My Favorite War* is one of those rare jewels. It has everything a page-turner should, and it also has 'layers' . . . Farley combines fresh images, global knowledge and crisp writing with unpredictable action . . . When the book was approaching its climax, I braced myself, not wanting to let go of the story or the people."
—*Washington Post Book World*

"Farley steers through his right-on material with wit and tight narrative control. He has an original, amusing voice and a social conscience to rival the great John Pilger. As a satirical anti-war novel and a snapshot of contemporary America, this is a class act."
—*The Times* (of London)

"Cynicism and sharp comic observation of middle-class America are the main cut and thrust of the novel . . . Witty, angry, fresh."
—*Time Out London*

Kate Simon

C.J. FARLEY has worked as a senior editor for the *Wall Street Journal* and *Time* magazine, and is the author of the novels *Game World*, *Kingston by Starlight*, and *My Favorite War*. Farley served as consulting producer on the Peabody-winning HBO documentary *Mr. Dynamite: The Rise of James Brown* and wrote the best-selling biographies *Aaliyah: More Than a Woman* and *Before the Legend: The Rise of Bob Marley*. Farley, who was born in Kingston, Jamaica, is a graduate of Harvard and a former editor of the *Harvard Lampoon*. He is currently an executive editor at Audible.

AROUND HARVARD SQUARE

by C.J. FARLEY

This is a work of fiction. All names, characters, places, and incidents are the product of the author's imagination or are used fictitiously. Any resemblance to real events or persons, living or dead, is entirely coincidental.

Thanks and appreciation to the poetry of Claude McKay.

©2019 C.J. Farley
ISBN: 978-1-61775-714-3
Library of Congress Control Number: 2018960508

All rights reserved
First printing

Black Sheep
c/o Akashic Books
Brooklyn, New York, USA
Ballydehob, Co. Cork, Ireland
Twitter: @AkashicBooks
Facebook: AkashicBooks
E-mail: info@akashicbooks.com
Website: www.akashicbooks.com

For Dylan, Emma, Astrid, Obadiah, Elisha, Jack, Morgan, and Sarah

CHAPTER ONE

LOST ONES

My freshman year at Harvard was hilarious until somebody died.

This all happened before the White House went black, before the sky fell and the seas rose, before machines took the wheel and the world beamed up to the cloud. Phones were humongous, TVs were tiny, and every time a computer connected to the Internet it sounded like balloon animals fucking. I had come to Cambridge hoping to bust out of my personal recession, to find some perestroika for my soul. Have you ever been down so low that hip-hop samples make you sob with nostalgia? Have you ever been so sick of living that you start to feel good about how bad the people who love you will feel when you die? Have you ever felt so broken and bleached you begin to cherry-pick tragic figures in the news—an Olympic figure skater assaulted by a rival, a former football great charged with double murder, a rising rock star who put a bullet where his music used to be—so you can try to feel a relative sense of happiness to lift you out of your infinite sadness? Have you ever been in so much pain that all you want is more suffering to prove the entire galaxy is conspiring against you?

I needed to go back to Go, I needed to return to the Original Position, I needed to be green again. Everything around Harvard Square was green but me. Harvard Yard was green and the ivy wiggling up Wigglesworth Hall was green and all the newly arrived freshmen and freshwomen from Honolulu, San Francisco, and Ashtabula—they were all green too. All the eager new students were like the kid in that E.G. Morris book *Around Harvard Square* who discovers a fantasy world where every step is a leap, every jump is like flight, and that gravity has become a law, like jaywalking or downloading pirated music, that only suckers follow.

You might have seen me first, dragging a green garbage bag with all my stuff across the grass sea of the Yard, through the froth of freshmen, in front of the classical columns of Widener Library, down Massachusetts Avenue with its airspace clogged with helicopter parents, near that pretentious bookstore where half the employee picks are in French, across from that video place where the new releases are always rented, past striking food service workers chanting, *Hey, Harvard, you can't hide, we can see your greedy side,* over homeless people snoring on sidewalk grates, beneath a cloud of pigeons dropping shit the way social climbers drop names, up the wide steps of North Peerpont dorm, all under the penitentiary gaze of the John Harvard statue.

I seem to remember that L-Boogie song was blaring out from somewhere, it seemed to be playing everywhere that year, from headphones and boom boxes, from sushi bars and passing station wagons, it was one of those tunes that when you hear it you just know you are going to be hearing it again and that it's gonna spread like avian flu. Rap was already old by then, but like a Gen Xer in a skimpy swimsuit, it saw itself as forever young, and that song gave me a new hope that hip-hop hadn't been completely co-opted into corporate crap yet, so maybe I had a shot too. I had gone solo to my senior prom, and I asked the deejay to play that song, and it cleared the dance floor because nobody in upstate New York knew what to do with their hips when it came on, and I was left alone on the festooned basketball court hobbling on my crutches to the beat, and thinking back on that, I was back in my infinite sadness.

From the steps of my dorm I could see the *Harvard Harpoon*, the school's legendary humor magazine, rising above the music and the Yard, a castle in the clouds. The sunlight made me squint and everything blurred and divided, and for a moment there were two towers, like the world was splitting and the multiverse was revealed. I could picture all the Harvard lives I could lead—lugging a stack of books by critical race theorists up the stairwells of Emerson Hall, stumbling sloppy drunk down the sidewalk in front of the Frog Club, rowing down the Charles in the cool of a misty morning. The sound of police sirens, growing closer, oscillated across Quincy Street and derailed my train of thought. At the end of high school, my life had become something warm and moist that you pick up with a plastic bag in a public park. I was rancid, I was radioactive, I was contagious, I was a scabless wound glistening after a bandage is ripped off too soon. I didn't know it then, but everything was going to be green again. What you and I did that semester, what all of us did that last wild night, spilled more secrets than Harvard has ever seen, and that's saying a lot. But at that moment I was just another freshman who was too smart for his own good and too stupid to know it. The aroma of cappuccino wafted over the Yard from a café on Mass Ave. and it smelled like the whole campus was waking up. I had arrived at the one place where I could be exactly the person I wanted to be: anybody else.

CHAPTER TWO
REPRESENT

On an outdoor basketball court next to my assigned dorm I saw two jocks playing keep-away from an overweight kid. The jocks were tallish and biggish and talentedish, but in an Ivy League kind of way, which meant they could pass and shoot, but were slow and couldn't jump over a term paper. I pegged them for wannabe jocks who had been cut from JV and had to settle for intramurals and rapping to girls in bars that they could've would've should've been on the team but politics, man. People say you can learn a lot about a person from walking in their shoes, but I've discovered you can find out more from the shoes themselves, and forensic sneakerology is a hobby of mine, an outgrowth of all the time I've spent on basketball courts, in locker rooms, and window-shopping at athletic gear superstores. The high-priced kicks these jocks were styling, one pair with patent-leather mudguards and the other with air pumps that make the shoes snug around the ankles, were more for players who were trying to show off than show up.

The overweight kid they were playing was a hot mess. I really felt for him because he had reached the stage where healthy activity was probably bad for his health. Rivers of perspiration ran down his forehead like the levees had broken along his hairline and the polo shirt draped over his torso was drippy like a dog's tongue. He was wearing low-tops with no midsole padding that were for wrestling, not basketball, so every time he jumped the landing must have been hell on his ligaments—not that he had much of a vertical.

The jocks were throwing the ball back and forth as the obese kid waddled forth and back between them trying to get it back. The kid was attempting to maintain his dignity and pretend like he was in on the joke, which is as impossible to do as keeping a smile on your face during a dental procedure. A boom box in the grass near the court was blaring that song by that Seattle band Mookie Blaylock that was so full of crap it could have generated methane. The song kept playing and the jocks kept keeping away and the increasingly desperate chubby kid, blushing highlighter orange with exertion, finally just collapsed in on himself like a pumpkin two weeks after Halloween.

One of the jocks spun the basketball on his middle finger and broke me off a sneer. "You don't want none of this, my man."

Oh hell no. If there's one thing you need to know about me, it's that I'm a baller. I dunked my first basketball when I was eleven. I got called up to varsity when I was twelve. I racked up fifty points in a single game my junior year and I would have scored more if the other team hadn't forfeited at halftime. Senior year I led my team in points, rebounds, assists, steals, blocked shots, and raffle tickets sold for the end-of-season dinner. I break ankles, I break backboards, I break presses, and I don't break a sweat. If you're coming to see me play, bring popcorn; if you're playing against me, bring lunch money 'cause I'm taking you to school. My game is no joke.

I put down my garbage bag and helped the overweight kid to his feet. I had stopped taking my meds, so I knew what I was doing was a mistake. I was getting pulled into something I had no business being a part of and that I told myself I would no longer do, but I couldn't sit on the sidelines. This is the attitude that got me into trouble, and the kind of thing that got me that goddamn nickname. I don't know what happens to me but I'm not myself, or maybe those are the times when I'm most myself, I don't know. I could almost see a ref making that T sign with his hands, the one I had seen too many times. I heard myself challenging the jocks, "Yo, me and white Biggie Smalls—we got next."

The jocks sized me up. I'm tall but skinny with big feet and a big head; basically, I'm a human barbell. Guys who lift weights underestimate me because they've just spent the afternoon benching things that look just like my body.

The chubby kid whispered in my ear, "I'm not much of a player."

I was sure that was true. I didn't know where this kid was coming from, but I could tell he wasn't going anywhere fast. No worries—my plan was to end this game quickly with shock and awe.

One of the jocks squinted at me. "Did we see you this summer?"

Uh-oh—I may have been made. "Me?"

"At the thing for incoming freshmen considering a major in literature."

I smiled. They were lit majors? Maybe we did have a shot.

"I'm a philosophy major, motherfucker," I shot back.

One of the lit-jocks threw me the ball and the other started in trash-talking about how he was gonna teach me a lesson like Humbert Humbert schooled Dolores Haze, that he was gonna knock me back into last year's Bloomsday, that he was gonna blow me away like Ignatius J. Reilly's flatulence.

I dribbled parabolically along the three-point arc looking for an opening.

I had no business being here, but I have to admit, even though it had only been a few months, I missed the competition, that goose-bumpy feel of the ball against my fingers, that coital squeal of sneakers on the court, that moment of levitation above the hoop. I took one power dribble past my defender, and rose up to the rim to slam the ball home like I had done so many times in high school.

This wasn't high school and I wasn't me. As I powered upward, my right leg collapsed like someone shouted, *Jenga!* The first lit-jock easily blocked the ball from behind, and the second one body blocked me into the ground. I tumbled off the court and landed face-first, scarfing up a mouthful of grass and dirt.

A throng of students had begun to gather around the court, mostly girls. This was going to be a public execution. I struggled to my feet.

"This is not how I pictured my first day at college," I muttered.

The chubby kid shrugged. "This is exactly how I saw mine."

The jocks beat us 10–1. The chubby kid scored our only point, a set shot from way outside when the lit-jocks were double-teaming me. He actually showed pretty amazing shooting form, shoulders square to the basket, right foot slightly ahead of his left, and after the ball left his fingertips, his follow-through was smooth and sweet. I had played like a punk, waving weakly in the wind like one of those towering inflatable men outside automobile dealerships. Now it was game over and the chubby kid looked at me with tears in his eyes. I had judged him by his size and he had sized me up too and we had let illusions divide us. If I had just let him take his shot, he would have hit it. If we had run some pick-and-rolls and worked as a team from the start, we might have done some damage, but now we were just done and my right knee was a white-hot pulsar of pain. I pulled my T-shirt up over my face to hide my identity as the crowd of girls dispersed, the public execution having been executed.

"We did you like Macbeth did Duncan," the first lit-jock taunted.

"Like Seymour Glass did himself," the second lit-jock cackled.

The speakers were still blaring that crapalicious Mookie Blaylock song. The lead singer was yowling like he was lost in the woods of the Pacific Northwest.

I hated that we lost the game, and in such a humiliating way, but at least I wouldn't be seeing my tearful teammate or the lit-jocks ever again, because Harvard is a big place and if any of them crossed paths with me on campus, I would just head the other direction.

I picked up my garbage bag and, hunched and limping, Quasimodoed away.

* * *

North Peerpont Hall has an old-world decor that's charming, and a complete lack of elevators, which is less so. My dorm room was on the seventh floor, through twin ivory columns in the lobby, up marble steps, past stone busts of illustrious alums from bygone classes, like novelist Heinz Beck, activist Jack Reed, and a bunch of other public-intellectual types whose names might not be on the tip of your tongue but whose faces would be when they ended up on postage stamps. You couldn't pass through the building without passing through the past. How many future Pulitzer Prize winners and Nobel laureates had ascended these same stairs on a journey to even higher heights? And how many budding white-collar criminals, ozone-hole deniers, and unindicted coconspirators had descended those same steps on their way out to plague the world?

On my way up, I heard music burbling from the basement—Caribbean cadences playing in the lower frequencies, half-heard notes that hovered and hummed like hummingbirds—but the higher I got, the more the rhythms receded. On the third floor my plastic bag ripped, and by the sixth, I was leaking possessions down the steps and along the hall, a sneaker here, a toothbrush there, *Star Wars* memorabilia everywhere. As I pushed through the double doors leading to the seventh floor, I noticed somebody had written in black marker near the door, *Ubersectionality is better than sex*. I made a mental note that whatever *ubersectionality* was, I needed to get myself some.

I walked toward my room and heard the chubby kid from the basketball court huffing and puffing behind me like he was steam powered. He was cradling stuff in his arms that had fallen from my bag. "This garbage?" he wheezed.

"Recyclables," I lied, not wanting to look like a total pauper, which I totally was. My dad—who wasn't that focused on finances or much of anything these days—had given me a couple crumpled Hamiltons to last me a week until I hooked up a work-study job. I was going to be snacking on a lot of cereal if I wanted to eat anything between meals because I couldn't afford anything else. My dad always told me cereal was the one food you could count on because the sell-by dates were set so far into the future the sun would be burned out and Christ would have returned by the time any box went bad. When I was a kid, this seemed cool, but now that I was an almost-adult, seeing my dad with a bowl of soggy flakes, struggling to fill out puzzles on the back of the box, made me as sad as the same cereal used to make me happy.

Some people in my neighborhood thought my dad had money because I was going to Harvard, but in reality my ass was ashy and broke, and not broke like white-people broke, like I can't donate to NPR on the tote-bag level broke. I mean Black broke, like the lights in my house got turned off broke, like eating sardines for dinner again broke, like wearing high-water pants all through ninth grade and trying to rock the shit like it's a thing broke, like when Mom died it took us eighteen months to afford a headstone broke. The kind of broke I come from is the kind you can fall right back into, because my kind of broke never gets unbroken. Superglue can't fix Black broke.

The kid put down all the junk he was holding, including a basketball and a boom box. "I'm Tilfer," he huffed, and after a beat or two he gave me an odd look. "I feel like I've seen you before . . ."

I knew what was coming and I waited for it like that gross granular wind that follows a big truck passing you on a gravel road. I was about to get officially recognized, and I was enduring the traditional pause before he referenced some game he saw me play where I hit a last-second three pointer or slammed home an alley-oop. We had just gotten our booties handed to us on the basketball court, so the idea that I was some sort of hoops star was gonna be hard to explain.

I decided the best approach was to switch the subject: "So what's with the reggae?"

Tilfer blinked blankly like a cursor.

"In the basement, I heard someone playing reggae really loud."

Tilfer's eyes opened wide. "There's a crazy person living down there."

"What?"

"My brother was in this dorm when he was a freshman and he told me that every couple years some psycho requests a room down there. It's gross—that's where the garbage chute empties out. Hey, are you sure I don't know you from someplace? Do you ever go to Southampton?"

I tried to shake loose from the conversation before recognition required explanation. I turned toward my room, stuffed my hand into my pocket for my key, and came up with lint, an old breath mint, and an empty plastic baggie that had once been packed with pills. I was always finding random shit in my pockets. After giving myself a pat-down, I realized I had left my key in an envelope, which I had stuffed in my bag, which I had left in the hallway behind me.

I turned around and Tilfer was shoving everything I owned in this world into the garbage chute.

"Hey!" I called. "That's not garbage!"

Tilfer finished forcing the bag into the trash—*thruppp!*—then turned to me. "I'm sorry," he said. "Was that bag recyclable?"

I couldn't tell if this kid was messing with me or if there was something genuinely wrong with him. I didn't have time to think about any of this. Maybe it wasn't too late to rescue my stuff.

I ran down the hallway to the stairwell, leaping down the stairs three, four at a time, cursing and mumbling, slipping, falling, tumbling and stumbling down the rest of the flights to the basement as my knee gave out, bending backward like a flamingo leg. I fell down the last step face-first, landing in front of the marble bust of V.C. Peerpont, patriarch of the family that had built the dorm. I recognized the face because the statue was clearly fashioned from the only known snapshot of the reclusive Peerpont, who had never sat for a formal photo or an interview but was widely assumed to be the real genius behind the pseudonymous E.G. Morris book. The statue's eyebrows arched in permanent disapproval, the proud lips pursed like he was sucking on a lemon, and a large mole dotted the left nub of his cavernously cleft chin like punctuation on the end of a declarative sentence. The legendary head was cracked down the center, probably explaining the busted bust's banishment to the basement. On the pedestal was inscribed: *What you laugh at is who you are.*

I looked up at the marble head looking down at me—I would always be here and he would always be there. He would be remembered forever, which was even better than living forever, because memories never got arthritis. I would be forgotten fifteen minutes after I was dead, which was worse than dying, because if nobody remembered anything you had done, everything you did was a waste.

The basement was unlit except for the furnace which bathed the bust and all the surrounding piles of garbage in a crimson glow. There were heaps of refuse everywhere and everything stank and every few seconds I'd hear a fleshy thud like a basketball player taking a charge as more garbage slid down the chute into a large collection area. I breathed in deep that too-familiar olfactory triptych of trash collection: decay, disinfectant, defeat. That's when it hit me that I wasn't at the beginning of something; I was at the end. I had just gotten beaten at basketball by bench-warming literature majors. I had lost parts of my life I was never going to get back. I'd never find my stuff and my key was gone. At that point, at my lowest level, all I saw was red. Red like brake lights, like rabbit eyes, like a shot clock running out. Red filled my vision and my thoughts. Everything I owned was gone and I was too broke to replace any of it. I couldn't even open my dorm room door.

I heard a blast of reggae.

"Is anyone there?" I called out.

No answer but the music.

I tried again: "Hello? Did you see a garbage bag full of stuff come down here? I know that's not very specific, but this bag had a key in it . . ."

Behind me, I heard a metallic clink. I turned around and saw my key lying on the basement floor.

"Thanks!" I called out. "Um . . . did you find any more of my stuff?"

A few *Star Wars* commemorative hand towels landed at my feet.

Then silence.

I sniffed the air. Was that curry? The smell was warm and spicy and sweet and cut through the stench of the garbage. Someone down here had definitely been cooking curry, maybe chicken, maybe goat, maybe a vegetable stew, but definitely curry. The aroma made my mouth water and my stomach growl and I remembered vacations at my grandparents' house in the Blue Mountains of Jamaica. They had a pet goat one summer, at least I thought it was a pet, but the fact nobody had given it a name should have tipped me off that everyone else knew it was for supper. I didn't eat dinner that fatal, fateful night, or the left-overs the night after, but I still had a taste for curry, as long as it wasn't made with anything I had once fed from a baby bottle.

My eyes began to adjust. Part of the wall had been painted underwater blue and the artist, whoever they were, had begun to sketch manta rays diving beneath the waves, blue giving way to deeper blue. The mural looked like the paint was still wet and I couldn't tell if it was because of the skill of the artist or because it had actually just been painted. Across the bottom of the mural, in black letters, were the words, *like hogs hunted and penned in an inglorious spot.*

I heard a whirring around my ears like a big bug or a tiny helicopter.

I heard the onomatopoeic *THOOM* of a door closing somewhere in the dark.

That was the first time we didn't meet.

CHAPTER THREE

C.R.E.A.M.

As I pulled out the key to room 714, my dorm door opened and banged me in the nose. A kid with a ponytail and a patch over his right eye peeked out of the half-opened doorway. He was wearing a T-shirt with a picture of the Terminator that read *Judgment Day*, and high-tops from a Shanghai footwear company with patent-leather toe caps and translucent outsoles limned with LEDs that flashed when he tapped his feet. He smelled like he was maybe a smoker, and a sneaky one at that, because floral notes of air freshener commingled with a darkly ashy scent encircled him like Saturn's rings. He was holding a Mee Corp. DiscMan and I could hear music humming from the black headphones around his neck that sported ear pads bigger than Princess Leia's buns. I couldn't quite catch the song, which was definitely something I had heard before, but the melody and the title were just a bit beyond my recollection. The kid muttered something in another language under his breath.

"Hey, I'm your . . ." I began.

Dude didn't even wait for me to finish. He slipped his headphones over his ears, almost completely muffling the music he was playing, and pulled away from the door without even a word of greeting to me.

"Ass hat," I muttered.

I followed him inside but the kid had disappeared. Another guy, tall and tan with a tangle of brown hair and eyes as green and bright as new money, jogged over to me with the jaunty air of someone who had just leaped over the net after a tennis match. He smelled of perspiration and victory. He was one of the lit-jocks who had handed me my ass in basketball. He smiled and rolled up the sleeves of his *Property of DHA* (Department of Harvard Athletics) sweatshirt. "I didn't know we were roomies!"

"Neither did I," I replied. "I don't even know your name."

"*We are named before anyone knows who we are*."

"That's from *Around Harvard Square*, right?"

"Nice!" he laughed. "I'm Davis, by the way."

I held out my hand for a handshake and he jabbed out his fist for a fist bump and we met in the middle for something that resembled a game of rock-paper-scissors in which neither party knows the rules. I'm terrible at figuring out what kind of greeting people are expecting until it's too late—an old white guy tried to give me a high five once and I ended up slapping him upside the head.

Another kid, blue-eyed, blond-haired, strode over holding a copy of Willem R. deGroot's *Most Excellent Fancy*, one of those 1,000-page novels everybody pretends to read but, like Zeno's race, nobody ever finishes. Yep, this kid was the other lit-jock. He was still moist from a quick shower and his tastefully muted cologne made me think of cedarwood humidors and that triangular tuft of hair between a man's pectoral muscles.

"I'm Dorian," he smiled. "Back for more, bitch?"

Davis and Dorian slapped my back and punched my shoulder like we were all characters in a bromance novel. It was late morning and the sun was streaming through the common-room window and we had a whole day before any classes so we had plenty of time to shoot the shit. Our room was a suite, with two bedrooms off a common area, and I noticed that D^2 had both emerged from the same door.

"You guys already picked rooms?" I asked.

"Dorian and I are both rowing crew, so it made sense for us to bunk up," Davis explained.

"That cool with you, player?" Dorian asked.

I thought it was bad form to pick rooms and bunkmates before all parties had arrived, you learn that stuff in summer camp, but Dorian and Davis were such affable dudes that I didn't want to insist on a point of order on my first day. My new roommates spoke with the trusting familiarity that comes with having lived a life, like Luke on Tatooine or Bilbo in the Shire, where no true troubles had ever seemed to come close, and their chummy oversharing, on balance, seduced more than it repelled. Before I even had time to dwell too much on the room thing, Dorian and Davis were teaching me an elaborate handshake they had created.

Dorian winked. "This can be our thing. We can do it when we see each other in the dining hall or at parties or whatever."

I had never shared a secret handshake before—it felt good, like I was being asked to be part of a team again. Plus, I appreciated the handshaking practice.

Dorian's eyes narrowed like venetian blinds. "Hey, do I know you?"

"Yeah, we played ball today."

"No shit. I mean before that."

Getting recognized was the last thing I wanted to happen right now because recognition would require explanation.

Davis looked at me hard. "Did I see you on the Vineyard?"

"Like at a wine tasting?" I replied.

D^2 laughed and nudged each other with their elbows.

"Not *a* vineyard. *The* Vineyard," Davis chuckled.

Oh—*Martha's* Vineyard. Damn—if I wasn't such a country mouse, I would have known that. I had heard of the place, I wasn't a total Visigoth. But at least I had diffused the whole recognition thing. I tried to make a recovery and drop a name I had heard in the hallway from Tilfer. "I'm more of a North Hampton guy."

Dorian smiled. "Is that near *West* Egg?"

"I didn't have you pegged as a *North* Hampton guy," Davis winked.

"Well, South Hampton has its merits too," I bumbled. "But I'm usually partial to northern things. North is definitely my favorite Carolina. I'll take North Dakota over South Dakota any day of the week. I'm not certain why there are two Dakotas, one Dakota is plenty, but I digress. Definitely North Hampton is my jam."

Davis gave me a look. "Where are you from?"

"New York," I answered. "Upstate New York."

"Like Westchester?" Davis asked.

"Knockport," I said. "It's on the Erie Canal."

"The whaty-what canal?" Davis asked.

I sang, "*I've got a mule and her name is Sal, fifteen miles on the Erie Canal . . .*"

Davis looked at Dorian as if to say, *Is this motherfucker for real?*

Dorian smiled. "The Erie Canal is not upstate. It's Canada."

"Actually, the Erie Canal was the biggest public works project that America—"

Davis laughed. "We're just fucking with you, Upstate. Just FYI, nobody goes to Northampton—it's pretty much fictional, like West Egg. Do you not get out much?"

"I almost took a school trip to China once," I replied. "I saw my grandparents in Jamaica a bunch of times. But no, I don't do too much traveling, and yes, I know West Egg is not a place you can go."

Dorian shared a look with Davis. "Listen, Upstate, if you want a real trip, you should come with us."

"You should definitely come with us," Davis agreed.

"Where?" I asked.

"To the Vineyard," Dorian answered. "It'll be cool."

"What about . . ." I began.

"Classes don't start till Monday," Dorian said, "so a bunch of us were going to pop up."

"There's gonna be a lot of cool people there," Davis winked.

"So it's settled." Dorian clapped me on the shoulder. "You're going to pop up with us."

I was trying to figure how I was going to swing this trip to the Vineyard. I didn't have any money to pop up or pop down or pop anywhere really, lack of funds was why I had to skip that trip to China back in high school, and this Vineyard excursion sounded pricey because the two guys who were inviting me looked pricey. Yeah, maybe they were kinda full of shit, but if I was going to get along with the different sorts of people I was going to meet at college, I was going to have to learn to see the glass of shit as being half empty and not half full. In any case, it was cool that I had been on campus less than an hour and I was already getting invited to cool places. Maybe Harvard wasn't as cliquey as I imagined.

"Upstate, we are going to get you *so* laid," Dorian declared.

"You're still a virgin, right?" Davis asked me.

"Um . . ."

One of the bedroom doors slammed open. The rude kid I had run into when I first entered wandered into the main room, still sporting his Princess Leia headphones, still playing that song I was struggling to identify. I could hear the rhythm muffled by his ear pads. I knew this group, definitely, and I could almost picture them in my mind, but the name kept receding just as I reached out to grasp it, like Gatsby's green light. The kid with the headphones looked at me looking at him and retreated into his own room with a slam of the door.

"We're not certain that one speaks English," Dorian whispered. "He's been listening to classical music since we got here."

"Asians are like 1 percent of the USA and 51 percent of Harvard," Davis added. "Where's the diversity?"

I didn't like the turn this conversation was taking, an off-ramp onto Xenophobia Avenue. Sometimes, when you're talking to certain white people, they'll say microaggressively racist stuff, like they're probing your defenses. If you call them on their shit, they'll be on their guard around you from then on out, and who knows what they're saying behind your back. If you say nothing, the microaggressions gradually go macro and pretty soon you can never say anything again because you've let too much go already. The guy who coined the term *microaggression* was an African American Harvard grad, so I'm sure he knew Ivy Leaguers were masters at these kinds of racial Jedi mind tricks.

"I gotta take a dump," I blurted.

I ducked into the bathroom and saw a door leading into the bedroom that Dorian and Davis had taken over. Time for some snooping. I snuck into their room but didn't discover much. There was mostly athletic gear, bottles of musky-smelling body wash, today's edition of the *New York Banner*, and a yellowed paperback edition of Alisa Zinov's cult novel *Selfishness Is Next to Godliness*. I returned to the main room.

"You were in there a while," Dorian joked, "are we gonna need fumigation?"

Davis laughed. "The Vineyard is waiting, so we should roll."

Dorian held out his hand for our secret handshake. "Ready to pop up, player?"

So there it was—two roads diverged in a yellow wood. I could head off with Dorian and Davis and find out what their world had in store for me. I could glimpse a future of private parties and private jets and the private parts of public figures. But I couldn't get that song on that kid's headphones out of my head. What was the name?

"I don't know about popping up," I said.

Dorian's mouth didn't seem to know what expression to make and settled on something that looked like a tilde. "I can pay your way, if it's a money thing."

"It's not really a money thing."

"We need you to pop up," Dorian pleaded. "What are you gonna do—stay here with the Chinese exchange student and bake fortune cookies or some shit?"

The mask had slipped—micro had gone macro. I knew something was bugging me about these motherfuckers. "Fortune cookies aren't a thing in China," I muttered.

"What?" said Dorian.

"They were invented by Japanese Americans. If you asked

for a fortune cookie in China, a lot of Chinese people wouldn't know what the fuck you were talking about."

"Thanks for the history lesson. Are you popping up or what?" Davis asked.

"Don't try to do Harvard alone," Dorian warned. "It's almost lunchtime—do you even know anybody? Are you gonna eat in the dining hall by yourself like some loser? Just come pop up with us, man. You look like you could use some friends."

I waved them both off. "Thanks, I'm good."

Dorian and Davis looked at each other; there was a flash of something desperate in their eyes, but then they both put their masks back in place.

"I guess homey don't play that," Dorian smiled.

D^2 retreated to their bedroom, grabbed their gear, and left. I could hear one of them whistling that crappy Mookie Blaylock tune as they headed down the hallway. I hate that song—it wants to make you think it's all edgy and dangerous and all it's really doing is taking up space that could have gone to music that *is* edgy and dangerous, which is just about the most unedgy and un-dangerous thing any band could do.

I headed off for lunch alone.

CHAPTER FOUR

GEEK U.S.A.

All Harvard freshmen eat together at J.D. Hall, which forces nerdy kids who ate lunch alone in high school to relive in college that life-affirming experience of desperately searching for a group that will let you have a place at their table. J.D. Hall isn't really officially named J.D. Hall, but for some reason lost to living memory, that's what a lot of kids call the place. Hundreds of first-years pass through the hall every day, so the service is about as warm and personal as one of those stops along the interstate where they cram a dozen chain restaurants into a single crappy food court. My first day, the service was probably crummier than usual because the food workers union was pushing for a new contract and threatening to strike and the staffers on duty were all on edge. A half-dozen sign-carrying union members milled about on the steps outside the hall, handing out flyers in English, Spanish, and Mandarin about how they were being screwed on health care benefits, work hours, and wages.

Inside the building, I joined the hot-food line and choked back a gag as I got a whiff of vats behind the counter that were brimming with what might have been porridge or soup or eggs. Any food, served up in massive enough amounts, becomes gross. Escargot may be a delicacy, but if someone rolls up with two tons of it on the back of a flatbed truck, those snails are going to make you lose your lunch. As I dealt with the smell, I didn't even notice you, in your white food-service apron and your white food-service cap, ladling out what could have been grapefruit juice or porridge or a milkshake. I don't know if our eyes met through the plastic angled sneeze shield, I doubt if our fingers touched as you handed me a biscuit as yellowed and hard as a urinal cake, and we certainly didn't introduce ourselves or have a single human moment of interaction. So maybe I never saw you and you never saw me.

But I did notice that the dining hall staff had left out some mini cereal boxes from breakfast. Mini cereal boxes at college are like cigarette cartons in prison. I checked the sell-by dates—yup, these things would be good until graduation. Hell, they'd be good until my grandchildren graduated. I piled five boxes on my tray and stuffed one more in my pocket. It wasn't a good look—the bulge in my pants looked like a rectangular hard-on—but I was willing to trade cool points for cereal.

I edged out into the Valhalla-vast dining area. There were rows of sturdy wooden tables that could have entertained Beowulf and all his bros; above them were huge wooden trusses that wouldn't have been out of place in the belly of a Viking ship; the walls boasted stained-glass windows that shimmered in the sunlight like sails rippling in the wind. Lines of lab-coated food service workers, toiling as hard as any transatlantic oarsmen, filed through the huge hall, pushing wheeled carts laden with tubs of more soup-slash-eggs and grapefruit juice-slash-porridge-slash-milkshake. I noticed one white girl among the workers—she stood out because she had green hair—and when she saw me looking she smiled, put a finger to her lips, and vanished into the kitchen.

As I walked through the hall, I marveled in dismay, if one can actually marvel that way, at how most of my classmates had already fallen in with groups of friends. Every seat was taken, every table was filled, plans for the evening were already being made, and I was already left out. I thought back wistfully to the days, not too many nights ago, when I was the captain of a team, with all my teammates huddled around me, and how all that was a memory I couldn't save, like when the first snowflake of Christmas melts in your palm.

I've never been great at making friends. I forget people's names right as they are telling them to me. I'm terrible at sharing anything personal—never have I ever played "Never Have I Ever." I once bought a Tamagotchi on a keychain to practice the whole bonding thing and it died in a week—I can still hear its digital death beeps in my head. I actually connect better on a friendship level with girls than with guys, which sounds terrific but it sucks because being in the friend zone with a girl isn't the same as being a real friend, and all her friends end up putting you in the friend zone too, and everything falls apart the second she gets a real boyfriend because of course her new guy doesn't want her hanging out with you anymore and she feels guilty and weird and so you've just lost a friend and a potential girlfriend both at once.

In the mass of people in the hall I recognized a familiar face at a far table in the corner. It was my eye-patched roommate in the Terminator T-shirt.

I walked over to where he was eating alone and stood there holding my tray like an idiot for more than a few seconds before I decided to say something.

"The Tranzlator Crew," I said.

The kid just looked at me with his one eye.

"The music you were playing on your headphones back at the room, I finally remembered who it was. L-Boogie was with the Tranzlator Crew before she went solo. I used to play that album all the time when I practiced free throws."

Still nothing, like those stretches on I-90 when the car radio can't find a station.

"你会说语吗," I said.

The kid stared at me for a beat and then started laughing. "Your pronunciation is wack," he said, without any trace of an accent.

"You speak English?"

"Of course I do, you fucking racist."

"Dorian and Davis said you were an exchange student."

"Those jerks assume anyone Asian can't speak their language. I'm from China but I'm fluent in four languages—I've read Vladimir Sirin's work in Russian! Where'd you learn Mandarin?"

"I took four years of it in high school."

"You can fuck up vowels and consonants, but do that to tones and nobody will understand your ass. I'm guessing you had no Chinese people in your school."

"I'm from upstate New York—even our Chinese restaurants are run by white people."

The kid laughed again. "Hey, sorry if I was rude back at the room—I thought you were with those white-privilege ass hats."

"I just met them like you did."

"I heard them talking shit about how Final Club members don't have a racist bone in their bodies. Maybe—but they got major organs that are prejudiced as fuck."

"What's a Final Club?"

"If you don't know, you don't want to know, you know?"

"Uh . . . okay. I'm Tosh, by the way."

"You can call me Lao. Why don't you sit down? Someone told me there's gonna be some drama at the dining hall later."

I sat down next to my new roommate. He had a single small dish on his tray on which were scattered a few lonely cauliflower Afros.

"You're not hungry?" I asked.

Lao pushed away his plate. "Robots fucked up farming. For real."

"You lost your appetite . . . because of robots?"

"My family has a farm near Zobeide. The more automated our place got, the less there was for anyone to do."

"And you blame . . . robots?"

"Robots plant, prune, and pick better than us, they're developing thermal, multispectral, and hyperspectral sensors, and they sure as hell don't need health insurance. A lot of farm equipment doesn't even have seats anymore because drivers are obsolete. Just thinking about it makes me wanna hurl."

"So what do you grow on your farm?" I asked.

Lao didn't answer because he was looking over my shoulder. "You know how I told you someone told me something was happening? That someone just walked in."

CHAPTER FIVE

TERRITORIAL PISSINGS

I turned in my seat to look and I saw a student with short black hair emerge from the cafeteria line wearing a black collared shirt and black jeans. I couldn't tell, from this distance, whether the person was a boy or a girl, and I had my doubts whether proximity would resolve my uncertainty. I was aware from my shoe knowledge that only boys wore curly toed jutti slippers, and this someone had on a pricey-looking pair in dark green. He/she looked this way and that for place to set down their tray, uncertain where to go but too proud to show too openly they didn't have a place. They approached one table but when they got close, a blond girl put her bag on the open seat. He/she headed for another table but it was bad timing because the guys there were finishing up. On the hunt for a spot, his/her gaze swept across mine and he/she came over to where we were.

The newcomer plopped down a tray full of Rainbow-Flavored Sugar Kombos at our table, slung their aquamarine backpack over a chair, and sat opposite Lao and me. They didn't say anything for the longest time but instead got a book out of their backpack titled *Schrödinger's Kittens and Spacetime Physics* and started underlining things with a neon-green highlight pen.

"Hello again," Lao said.

The newcomer acknowledged him with a nod but went back to underlining.

"I like your jutti slippers," I said.

A smile flickered on her/his lips but she/he didn't look up from the book.

"What are you even studying?" Lao asked. "Classes haven't even started yet!"

She/he looked up. "So you don't know about . . ." The voice gave it away—she was a girl, all right. I don't know how I missed it before—maybe the short hair threw me off. Some people have a rhythm to the way they talk, but she had a beautiful melody and I could have listened to her read a terms-of-service agreement. But she trailed off with a shrug like she had decided halfway through whatever she was about to say that she couldn't be bothered to complete her thought.

"What?" Lao asked.

"I was just doing . . ." Again, she faded out.

"Come on, please finish what you were saying," I said.

She finally looked at both of us. "The supplemental optional summer reading, silly! You did do the supplemental optional summer reading, didn't you?"

Lao and I looked at each other.

"The key word is *optional*," Lao said.

"Not to mention *supplemental*," I said.

"Not to mention *summer*," Lao added.

Her name was Meera, and she said she was from India. She and Lao had met in passing at a mingle for incoming foreign students. We talked for a bit and it quickly came out that she had an odd habit of pausing in the middle of her sentences like there was a modem in her brain struggling to make a dial-up Internet connection. "I grew up in New Delhi, but . . ." she began before hesitating.

"You were raised in New York?" I guessed.

"You moved to London?" Lao said.

". . . I live in Mumbai for work," she finally finished.

"Mumbai? Is that near Bombay?" I asked.

"Mumbai's what we call Bombay. Like how Constantinople is now Istanbul."

"Or how Manhattan became Gotham City," I said.

"No, not like that at all, actually," she said. "Because Gotham

City is where Batman lives and real people live in Mumbai."

"Wait—you have a job?" Lao said.

"Worse," she sighed. "I have a career."

"Really? What do you do?"

"Nothing too interesting . . ." Meera began, and neither Lao nor I wanted to guess at what her job was because we had no clue, so all three of us went back to sitting in silence and she went back to flipping through her textbook, and frankly, it was a little weird. She was good at this dangling-info thing because she would not break, she would not divulge the end to what she had been saying, and if we wanted to know we were going to have to break first and ask her. Suddenly, after what seemed a couple hours but was probably less than twenty seconds, she snapped her book shut. "How about we play a game?"

"What kind of game?" I asked.

"In my line of work, I used to meet new people all the time and you had to get comfortable with them really quickly. So I used to always do a little quiz. Here's the question: if you could only eat one food for the rest of your life, what would it be?"

My anti-sharing lock kicked in, so I said something bland: "Um, hamburgers."

Meera looked disappointed. "Really?"

"Why does it matter?"

"What you eat says something about you. I read immigrants are much healthier when they eat their home cuisine. Once they start buying french fries and hot dogs and sugar cereal with crazy flavors and crazier names, they're lost."

"But you got a bunch of Rainbow-Flavored Sugar Kombos just like me," I said.

Meera laughed and rattled a box of her cereal. "This isn't for me—I feed this to the birds in Harvard Square. They love it, but it makes them poop something awful—"

"My turn," Lao interrupted. "I have a thing for *shuang pi nai*—it's this traditional custard from Guangzhou. I don't know the whole recipe, but it's got egg whites, water buffalo milk, and some other stuff."

Meera punched me in the shoulder. "I grew up drinking buffalo milk! It's so hard to find good fresh milk in some parts of India. The milkmen add sugar and water and powder to it and it tastes all yucky. I learned how to milk buffalo when I was a kid, and trust me, it's even more difficult than it sounds!"

"So what would you eat if you could only eat one thing?" Lao asked Meera.

"That's easy—*dhokla*!" Meera replied.

"No idea what that is," Lao said. "But I want to know everything."

"Key ingredients: fermented rice and chickpeas. Like Rice Krispies Treats, but spongy and savory. I'd pack it in my lunch and boys at school would try to steal it!"

Lao smiled. "I'm thinking there's a story here."

"Can I change my answer?" I cut in. "Maybe to Jamaican beef patties?"

The chatter in the dining hall suddenly picked up all around us.

Lao shushed us. "You know that thing that was gonna happen? It's happening."

"I've been waiting for this!" Meera said.

"Could one of you tell me what's going on?" I asked.

Meera winked. "You'll see . . ."

A gaggle of five upperclassmen in matching suits and bow ties sauntered into the center of J.D. Hall. One of the guys told the crowd to quiet down and another blew a note on a pitch pipe and all five began to croon an a cappella song.

I groaned. "This is what we've been waiting for, this barbershop bullshit?"

"Just hold on—this is comp season," Lao explained.

"Whaty-what season?"

"Shhh!" Meera scolded.

The song dragged on until finally one of the singers exclaimed, "Thanks for listening! If you want to join us, *just stop by our table outside the hall!*" They sang that last line in five-part harmony, stretching the final "*haaaaaaaaaaaaall*" like a piece of old-fashioned taffy. Then the preppy quintet sauntered away.

"We're supposed to be impressed by that?" I asked.

"That was just the opening act," Lao replied.

A boy with rolled-up shirtsleeves and alligator-skin boat shoes strolled to the front of the room clapping his hands slowly and with palpably increasing sarcasm. He was short and slight with patchy brown scruff on his cheeks that seemed as poorly maintained as the front lawn of a crackhouse. "Wooo! Let's give it up for Choral Fixation!" he smirked. "How much do you want to bet that every member of that group will die a virgin?"

The crowd fell silent.

"I know many of you were expecting a certain alleged humor magazine to give a presentation. Well, Dean Kinney just let me know that that magazine has been banned from recruiting after last year's shitshow with the alligator. The alligator's not fucking coming either."

He pointed to his alligator-skin boat shoes. There was a gasp from some onlookers and some boos as well, and the boy held up his middle finger.

"My name is Morven S. Morlington and I'm the managing editor of the nation's oldest student-run newspaper, the *Harvard Magenta*. I know journalism is old-school. You know what's not old-school? Getting a goddamn job. After I get my corner office at *Facts* magazine, while the virgins from Choral Fixation are singing on street corners, and the jackholes from the *Harpoon* are telling fart jokes to their parole officers, I'll be sleeping on a bed of gold like a goddamn dragon."

A few freshmen applauded, and the boos started to fade.

Morven's voice grew louder: "You're going to hear from a lot of groups today. Fuck 'em—you're not here for punch lines or five-part harmonies. Go to Dartmouth if you want that punk-ass shit. Join the *Magenta* . . ."

Just then every light in J.D. Hall went out.

Meera whispered in the darkness, "It's happening!"

A spotlight fell on the side of the dining hall and the white girl I had spotted earlier glided into the center and stripped off her food-service coat to reveal casual clothes underneath. Her green hair dropped dead straight to her bare bony shoulders, which looked sculpted from the ivory tusks of poached elephants. Her nose was long and thin and her high-rise cheekbones gave her the air of a Disney villainess, but her look was softened by thick black glasses like you'd see on the sexy librarian in the rare books room. She was wearing a pair of Rollerblades and a ring of keys jangled from her belt. "This is going to be really short," she drawled in a New Orleans accent, before flashing a crooked smile and adding, "That's what she said!"

Only a few students laughed, but the girl chortled at her own joke.

"I hate when people talk about me behind my back," she continued. "So I wanted to tell you myself that everything you've heard about the *Harpoon* is true. We're all juvenile-delinquent weirdos. I was breastfed until I was thirteen, which was really traumatic because my mom died in childbirth. I hand out my used bikini-wax strips as fake mustaches on Halloween. When I reach orgasm, I make the same sound as a fax machine—and if the sex is really good, a fax will slip out of my vagina. Usually it's from my dad, reminding me to use a condom."

Some freshmen giggled but most seemed in various states of what-the-fuck.

"If you do join us, it's gonna screw up your grades, your social life, your future, your cholesterol. You know how prescription-drug ads have a long list of side effects that sound way worse than the condition they're supposed to treat? That's us! We cause nausea, dry mouth, erectile dysfunction—and if you still want in, that's on you."

There was the sound of a commotion at the far edge of the hall. That diminutive *Magenta* editor was back with a bunch of uniformed campus security guards and they were making a beeline toward the spotlight.

The editor jabbed a finger. "She's not supposed to be here!"

The green-haired girl smiled. "Here's the punch line."

She began to throw flyers and the freshman got out of their seats to try to grab them, blocking the security guards. Then she spun around on her Rollerblades and the lights went out again.

When the lights came back on, the green-haired girl was gone and the *Magenta* editor started screaming, "Motherfucker!" about a hundred times in a row. The campus security guards shrugged and began filing out of J.D. Hall.

I realized I was clutching one of the *Harpoon* flyers in my hand.

On it there was a picture of a castle with calligraphic text announcing that the *Harpoon* comp would start in three days' time at midnight.

Below that, in bold letters, was an invitation and a warning: *Join, or Die.*

CHAPTER SIX

BALLAD OF BIG NOTHING

I didn't have a work-study job yet, which meant I couldn't afford a long-distance calling plan, which meant I had to use the pay phone on the first floor of North Peerpont Hall like I was an inmate at a prison. The phone was installed in a skimpy half booth, which didn't provide much privacy, so I only used it late at night when my roommates weren't awake to witness the broke-ass kid from upstate New York pumping coins into a box like I was a retiree playing the slots in Vegas.

While I was steeling myself to make my call, the phone rang and I answered it.

"Hello?" I said.

I heard Darth Vader–ish heavy breathing, then a light voice like dry leaves blowing across a road. "I was wondering if you might be interested in a little . . . action."

"What kind of action?"

More Vader-ish breathing, then two punchy syllables: "Bee-jay."

I hung up the phone. What the fuck? I picked up the receiver again and dialed the number I had come down here to call. As I waited for somebody to pick up, I noticed someone had scratched these words into the glass of the half booth: *Ubersectionality is what you see when you stop looking.*

After eleven rings, I heard a too-familiar voice: "What's up?"

"What took you so long to answer the phone?" I said.

A heavy sigh. "Hey, Tech."

"Don't call me that."

"So sensitive!"

"Don't be a jerk."

"You phoned me. What time is it?"

"Oh my god, are you just getting up now?"

"You know, late night."

"Getting up at nine p.m. isn't a late night, it's nocturnal. You a raccoon now?"

"At least I'm here."

"Were you out with Ben?"

"Where have you been? Ben and I haven't been a thing for like forever."

"Too bad. He was the only one of your boyfriends I actually liked."

"All he cared about was his damn bank job. I'm trying to get paid."

"Not the dogs again."

"I have a system."

"Everyone has a system until they lose everything."

"Well, not all of us are at Hah-vard."

"Just put Dad on the phone."

"He's out."

"What? Where?"

"I don't know, getting a Happy Meal or some shit."

"Are you kidding me? With his blood sugar?"

"A lot of retirees hang out there. It's the only place open late in this shit town."

"I told him to stop it with the fast food."

"I guess he forgot."

"Did you forget too?"

"I got my own shit to do."

"There's always some excuse with you."

"At least he's out of the house."

"Did he drive?"

"How else is he gonna get there?"

"Really? You gotta do better than that."

"I told you I have shit to do."

"You're the older sister. You should be handling things."

"Maybe you should be in Knockport more."

"I'm in college, you idiot."

"There's always some excuse."

"Fuck you."

"Even when you were here, you weren't here. That's why we're in this mess."

"That's so fucking weak. Just tell Dad I called."

"He's not gonna remember to call back."

"Remind him."

"I told you, Tech—I have shit to do."

"Just remember to remind him."

I woke up in the dark later that night and the mattress above me was rocking. As the squeaking became louder, the parallel feelings that 1) *I know what's going on*, and 2) *I absolutely don't want to know what's going on*, grew exponentially. When the moaning started, quietly at first, and then at roughly the volume and intensity of the grunting during a long rally at a women's Grand Slam tennis quarterfinal, I almost involuntarily said something to make the noise stop. "Hey!"

The rally ended.

I heard Lao's voice in the dark. "What are you doing up?"

"You woke me up. You were moving around so much I thought the top bunk was going to collapse! What are you doing up there?"

Lao was silent for moment before he responded. "Jerking off."

"Dude, TMI."

"What, you don't jerk off in America?"

"Of course, but we don't talk about it! Americans don't talk about race, money, or jerking off. Come, learn the rules!"

"Jerking off is totally natural, man. Did you know wolves, brown bears, and bottlenose dolphins masturbate? Even Tibetan macaques do it!"

"What's a Tibetan macaque?"

"It's a Chinese monkey that's so ugly a Tibetan macaque wouldn't fuck a Tibetan macaque, which is probably why they're always masturbating."

"We're not animals. You couldn't jerk off in the bathroom?"

"I have a towel."

"Not one of my *Star Wars* commemorative hand towels?"

"Relax, I would never ejaculate on anything from the first two movies."

"Okay then, have at it. But for the record: ew."

"Why the fuck did you bring *Star Wars* collectibles to college? Did you pack your Dungeons & Dragons gear too?"

"Why—are you gonna whack off on my dodecahedron dice?"

"No need. When you said *dodecahedron*, I think I came again."

"You're twisted. I got a prank call from a perv tonight. You two should meet."

"You got a call from the Action Man?"

"You know him?"

"I don't *know him* know him, but he calls all the freshmen. The story is he's a professor who lost a book he was working on in a house fire and then lost his mind."

"I gotta take a walk. You can go back to doing whatever you were doing."

Lao slid off the top bunk. "I'll keep you company. Now I'm out of the mood."

I went into the main room and I noticed that the light was on in Dorian and Davis's bedroom. I peeked inside and saw they had stripped their beds, emptied their drawers, and were stuffing jock straps and tube socks into their bags.

"Hey, Upstate!" Davis called out. "You missed popping up to the Vineyard."

"Wish we could have hung out more," Dorian added. "I swear I know you from someplace."

"You guys going somewhere?" I asked.

Dorian zipped up his suitcase. "We got punched, my man."

"Punched?"

"God, are you new to this planet?" Davis laughed. "Punched is when you get chosen for a Final Club. They only pick the best of the best."

Davis held out a manila envelope with a logo of a frog on one side and a broken wax seal on the other. Inside was handwritten note, but Davis and Dorian wouldn't let me read it. "That's for Final Club candidates only," Davis winked.

I had been told that Final Clubs were super-secret, ancient societies that were like fraternities on steroids if fraternities weren't already on steroids. I had overheard other freshmen whispering the names of Final Clubs like they were sharing state secrets: the B.C., the Pork, the Tarquin, the Hylaeus, the Rhoecus, the Romulus, and the most mysterious of them all, the Frog Club. I hadn't realized any of these groups were still operating on campus. "I thought Harvard banned Final Clubs."

D² smirked.

"They didn't get banned," Dorian said. "They just got more secret."

"And that means they got *better*," Davis added.

"Do the clubs even admit . . . black people?" I blurted out, and I instantly regretted saying anything. See, I have two rules about talking about race with white people, and I had just broken both of them.

Davis and Dorian laughed.

"The Final Clubs are the opposite of racist," Davis argued. "It's all about who you know, not who you are. I mean, the Frog Club is pretty much all white but that's not something the members talk about or notice necessarily."

"The Frog Club is color-blind," Dorian said. "Froggers see everyone as human colored."

"What color is that?" I asked.

Dorian shrugged. "You know, flesh-toned."

"What he's trying to say is that people are like Swedish Fish,"

Davis said. "They're different colors, but they all taste the same, basically, and at the end of the day, they're all Swedish. Which is to say, African, since all humankind is from there."

Dorian nodded. "This summer, as part of the immersive lit program, we did a unit on African American nonfiction, so this is shit we've thought about. I mean, those Tuskegee experiments were terrible."

"Horrible," agreed Davis.

"And so racist," Dorian said.

"The Tuskegee airmen, on the other hand . . ." Davis began.

"They never lost a bomber," Dorian said. "Not one."

Davis clapped me on the shoulder, and Dorian did our secret handshake with me. "All righty then!" They both exited the dorm.

Pulling on his eyepatch, Lao emerged from our room. "Those assholes are the worst kind of racists," he groused.

"There's a good kind of racist?"

The only thing Dorian and Davis left behind was a bottle of red pills they must have dropped on the way out.

"What are those?" Lao asked as I picked up the bottle.

"Prescription meds. But I don't think they got them from a doctor."

"What were Dorian and Davis doing with them?"

I stuffed the pills in my pocket. "I'm sure nothing good."

CHAPTER SEVEN

IF I DIE 2NITE

It was so late it was early; sleeping was useless because it was almost time to get up. I had to get out of the room and out of my head and so I pushed through the double doors of North Peerpont Hall, walked past that Chinese restaurant which serves spring rolls that look like limp uncircumcised penises, and ventured onto a dark stretch of Holyoke Street. Groups of street women had taken to sleeping on the grates around the Yard, counting on warm air rising from underground to keep them from catching a chill as autumn arrived.

To keep up with me, Lao was walking double time. "So what's the plan?"

"Can we walk in silence?"

"If we're up and about, we should at least do something. I heard the dining hall workers are getting together with students who support their strike. They're calling themselves the Student Labor Action Movement."

"SLAM?"

"There's a secret meeting tonight at Adam House."

"If it's so secret, how come you know about it?"

"The point is, we should go."

"I'm not trying to get thrown out of school."

"Maybe you should try out for the *Harpoon*. That would loosen you up."

"I'm definitely not comping for the *Harpoon*."

"You don't have to decide now. You want to get high first and think it over?"

"Are you serious? I don't do drugs—illegal ones."

"Marijuana is not a drug, it's a natural herb. We've been using it for medicine in China for five thousand years. Legalize it, don't criticize it."

"Hold up—does your family farm grow medical marijuana?"

"I have import licenses and doctors' notes for all of it. I got all different kinds: Shanghai Special, Dragon Haze, Hindu Kush. All totally legit. Well, mostly. In some states. Okay, it's technically illegal, but so are lots of things, like polygamy."

"Polygamy isn't technically illegal, it's *actually* illegal. I'm not going to risk my college career doing anything against the law. I'm from upstate New York."

"Your loss." Lao lit up a joint, took a drag, and exhaled smoke. "But you should really give some thought to the *Harpoon* comp."

We both fell silent as we realized we had wandered onto Bow Street, or maybe Lao had guided us there. The *Harpoon* crouched in front of us like a monster made of bricks. The tower windows looked like eyes, a glowing green lantern grew into a nose, and the door was a sphinx's grin. As we walked, Lao was talking about stuff he had learned about the *Harpoon*, that inside the building there were any number of trapdoors, secret rooms, and hidden passageways, most known only to members, and some still waiting to be discovered. The construction of the place in 1909 had been funded by the media mogul who had inspired the character of Charles Foster Kane in the movies, and this real-life Kane had hosted massive beer bashes in the Square, sent chamber pots brimming with fresh-steaming piss to his professors (with their faces engraved on the bottoms), had his booty booted out of Harvard his sophomore year, and went on to underwrite the construction of a castle to house the college's humor magazine as a final shot at his former school. What better place for a disgruntled dropout to donate his wealth than an institution devoted to ridiculing his ex–alma mater and everything the place held dear? The *Harpoon* castle was a last laugh memorialized in architecture.

From outside the castle, as Lao talked, I could almost hear the laughter echoing through the corridors; I could imagine a mope-rock song by that band Tristessa tinkling the stained-glass windows. I could visualize the stone ballrooms inside glittering with green light, see the throngs of guests in tuxedos and shimmering gowns. I could almost smell the food being heaped onto trays, taste the wine being poured into goblets. I found myself dreaming about the erudite banter, the endless pranks, the dancing, the singing, the toasting . . .

"So are we gonna do this or what?" Lao asked.

"Comp the *Harpoon*?"

"Fuck yeah. Let's do it. Dorian and Davis and douchebags like that have their Final Clubs and we need a place too. "

"We'd just get cut. It's impossible to make the *Harpoon* staff."

"Yeah, it's so impossible people do it every semester."

"Not people like us."

"The *Harpoon*'s a meritocracy, man—if we're funny, we make it on. You know how hard it is to find a place like that?"

"It's like Shangri-Ha. See what I did there?"

"Oh my god. Maybe we shouldn't do this."

"Well, I don't want to comp anything—I want to stay in my lane."

"Did someone damage you in high school?"

"Who said I was damaged in high school?"

"Your whole attitude says so. You're like one of those people driving around with a plastic bag duct-taped to where his driver's-side window used to be."

"So why would the *Harpoon* want someone like me?"

"The *Harpoon* has a history of signing up damaged people. Comedians are more fucked up than rock stars!"

"I don't get why you want to join the *Harpoon* so badly."

"Let's just say I have family ties."

"From China to Cambridge?"

"You're missing the point, man. Robots are taking over."

"Enough with the robots, dude. I mean really."

"You ever heard of Moore's Law?"

"Anything bad that can happen, will happen?"

"That's Murphy's Law."

"In the criminal justice system, the people are represented by two separate yet equally important groups . . . Dun! Dun!"

"That's *Law & Order*. Moore's Law says computer speed doubles every year."

"Two, four, eight, sixteen . . . Is that true?"

"It's been true every year since it was said like thirty years ago."

"So R2D2 is cute with the beeps and shit, but R4D4 is gonna take my job?"

"And R8D8 takes your girl, and R1024D1024 takes over the world."

"So Murphy's Law."

"No, not Murphy's Law. This is serious—everything seems cool now, with our PCs and shit, but one day everything is gonna double and the HAL 9000 is gonna lock the pod bay doors on our ass. I have my own law: anything a robot can do, it will eventually do better than us."

"A computer is never gonna be able to drive a car or hold a conversation."

"You heard they can beat us in chess, right? People thought that would never happen—and the smarter they get, the more we depend on them."

"Dude, this sounds like Y2K paranoia. Just take a Xanax or something."

"Y2K is for real and it's just the start. The new millennium is gonna spark a global shutdown of computer networks and everybody's gonna realize we're past the point of no return. That Terminator shit isn't fantasy, it's prophecy. For real."

"So what's your—"

"My point is let's comp for the *Harpoon*. I don't know if computers will come alive, but I know one thing they'll never know is that life's a joke. Why waste time doing stuff in college that's gonna be automated by the time we've graduated? Let's do the one thing humans can do better than machines—make fun of shit. Are you with me?"

He stared at me with his one good eye and held out his hand for me to shake, but I couldn't stop thinking about what a bad idea comping for the *Harpoon* would be, and I couldn't help but remember where his hand had been earlier.

Lao thrust out his hand again. "Are you gonna leave me hanging?"

CHAPTER EIGHT

SUBTERRANEAN HOMESICK ALIEN

I was ten minutes early and room 237 in Emerson Hall was already packed. The morning was bright but cold and most of the students had come to class armed with cups of steaming cappuccino. Emerson is a prewar building, and by prewar, I mean it was built pre the First War to End All Wars, which on the Harvard campus makes the place an architectural adolescent. There's an inscription above the entrance reading, *What is man that thou art mindful of him*, and at first I had no idea what that meant, but I figured since Emerson is the philosophy building maybe it was supposed to inspire soul searching. I hustled through the hallways which were all dark pine, white plaster, and brown oak, and once I got to the classroom, I found most of the seats were taken and I had to settle for a place near the back. I was surprised a philosophy class would attract so many people so early in the morning, but I shouldn't have been shocked since the professor was Hyacinth "The Chair" Bell.

Lao and Meera slid in on either side of me like bookends.

I nodded in greeting. "I didn't know you two were gonna be here."

"I'm gonna major in economics," Lao replied. "But Meera dragged me along."

Meera nodded. "I'm gonna double major in physics and computer science, but I just love Professor Bell's whole . . ."

"Curriculum?" I suggested.

"Joie de vivre?" Lao proposed.

Meera's dial-up connected—*bing bong bing!* ". . . concept of ubersectionality."

"I keep seeing that word," I said. "Don't you mean *intersectionality*? That's the idea that issues like race and sex overlap."

"Thanks—I sure appreciate it when a man explains feminist concepts to me! Yes, I mean *ubersectionality*. In physics they've been trying for centuries to come up with a Theory of Everything, but so far they've only got partial answers—general relativity, quantum mechanics, string theory. Those theories only explain part of how the universe works—and they're not even completely compatible, really."

"So she's trying to do something bigger than the Theory of Everything?"

"Professor Bell is searching for *the* Unified Field Theory that will bring together every scholarly discipline from philosophy to physics to feminist studies to psychohistory! There's fancy logic symbols that explain it—"

The clock on the wall struck eight a.m., the door banged open, and the chatter stopped. The Chair strode to the front, wearing the clunky comfortable cross-trainer sneakers you wear when you could give a fuck what people think about what you're wearing. Across the blackboard were written the words *Much have I travell'd in the realms of gold*, but the letters were half-erased and faint. There was a TV next to the blackboard, and a girl in a long-sleeved blue dress danced across the screen before the Chair clicked it off. The professor surveyed the class, her dark eyebrows hovering above her sea-green eyes like storm clouds.

"I'm supposed to be a walking cliché," the Chair announced, and her voice had the steely ring of steak knives rattling in a drawer. "*Prickly professor mistreats students until they learn the secrets of life*. Well, I'm only teaching this class because it's a requirement if I want to be considered for tenure, but I'd rather not teach all of you. The smaller the class, the fewer papers I have to grade." She began handing out stacks of books, gesturing that she wanted them passed around the room, from the front to the back.

Lao took three and handed one copy to Meera and another to me.

When I saw it up close, I realized it wasn't a book, it was a massive reading list. The top of the packet read, *Philosophy 107: Is Life Worth Living?* and below was a list of at least a hundred books. There were a lot of famous authors on the list, but the Chair had selected super-obscure works by each of the writers, including *Herod the Great* by Z.N. Price, *The Ivory Tower* by Mademoiselle Caprice, *The Dark Tower* by N.W. Clerk, *The Owl in Daylight* by Jack Dowland, *Fasti* by Publius Ovidius Naso, *The New Shadow* by Oxy More, *The Black Man and the Wounded World* by Willie DuBois, *Maria, or The Wrongs of Woman* by Mary Cresswick, *A Smoking Room Story* by Eric Blair, *All the Dark and Beautiful Warriors* by Emily Jones, and *Harlem Glory* by Rhonda Hope.

That was just the first three weeks of the course.

Ohh heeelllll nawwwww.

Lao was on my wavelength. "I'm out, brah."

"I'm with you." My knee had begun to throb and I felt a headache coming on.

"Don't you want to at least hear what she has to say?" Meera pleaded.

"We've heard enough," I replied. "Look at this list—if we read even half these books we'd have no time to study for anything else."

"So you're afraid of a little reading?"

"My dad can barely afford to send me here. I can't afford to flunk out."

"Her ideas are worth your time! Did you read her *Harvard Square* study?"

"Everyone's read that," Lao said.

"Remind me, what did it say again?" I said.

Meera's eyes were bright. "*Around Harvard Square* isn't just a novel, there are all these philosophical themes and hidden meanings. Did you know most of the authors mentioned in it are pseudonymous and the book titles are imaginary—kind of a dream within a dream? It's like the author, by renaming everything, was making it all part of the dreamscape. The Chair argued she could use the book as a parable, proof of her Unified Field Theory, to explain the underlying principles of human existence. I heard she's on the hunt to unmask the real author when she expands the paper into a book! If she ever finishes—she's been working on it for almost twenty-five years."

"Why would any of this make me want to stay for this class?" I said.

"She's not a member of the academic boys club. You know why they call her the Chair? Because she lost the vote to become chair of the department and the male professors started calling her the name to mock her—but she turned it around and started calling herself that! They've been trying to push her out for years, but she always stays a step ahead. Everything she does is for a reason. Maybe all these books on her list somehow tie into her theory of ubersectionality."

"Or maybe she's an academic sadist."

"Either way, don't you want to find out?"

I was curious, but still suspicious, and my knee was really hurting. I was about to leave anyway when my eye passed over one title on the list—*God's Own Straight Man* by David Wilson—and something clicked.

Lao was moving toward the door. "You with me?"

I flopped back into my seat and stretched out my leg. "Let's give it more time."

"You're going to leave me hanging like you did at the *Harpoon*?"

"I explained that last night. The *Harpoon* isn't for people like us."

"We don't even know what kind of people we are yet."

"I just have a feeling about this class." I pointed to the title that had caught my eye. "*Battle Royale* is the only novel David Wilson published in his lifetime."

"So why is *God's Own Straight Man* on this list?" Lao asked.

"It's unfinished—he spent decades on it, but died before he was done. There's been some excerpts, but the bulk of it was never published. I wrote Wilson a fan letter once."

"*Falcon Yard* is the novel Victoria Lucas was working on when she committed suicide," Meera added, pointing to another book on the list. "I read somewhere that her husband Daniel Hearing burned the manuscript after she died because it was about their marriage. Men make *terrible* executors and even worse literary critics."

"A lot of these are unfinished works," Lao said, flipping through the packet. "Like *Dying Is Fun* by Vladimir Sirin. He's kind of a personal hero of mine—grew up speaking one language, became a master of another. I read a bio on him and he never finished this novel, it was just a bunch of notes on index cards beside his deathbed."

"So Professor Bell has been working on a book?" I asked Meera.

"She's been at it for twenty-five years."

"This list is full of people who didn't finish what they started—that's the ubersectional connection here. We need to finish class."

Other students headed for the lifeboats. There was a trickle at first, and then suddenly there was a flood. The departed left their copies of the reading list stacked up in the front of the room, a leaning tower of homework. Within a few minutes there were only a dozen students left.

"Please pass your reading lists to the front of the room," the Chair announced to the sprinkling of students who remained.

When she had collected them all, the Chair picked up one of the reading lists and theatrically threw it into a nearby waste bin, where it landed with a metallic clatter. "Ms. Pallas? Can you please dispose of the rest?"

As if on cue, a mousy-looking woman with a blond bob who I think was the philosophy department's office manager rolled into the classroom with a cart and wheeled away the mountain of reading lists.

The Chair shut the door, turned the lock with an ominous iron *ch-Tunk!* and then turned to the class. "The good news is that reading list was your first test, and you passed. There will be no formal reading list for this class. We're not focusing on homework, we're focusing on how your mind works."

The beginnings of a cheer began to rise from the remaining students, but the tropospheric elevation of one of Bell's storm-cloud eyebrows quieted the room.

"The bad news is you should have all left when the getting was good. There will be no easy As in this class and no easy Bs, Cs, or Ds. I'm giving every one of you an F, and that mark will remain on your transcript until you prove to me that you deserve a better grade. There will be no dropping this class, no grade inflation, and no escape. I have no future plans, my only focus is this moment, this class. The only way for you to get out of the F that I gave you is with another F-word: hard *fucking* work."

The class fell completely silent.

"Oh, do I have your attention now?" the Chair growled. "Good, because the first thing I hope you learn in this class is I'm not here to teach you anything. Facts and dates and theories—that's all busywork and bullshit. If you finish this semester a little more confused about your life, a little less sure about your place in society, a little angrier about how fucked up everything is, I'm going to count that as a win."

Professor Bell began to cough, and after a few moments of hacking she gathered herself. "Did any of you notice the quote above the entrance to Emerson? It reads, *What is man, that thou art mindful of him?* That's Psalm 8:4, and the point is, God's big and we're small. It's like the architects wanted to remind us we're ants and nothing about us matters. But what the inscription doesn't say is that the next verse—" She began to cough again, this time longer and more violently, until at last she pulled out a hand-rolled joint and took a long drag, which seemed to steady her. "I have a prescription for this," she rasped. "That's it for today. Feel free to meditate."

She walked to the side of the classroom, turned down the lights so everyone was in near darkness, sat down cross-legged in a corner, and closed her eyes.

The warm aroma of the Chair's joint wafted around the classroom, and Lao waved some of the smoke toward his nose. "Kind of a pinecone scent, with vanilla notes and an oaky finish. Aquaman Splash, maybe? No, no . . . I've got it: Purple Haze! Not the high-quality stuff—she must be buying off the street or, worse, getting it from a doctor. Smoking medical pot is worse than eating hospital food."

Meera was in shock. "Did she say we start out this course with an F?"

"She also said we can't drop the class," Lao responded. "Tosh, remind me—why did you want us to stay again?"

I didn't answer because it felt like somebody was stabbing steak knives under my kneecap. I lurched out of my seat, exited the classroom, and limped into a bathroom in the hallway. I entered a stall and latched the door. The pain in my knee was intense and my heart was pounding against my chest like a basketball bouncing against a wall. I tried to think about anything other than my knee. I thought about all those unfinished manuscripts by all those great writers. I thought about how my basketball career had been left unfinished just like that. The sign above the building was right—I was a nobody, I was a nothing, and there was no reason to mind me. My heart began to gallop even faster and I felt I just needed to slow it down to stop the stall I was in from spinning. I pulled the red pills I had found in Dorian and Davis's room out of my pocket. They were calling to me like Frodo's ring.

I noticed something scratched into the stall door: *For thou hast made him a little lower than the angels, and hast crowned him with glory and honor. —Psalm 8:5.*

That was the verse that the Chair had started to talk about. The passage wasn't really about how small we are, it was a pronouncement that we're close to divine and destiny has designs on us. Was that a sign? After all I'd gone through, was I still meant for bigger things? My eyes dipped lower on the stall door. Beneath the Bible quotation was a cartoon of a penis and the words, *Ubersectionality will fck yr azz.*

Maybe I shouldn't read too much into stuff I read on bathroom walls.

I stuffed the pills back in my pocket and went out to find Lao and Meera.

CHAPTER NINE

1979

That night, Meera asked Lao and me to crash a party. Lao and I had been planning to spend the night in our room playing video games on the TV, but just as we started, Meera began lurking around like she had something to say. Finally she sighed, "I hate what's happened to video games."

"You haven't played this one," said Lao, joystick in hand.

"It's the latest from Mee Corp.," I added. "Somehow Lao got a beta version."

"Here's my problem with video games . . ." Meera began, but when Lao and I ignored her provocative pause, she decided to break form and finish what she was saying without a prompt, ". . . they're so sexist. They're worse than movies."

"Since when do you care about video games?" Lao asked.

"Why wouldn't I care? Because I'm a woman?"

"I didn't say that. I didn't even think that."

"You know who programmed some of the very first computers? Women at Harvard."

"Where'd you hear that?"

"I'm a science major. I hear things."

"I heard a black guy invented the video game cartridge," I said. "You never hear diddly-squat about that brother."

Meera shook her head. "The whole industry is problematic—just look at Lara Croft. If I'm going tomb raiding, I'm not doing it in a tank top and short-shorts!"

"It's a video game, it's not that deep," Lao said. "You don't get it, because you don't play them."

With an eye roll, Meera plugged in a joystick and sat down next to Lao. She made quick work of the game he was playing, decimating enemies, racing through levels, and reaching the final screen. She let the joystick tumble from her hands.

"How did you do that?" I asked.

"Don't get me started on body types," Meera said, continuing her rant, as if nothing had happened. "In game world, we all have big boobs, child-bearing hips, and waists too tiny to contain, I don't know, a uterus!"

Lao put down his joystick. "Now I'm out of the mood."

So we followed Meera outside. The night was cool and the stars were out and we got a head start on the drinking with some warm beer in plastic cups, but Lao started getting all worked up about where Meera was taking us—the Frog Club.

"So you have a problem with video games but you want to go party at a Final Club?" Lao groused. "I don't get it."

"Does it look like I'm dressed for a formal party?" said Meera, who was wearing a black sherwani jacket and black boots. "We're not attending it, we're crashing it."

"What's the difference?" I said.

"It's the difference between laughing with someone and laughing *at* them."

I raised a red plastic cup. "This all sounds like a rationalization, but it's a rationalization that allows us to drink, so I'm good with it."

The Frog Club was on JFK Street and it was easy to find because there was a steady stream of women in formal dresses walking up the sidewalks toward it. The club had high, ivy-covered brick walls and iron gates with metal frogs mounted along the top and the thudding drumbeat of that jock-rock Mookie Blaylock song booming from somewhere deep inside. Outside the building a half dozen workers in caps and overalls were spreading seed on the wide, lush lawn.

We knocked on the front door and there was no answer, which was annoying because we could hear voices and dancing feet inside. I looked up and saw various Frog Club fuckers leaning out of windows and hanging off ledges and tottering on the balconies, all hooting and hollering at the women down below them. Few things are more vomitous than seeing Harvard nerds act like they're party-school students.

I pointed at two assholes in particular who were spraying champagne from above on women below waiting to get inside. "That's Dorian and Davis."

Lao didn't even look up. "I guess they made the cut."

Dorian spotted me from above. "Hey, Tech!"

I tried to ignore him but he kept calling out to me, and Davis joined in.

"You know these guys?" Meera asked.

I shrugged. "They're our roommates, or they *were*."

"But why are they shouting that?" she said.

Dorian was leaning so far out the window that Davis had to grab the back of his tux jacket to keep him from falling out. "I found out about you!" Dorian was yelling. "Tosh 'Tech' Livingston! You were in the New York State finals!"

"What are they talking about?" Lao asked.

"No idea," I said nervously. "How do we get into this party?"

"I forgot," Meera said. "Nonmembers go through the side door."

"This is so fucked up," Lao grumbled. "This is back-of-the-bus shit."

Meera waved him off. "Remember, we're crashing, not attending."

Dorian and Davis were chanting now: "*Tech! Tech! Tech!*"

We walked around to the side of the building and we couldn't see or hear Dorian and Davis anymore. The queue of gift-wrapped women high-heeling their way up to the side door of the club was as long as lines at Disneyland. "And you think the women in my video game dress skimpy?" Lao cracked to Meera.

"Do you not like the way I dress?" snapped Meera. "Is it too boyish for you?"

"I didn't say that," Lao replied.

"I don't dress for the male gaze."

"I only have one eye. I have half a male gaze at most."

"I thought I'd escape all of this tree house stuff at college, but you still have the clubs, and *Magenta* has its 'Fifteen Hottest Freshmen' list . . ."

"You know, Final Clubs wouldn't exist if women stopped going to their parties."

"So you're blaming women for the Final Clubs? Tosh, do you agree with him?"

I put my hands up. "I'm just here to support you."

Lao pointed away from the club. "What's going on over there?"

Two Cambridge city workers had parked a sewage truck on a side street near the club. Some of the club members didn't like the optics of the workers and their vehicle and its formidable sewage-sucking pneumatic vacuum hose being so close to their fancy party and were leaning out of the windows and off the balconies and ledges to throw garbage at the guys who were just trying to do their jobs. Even the women in line were getting into the act, taunting the workers by flashing their bare breasts. The gardeners in overalls who had been tending to the Frog Club grounds continued spreading grass seed, seemingly oblivious to the class warfare all around them. I had a flashback to when I was a kid upstate—everyone treated the garbage guys like garbage and it pissed me off.

Meera walked up to the sewage truck and introduced herself to the two workers, whose names were Wojtek and Kostya. They had Eastern European accents and were a couple years older than me, but—small world—I had actually met Wojtek at a summer camp for promising basketball players five years earlier. I remembered he had a great crossover dribble and unexpectedly good hops, and he had managed to block my baby hook at least twice.

"My man Tech!" Wojtek said, giving me a big bro hug. "You ever fix that punk-ass hook shot you got?"

"You guys members of the club?" Kostya asked us suspiciously.

"We're not members," Meera replied. "And I'm not a guy."

Kostya's eyes opened wide. "No, you are not! I just . . ."

"Relax, I get that a lot," Meera said.

Wojtek and Kostya were working sanitation jobs until they put some funds away. Frog Club members always gave them shit on pickup days.

"Come the revolution," Lao told them, "we're killing club members first. That is, if the robots haven't gotten them already."

Kostya smiled. "I don't think we will have to wait for the revolution."

"What do you mean?" Meera asked.

"I service this street all the time, I know the people. The doormen—brothers from India, they go to graduate school. The house cleaners—a Colombian family, very nice, they go to my church. But these gardeners there now—I never seen them before, and I don't think they're up to anything good. Not that I give a fuck."

The gardeners were beginning to wrap up their work. I noticed then that they hadn't actually been spreading grass seed—they all had miniboxes of Rainbow-Flavored Sugar Kombos and they had been scattering the multicolored cereal all over the grounds of the Frog Club before walking over to a grape-colored van idling at the curb. I recognized the driver—it was the green-haired girl from the *Harpoon*. She noticed me and winked.

After stripping off their caps and overalls, the gardeners were dressed liked students—I remembered seeing a couple of them around the Yard. Two of the worker-students now opened the sliding side doors of the van—and about a million pigeons flew out. As party guests squealed and scampered away, the birds flocked to the yard of the Frog Club, pecking at the ground and gorging themselves on Rainbow-Flavored Sugar Kombos. In short order, the grounds of the club were a teeming mass of birds, flapping and fighting over scattered cereal. Members of the club began to throw things from the windows—water balloons, half-empty beer cans, and ceramic plates—trying to frighten the birds off the lawn.

"Have those birds been eating what I think they've been eating?" Meera asked.

"They gave them Rainbow-Flavored Sugar Kombos," I said.

"Things are about to get ugly," she said.

Dorian and Davis appeared at a window with a water hose and began to spray the grounds from the upper floor. The birds took to the air, cooing and fluttering and squawking—and shitting. The bird droppings dropped over everything—over the scattering party guests, over the Frog Club members leaning out the window and standing on the balconies and hanging off the ledges. It was a blizzard of shit, a storm of feces, a tsunami of excreta—and Meera, Lao, and I were covered in bird shit too. The droppings dripped on our heads, dribbled onto our faces, and coated our clothes.

Laughing, the green-haired girl and her companions drove away in the van.

After the shitstorm, Wojtek and Kostya drove us back to the Yard in their truck. "That was wild," I said, as they let us out in front of North Peerpont.

"That was nothing," Wojtek said. "Everyone knows getting *inside* the club is the real trick. I've been working that street a year now, and I've never been past the door."

Meera got out of the truck. "Thanks for the ride."

Kostya leaned out the driver's-side window. "Any chance I get your number?"

"I'm covered in bird dung and I look disgusting," Meera said.

"After you clean up, I call, take you someplace nice."

"I don't give out my number. Why don't you just give me yours?"

When we reached the room, Meera hit the shower first and I gave her one of my T-shirts to wear as a nightgown. Lao wiped himself down and pulled on a T-shirt reading, *The Future Isn't*

Working, with the image of a humanoid computer behind an office desk. The bird shit had gotten in my mouth and I brushed my teeth for ten minutes, changed my clothes, and tried to lose myself in homework. I came across an essay by the Chair in a book about ubersectionality I had picked up from the library.

"Most of us go through our lives on autopilot," the Chair wrote. Then:

> *We don't question the conventions of our societies or the everyday activities of our lives. This will be increasingly true with the rise of robots and artificial intelligence and electronic mapping technology. In the future, we won't even know our way home because we will trust programming to get us there. Ubersectionality asks you to stop, step back, and examine everything. Switch off the computer, shut off electric guides, take off your headphones. This is more than living what the Greeks called the Examined Life. This is the Explored Life, a journey, a quest up and down the forking paths your lives could take. Western philosophers encourage us to look within to discover who we are. Eastern thinkers recognize we can be many people and should open ourselves to possibilities. This is true independence, this is quantum freedom, this is the force that spins atoms and sets planets in their orbits. Only the imaginary is real!* The Book of the Tao *tells us,* The Way that is planned is not the way that . . .

I closed the book. "Argh! I can still taste bird shit on my tongue."

"I guess we deserved it for being at a Final Club party," Lao said.

Meera emerged from the shower, rubbing her short hair with a towel. "We weren't at the party . . ."

"This is going to be good," Lao said.

". . . we were just crashing," Meera finished.

"You keep telling yourself that," Lao said. "I'm going to play my video game."

"Is that one of my *Star Wars* commemorative bath towels?" I asked Meera.

"Is it not okay for me to use it?"

"Just don't use anything with an Ewok. Lao kind of marked his territory on those."

Meera plopped down on the couch. "I just wanted a peek inside the tree house. You think the *Harpoon* pulled that prank?"

"I know they did," I said. "I recognized some of them."

"I heard Poonsters have been trying to get inside the club for years," Lao said.

"I have so much supplemental reading to catch up on," Meera moaned.

I shelved my book. "Screw homework. I'm sick of getting shit on."

"So what should we do?" Lao asked.

CHAPTER TEN

COME AS YOU ARE

The castle was a dark silhouette against a gray sky. There was no wind and a chill hung in the night air. There were five minutes left before midnight and students hustled down sidewalks and through the castle's banana and plum-colored side door. Homeless people shuffled down the darkened streets as scraps of newspapers swirled around them. The university had recently installed rows of sharp spikes onto the heating vents all around the Square to prevent vagrants from resting on them. So sleep-deprived street people drifted by us as we hurried to our appointment. The meeting everyone had been waiting for was about to start.

Lao, Meera, and I walked up to the castle and Meera grabbed the golden gargoyle rapper on the door and knocked three times. The large, heavy door ground open and a guy who looked like he had time traveled from a Jazz Age party stood at the entrance. He was tall and buff and blond and his body language said he came from money, the way some people come from Pittsburgh or Shreveport or Cheyenne. He was wearing a tux with tails and frog flippers on his feet and one of those creepy bird masks with the long beaks that medieval doctors used to wear to protect themselves from breathing in the plague. He held the door for us with one hand and in the other he held a jewel-encrusted golden goblet which he swirled ironically, if it's even possible to swirl that way. Behind him, carved into a stone wall, was the *Harpoon* creed:

TRAGEDY IS COMEDY
MADNESS IS GENIUS
LIFE IS A JOKE

Birdman motioned for us to proceed to his right.

The interior of the castle had a faux-medieval feel, with stone floors and chandeliers with blazing candles, and mounted on the white-tiled walls was weaponry from various cultures and eras, from dueling pistols to ninja throwing-stars. A lot of Harvard buildings looked old, but this place seemed historic. Passing through the hallways felt like sneaking into a closed-off cobwebbed wing of a museum.

Meera touched one finger to the tip of a green-and-gold arrow on display in the anteroom. "Wit isn't the only thing that's sharp in this place."

We went through an adjoining chamber with a large Persian rug and oak cabinets stuffed with new and vintage copies of the *Harpoon* magazine and strolled into a snug circular library in which a dozen students were waiting, mostly freshmen with a sprinkling of sophomores and a dash of juniors and seniors. A tapestry hanging in one section of the room featured a jester in a tentacled hat, a bird with long legs, and an inkblot with bubble eyes. A lanky kid with a kamikaze bandanna on his head and limited-edition high-top sneakers on his feet looked me over as I walked in, and then looked away, as if dismissing me as a threat. In the flickering candlelight I saw various emotions and feelings pass across the faces of the people waiting, ranging from anticipation to fear to panic. Near the wall, waddling around in a shaggy cardigan, I spied Tilfer, and I pinballed through the crowd over to him.

"I didn't know you were funny," I said.

"I-I-I'm not," he stammered. "The *H-H-Harpoon* is a family thing."

"You okay? You sound weird."

"I'm h-h-happier than a d-d-duck eatin' cornbread." He

blushed like a baby's slapped bottom and shuffled away.

"You know that kid?" Lao asked me.

"Tilfer? I mean, kinda. He's in our dorm."

"That's Tilfer *Peerpont*. God had to take out a payday loan from the Peerponts to finish the fucking universe."

"Tilfer is V.C. Peerpont's son? How do you know?"

"My dad knew his dad. V.C. Peerpont is a legend and Tilfer's brother Spooner is on the *Harpoon* staff now."

"Are you sure about that? This does not seem like Tilfer's scene—he was stuttering and everything. A couple days ago he was like a different person. Now he's dropping *g's* and talking about ducks and cornbread. What the fuck?"

"Trust me," Lao said, "his family has this place on lock."

I browsed through the shelves as I waited for the meeting to start. The books in the library were mostly first editions, with fancy leather covers, raised spine bands, satin ribbon page markers, and gilded page edges. Virtually all of them were by *Harpoon* grads, like Jack Reed's *12 Nights Inside Mother Russia*, Heinz Beck's *Woonsocket Infidelities: Collected Stories*, and Natty Zuckerman's *All-American Whore*. There was also a copy, of course, of *Around Harvard Square*.

"Knock knock." A kid with close-cropped brown hair, an army jacket, and work boots had slid up next to me. The bottom half of his face was hidden behind a surgical mask.

"Can I help you?" I asked.

"Knock knock," he repeated.

"Um . . . who's there?"

"Mac."

"Mac who?"

The kid in the surgical mask bowed. "*Macbeth*, act 2, scene 3."

"That's not at all a weird thing to say to someone you've just met," I said.

"I was just posing a metaphysical question. The fact that it was in the form of humor, if anything, normalized it."

"Sorry, still weird."

"Well, you made it weird."

In an adjoining room, the mother of all grandfather clocks struck midnight.

Everyone looked around expecting something to happen. There was no air-conditioning in the castle, and with all the warm bodies, the place was getting stuffy. Somebody farted and everyone laughed, but as the stink lingered in the air with no signs of dissipating, things got unfunny real quick.

"When is this fucking thing gonna start?" Bandanna Boy declared to no one in particular, and then, because nobody was paying attention to him, he focused on me since I was the nearest thing with a pulse. "This is some bullshit, don't you think?"

I gave him a noncommittal look.

"You a freshman?" he persisted.

I nodded.

"So am I. There's only gonna be room for a couple of us, and I will straight-up murder anyone who tries to take my slot. It's survival of the funniest."

I didn't respond and Bandanna Boy moved away to bug someone else.

"What did he want?" Meera asked me.

"I don't know, but he's no freshman," I said.

"How do you know?"

"The kicks he's wearing were limited editions they made for the Harvard basketball team two years ago—cushioned midsole, four-direction traction on the outsole, mesh rubber tongue."

"Nobody should know that much about shoes," Lao said. "You need therapy."

"The thing I can't figure out is what a freshman is doing with some upperclassman's kicks. Those aren't the kind of things you just give away."

At three past midnight, Birdman swept into the room and set down his golden goblet on a shelf.

"I just figured out who that is," Lao whispered.

Birdman surveyed the assembled kids like a general reviewing his troops before stripping off his mask with a flourish and running one hand through his abundant blond hair. He had I-can-steal-your-girlfriend looks, with gray eyes and a thick jaw, but if you peered closely, you could see that his cheeks were dotted with faint acne scars like dimples on a golf ball. "I'm Spooner Peerpont," he announced. "I'm Ibis of the *Harvard Harpoon*. But you probably already know this, am I right?"

"Ibis?" Bandanna Boy interrupted. "What's that?"

"That's second in command, though that may change soon. Welcome to America's oldest humor magazine. We're a student-run publication that's been put out since 1876. I want to return this magazine to its glory days! The greatest writers ever have come from our staff—Heinz Beck, Jack Reed, Killy Trout, Dick Wharfinger, Hank Chinaski. Natty Zuckerman wrote the first line of *All-American Whore* with a used tampon he found in the bathroom upstairs. *Harpoon* writers founded *International Harpoon*, the magazine and movie company that earns this place millions every year in royalties. *Harpoon* writers have won fifty-four Oscars, thirty-four Emmys, and twelve Nobels. E.G. Morris was a *Harpoon* editor—"

Bandanna Boy broke in again: "Is it true that your dad V.C. Peerpont is really E.G. Morris and he wrote *Around Harvard Square?*"

"Nobody knows who E.G. Morris really is," Spooner replied. "A lot of smart people say Beck or Trout or some other *Harpoon* alum wrote *Around Harvard Square*. My favorite theory is the Action Man wrote it."

Bandanna Boy looked unsatisfied with that answer. "So what's upstairs?"

"Only *Harpoon* editors get to go upstairs. I'm not really taking questions . . ."

Bandanna Boy raised his hand. "What are the rules of the comp?"

Spooner looked annoyed but answered: "We're looking for writers, cartoonists, and business staffers. You submit three pieces in three days, business compers sell ads, then we vote. Survivors go to the next round."

"Can we hand in all three of our submissions at once?"

"If you want."

Bandanna Boy pulled out three sheets of paper. "Right now?"

Spooner sighed. "Throw 'em on the floor."

"What?"

"That's how it's done. Compers put their pieces on the floor, and editors write their comments on the back."

The kid gingerly placed his manuscripts on the floor of the circular library.

Spooner picked up the submissions and scanned them as the other students watched. Then he crumpled them up and began to rub his bottom with the paper.

Bandanna Boy looked at him. "What are you doing?"

"I'm wiping my ass with your work," Spooner explained. "Oh, and by the way, you can get the fuck out."

"What?"

"*GET* the fuck *OUT!*" Spooner screamed.

The kid stumbled backward and, whimpering slightly, backed out of the exit.

Spooner slammed the door in boy's face and turned back to the rest of us. "Anyone else got shit to say?" he asked. "No? Then let's do this."

The talk Spooner gave, like that one house in every neighborhood that displays a bonkers number of Christmas lights, was both illuminating and kinda fanatical. He was delving into the history of the *Harpoon*, how it started as an American response to the *London Charivari* magazine, how it first sold for a quarter from Whiton's cigar store at the corner of Main and Holyoke, and how it had played pranks on the *Magenta* over the decades, when there was a knock on the door.

Bandanna Boy was back—and he was holding a gun.

Meera squeezed my right arm and Lao grabbed the other.

"Who's laughing now?" Bandanna Boy sneered. He jammed

the gun into Spooner's side and marched him into the center of the library. The compers froze.

"That's my brother's brother's gun," Spooner said evenly. "You grabbed it off our walls."

"Yeah, so?"

"It's not loaded."

Bandanna Boy pointed the gun at the floor and fired a shot. The sound echoed in the small library and one of the compers fainted.

Meera leaned over to me and Lao. "I know how to take this guy out."

"Are you high?" Lao replied. "'Cause I am and I can still tell that's a bad idea."

"Quiet down, both of you," I said. "This isn't what it looks like."

But Meera had rolled up the sleeves of her sherwani jacket and was making moves like she was the hero of an action movie. There was a crack as the gun fired again, and faster than I could figure out what was happening, Meera had disarmed Bandanna Boy and pinned him down in an elaborate hold that looked like it hurt like holy hell. I hadn't noticed before how muscular her forearms were. Some compers screamed and then I saw why—Bandanna Boy's bandanna had come off and his head was gushing blood.

Everyone was going crazytown now and nobody knew what was happening or what to do. Spooner waved Meera away and bent down over Bandanna Boy, and after what seemed like forever he looked up, his bright gray eyes blurry with tears, like coins in a fountain. Compers began to cry along with him, and several of them hugged each other. A few kids dropped to their knees in disbelief.

"This freshman is dead," Spooner declared.

Some of the compers gasped, but Spooner held up a hand.

"We could all be looking at murder charges—or accessory to murder," he continued. "Murder is so hard to accessorize, am I right? Do you wear a necklace, do you wear a scarf? Do hoop earrings go with homicide? But I digress—we have to cover our tracks. Who is gonna help me move the body?"

Compers looked at each other.

Then Spooner began to laugh.

"What's going on?" Lao asked.

Meera's eyes narrowed. "I think this whole thing . . ."

"Is a prank," I finished. "Those sneakers were the tell. The kid in the bandanna was only pretending to be a freshman because he's already on the staff."

Spooner grinned and Bandanna Boy jumped to his feet and a bunch of other editors from the *Harpoon* staff came from upstairs and crowded into the room. Pretty soon the whole place was howling with laughter.

"You've been Harpooned!" Spooner announced. He patted Bandanna Boy's back. "This is Ruggles Hoyer—he's a junior and he got on last year. He was a jock, but now he's with me on the business staff."

"That asshole broke my arm," Ruggles moaned, nodding toward Meera. "Are you some sort of martial artist or some shit? I mean, what the fuck, dude?"

Meera put her hands to her mouth. "I'm sorry! I didn't know it was a prank."

Ruggles's mouth fell open. "What kind of reverse *Crying Game* shit is this? You're a girl?"

Just then a green-haired woman with a ring of keys on her belt entered the room. "I hope nobody was talking about me! I was finishing my Kegel exercises." She shot Spooner a pissed-off look that I don't think any of us were meant to see, but he didn't meet her gaze and she kept talking: "I'm Vecky Higginbottom, president—well, *acting* president—of the *Harpoon*. You've all been Harpooned! If you want to join the fun and join our staff, all it takes is talent—at making people laugh, cartooning, or selling ads. Your pieces are due over the next three days. No joke!"

After that, all the compers, rattled but weirdly exhilarated, began to disperse.

"Don't forget to sign the guest book before you go!" Vecky called out brightly, before grabbing a key off her ring, opening a massive wooden door, and slipping away upstairs.

Ruggles lingered behind and, clutching his arm, sidled up to Meera. "Good news—I think my arm's broken but it's not a compound fracture or anything."

"I'm glad to hear that," Meera replied.

"Sorry about getting so angry before—I really thought you were a dude."

"I get that a lot."

"Any chance I could get your number?"

"I get that a lot too," she sighed. "I don't really give it out. Sorry!"

Ruggles, rubbing his arm, retreated upstairs with the other editors.

Meera, Lao, and I all went over to a small wooden stand where there was a bottle of black ink, a long quill pen, and a large guest book. Most of our fellow compers had signed their names, and a few had also included a short quote or comment. I couldn't help noticing the quote that had been put down in bold strokes in the book just before me: *While round us bark the mad and hungry dogs, Making their mock at our accursèd lot.*

That was the second time we almost met.

CHAPTER ELEVEN

JÓGA

"So when were you going to tell us?"

The next morning at the dining hall, Lao and Meera were getting into it with each other over something when I put down my tray to join them. Breakfast today was worse than usual—the hot food was cold, the cold food was warm, and the food that was supposed to be room temperature wasn't even in the room because they had run out. SLAM had declared a strike at all the campus cafeterias and ringed the buildings with white-aproned marchers holding protest signs. The only staffers in J.D. Hall were a smattering of strikebreakers bused in by Peer-less Food Preparation, the contractor that oversaw campus food services, and the only food available was preprepared stuff straight out of boxes, bottles, and cans.

Meera sipped a juice box. "I don't see what the big deal is, really."

"What's going on?" I asked.

"Ask her," Lao said. "She's the one who nearly got us killed."

"Is that what you're arguing about?" I said. "The whole thing was a prank. Nobody got hurt or anything. I mean, besides the guy whose arm Meera broke."

"This isn't about last night," Lao explained. "It's about this morning."

"It really isn't a big deal." Meera shrugged. "Let's play a game. Would you rather have arms that can't straighten or knees that don't bend?"

"That's a tough one," I said. "I already have a fucked-up knee."

"Stop trying to change the subject," Lao told Meera.

"What was the original subject?" I asked.

"Remember that story I was telling about *dhokla*?" Meera said.

"Yeah, your favorite food. What does that have to do with anything?"

"You are starting at the absolute start," Lao groused.

"Shush—you are worse than some directors I know," Meera scolded.

"You know directors?" I said. "Like movie directors?'

"Just let her finish the story," Lao grumbled.

Meera plowed ahead: "When I was twelve, there was this bully, Darshit, who would steal the best thing out of your lunch. I was terrified he'd take my *dhokla*. So for six months I took *kalaripayattu*."

"What's kalawhatever?" I asked.

"It's like Indian kung fu," Lao explained.

Meera punched his shoulder. "More like kung fu is Chinese Kalaripayattu."

"So you take Kalawhatever," I said to Meera. "So you beat up this bully?"

"No, he beat the stuffing out of me. But years later I learned a few action hero moves which is why I could kick that guy's butt at the *Harpoon*."

"Wait—how and why did you learn action hero moves?" I asked.

"Skip ahead to now," Lao cut in. "I had thought she was some shy FOB from India. But after I saw her take out that guy at the *Harpoon*, I'm like, *What the fuck is happening*? So one of my weed clients is a grad student from Mumbai, and when he saw me walking home with her last night, he leaves me a message. Turns out, she goes by another name back home: Karisma Kamal. She's an actress."

Meera sighed. "I told you . . ."

". . . absolutely nothing?" Lao suggested.

". . . that I had a career."

"You got more than that going on," Lao said. "She's a Bollywood superstar."

"You said superstar, I didn't. I was a *child* star. I played boys in most of my films until they couldn't hide my curves any longer. I get maybe five fan letters a week—and all my followers in America are Indian expats."

"How many movies have you done?" I asked.

Meera rolled her eyes. "Can we move on from this subject? We should be focusing on what we're going to do about the *Harpoon*."

"I can't believe you still want to join the *Harpoon* after last night," I said.

"The number one thing I learned in Bollywood was never back down from a fight," Meera replied. "Well, actually, the number one thing was to not eat anything from craft services if it's been lying in the sun. But the number two lesson is the never-backing-down-from-a-fight thing. Yeah, last night was crazy, but that's what makes it interesting. Don't you want to see what's upstairs at the castle?"

Just then, all around us in the cafeteria, there was a swell of voices. The white-aproned dining hall workers who had been marching outside had forced their way inside and were streaming through the hall, pumping their fists, waving signs, and shouting. They were wearing white masks and one marcher untied their white apron, waved it over their head, and jumped up on a table.

"We are the invisible," declared the protester, whose dreadlocks spilled over their mask. "We fry the food, dust the portraits, guard the buildings, shelve the books. But still you do not see us. We are SLAM! We are invisible but we will not be silent."

Some of the masked workers began to shout.

"No justice, no food!"

"Sí, se puede!"

"Hey, Harvard, you can't hide, we can see your greedy side!"

I thought I recognized you then, as you led the chants and marched on the tabletops, but I couldn't place where I had seen you before. A chant rose up.

"Who's got the power? We've got the power!"

That was the final time we almost met.

I slipped out of the dining hall before my friends. Economics isn't my thing, but Lao had convinced me to take EC-107 with him and I had some reading to catch up on before class. I skimmed *The Economics of Latin America: Development Problems in Perspective* as I walked across the Yard: *A disproportionate increase in population in relation to the increase in total output negates the development effort in several ways. It pulls down per capita gains, leaving individual incomes . . .*

I felt something from behind me and turned and looked down to see Morven from the *Magenta* standing on the tips of his alligator-skin boat shoes and tapping me on the shoulder. Face-to-face, he looked even shorter. I should say face-to-*waist* because he barely came up to my belly button.

"Do you know who I am?" he asked.

"Why do people say that?" I replied. "If I know who you are, there's no need to ask. If I don't know who are, you asking is just embarrassing. It's lose-lose."

"I'll take that as a yes. I'm doing a story and you can help."

"Did I make the fifteen-hottest-freshmen list?"

"We don't publish that until February, but don't wait by the phone. This is about the *Harpoon*."

"I know next to nothing about the *Harpoon*."

"So that wasn't you at the *Harpoon* comp meeting last night?"

"What does that have to do with anything?"

"I heard shit got real. If you could fill us in as our inside source, we could hook you up. If your intel checks out, I could guarantee you a spot on our staff."

"That doesn't sound like being a source. That sounds like being a snitch."

"It's a fine line. There's some stuff going on at the castle that goes way back and this could be the path into it."

"Are you trying to get the *Harpoon* back for a prank? At the comp meeting they said the *Harpoon* and you guys are rivals."

"The *Magenta* is the oldest student newspaper—we have no rivals."

"So it's not true the *Harpoon* once nailed the *Magenta* furniture to the ceiling?"

"If the *Harpoon* had real guts, they'd break into the Frog Club."

"Did the *Harpoon* really run an advertisement for a male escort service in the paper and put your phone number in the copy?"

"They should have been kicked out for that but the Peerpont family probably paid someone off."

"What about the pig they released in your dorm room? I heard it was four hundred pounds and it shit on everything . . ."

"You think this is funny?"

"Well, yeah."

"If you laugh along with these people, you're just as bad. What's that quote from *Around Harvard Square*? *What you laugh at is who you are.*"

"Did you really make your boat shoes out of Vecky's gator?"

"If she hadn't used it for her *prank*, animal control wouldn't have euthanized it."

"Sounds like you're the one who went too far."

"Once you get entangled with these people, you'd be surprised how far you'll go. Your *Harpoon* friends are not the good guys here. They grab a fistful of cash from Hollywood and act like we're the preprofessional assholes. Spooner probably told compers the *Harpoon*'s won fifty-four Oscars, thirty-four Emmys, and twelve Nobels, right?"

"So?"

"They tell that lie every year! The shit about Natty Zuckerman writing *All-American Whore* with a used tampon? Total bullshit—how would that even work? He wrote it on a typewriter in Hilles

Library! The story about *International Harpoon* paying millions in royalties? The company is about to file for Chapter 11! The stuff about E.G. Morris being an alum? That's an urban legend—I hear he's from China!"

"How do you know any of this?"

"Look, I'm on your side, dude. The castle isn't the place you think it is—there's a civil war breaking out and their secrets are coming out. I've got a lead on someone who may know something and I need more. Are you gonna help?"

"I'm late for class," I said. "Out of curiosity, what's the name?"

"Rhonda Hope," Morven said. "Ring any bells?"

CHAPTER TWELVE

MUZZLE

The clock near the entrance to North Peerpont Hall read a quarter past midnight and I was standing in the half phone booth in the vestibule with a sock full of quarters in one hand. Before I could dial, the phone rang.

I picked up the receiver. "Fuckyouidontwannafuckinbeejay!"

There was a familiar voice on the other end. "Tosh?"

"Yeah?"

"It's Albert."

"Excuse me?"

"Albert McGunter. I taught you math in seventh grade."

"Mr. McGunter! Um, sorry about what I said. We've been getting prank calls."

"It's okay. I don't pretend to know what goes on at a place like Hah-vard!"

"How did you get this number?"

"I saw it on your dad's phone bill. I know you usually call around this time, so I thought I'd cut you off at the pass. I hope you don't mind."

"It's a little strange, but . . ."

"We're all very proud of your success in the Ivy League! I always told people you were more than just Tech the basketball player—you were my best student."

"Thanks, Mr. McGunter. Nobody calls me Tech anymore."

"Yes, I can understand that given what happened. How's your knee?"

"It's not great, but you know."

"That Fairport game was a tough break. Such a memorable championship . . . so sad it had to end that way. That was terrible, just terrible."

"Why are you calling, Mr. McGunter?"

"I ran into your dad buying a Big Mac."

"You're calling about a hamburger?"

"Well, it's more than that."

"I know—his blood sugar. I tell him not to buy fast food, I don't know why—"

"He goes there because it's familiar, maybe to have some human interaction. He talks to the cashiers, other customers. Most of them don't mind because they know you and your family. But that's not the whole story either."

"So what is it?"

"His credit card was declined. I was standing in the line next to him, buying a coffee. He was very agitated, really caused a scene. Nobody called you about this?"

"Wait—his card was denied? His credit card should be good. More than good."

"Well, I don't know if you know this, but his checking account is overdrawn."

"How do you know?"

"I quit teaching two years ago and I do financial planning now. I agreed to help your father sort through his bills after I witnessed his problem with the card. Did I tell you the police were called?"

"Wait—what?"

"It's okay, I vouched for him, they didn't even file a report. The important thing is he's gotta get his finances in order."

"He should have a ton of money in savings."

"He didn't mention anything about a savings account."

"This whole thing has to be a misunderstanding. I have friend at the bank, Ben—maybe he can help."

"Listen, I don't know if your father is capable of handling his own finances. As I said, I've been trying to help him, but I can only do so much. I saw stacks of unopened bills in his kitchen. I don't know if he should be living alone."

"My sister checks in on him like every day."

"Tosh, you might recall I had your sister in class too—I don't need to tell you handling something like this isn't her forte. I could help you more if you could convince your father to let me examine his bank records. I didn't even know about the savings account."

"He used to work for the town. There was this whole disability lump sum."

"Sorry, I'm having trouble hearing you. Are you playing music? I know this kind of thing is hard, and it's easier just to put it out of your mind. I can help, if you want. You should call your father and tell him to let me put his financial house in order. Do you know if he paid property taxes this year?"

"Mr. McGunter, I have to—"

"That music suddenly got really loud. Would you mind turning it down?"

"It's not my music. But maybe we should talk another—"

"There's nothing to be ashamed of, son."

"I'm not—"

"I know in situations like this we tend to blame ourselves. Your sister said his decline started when you were home and she—"

"Mr. McGunter, I just really have to—"

"Have you thought about a home health aide, or assisted living? When is the next time you're going to be in Knockport? We could meet and you could tell me more about the savings account. People in town remember how much you did for the basketball team and they want to help. You were a true student-athlete—when I had you for study hall, you'd sit and read poetry while other kids were gossiping!"

"I did read a lot of poetry, didn't I?"

"You sure did. But we should talk about your father. If you could just turn down that darn music, I could help you think through all this."

"Thanks so much for calling, Mr. McGunter. I just remembered there's somewhere I need to be."

CHAPTER THIRTEEN

DOO WOP (THAT THING)

The reggae beat boomed as I bounded into the basement. "Anyone here?"

There was no answer but the music swelled and the shadows deepened.

I couldn't see any doors, though Tilfer had mentioned that there was a room here somewhere, so I felt around in the dim light along the mural on the wall, down to the floor, and my fingertips brushed a square outline beneath my feet. There was a trapdoor in the floor. I pushed and something clicked and I pulled open a hatch which released with a burst of light and music, and I climbed down a ladder into a lower level.

When my eyes adjusted, I discovered I was looking around at a small room with pale lilac walls and a faded red floor. The reggae beat blaring from some hidden speaker echoed off every surface. Scanning the room I saw a blue washbasin, a brown wooden chair, and a chrome-yellow bed. The smell of curry chicken wafted through the air and I followed my nose toward a small kitchenette and my stomach began to growl in a Jamaican Pavlovian response. There was a small caldron of water boiling on the stove top, which was weird because the heating coils were all off. I couldn't find the curry, but I smiled when I saw rows of mini cereal boxes, presumably looted from the dining hall, stacked up on a cabinet. When I got closer I saw all the cereals were limited-edition Caribbean-themed variations like plantain-flavored Quisp and Cap'n Crunch with naseberries. Whoever lived here was good at swiping shit.

On the desk nearby, there were charcoal pencils, tubes of oil paint, and a few sketches of some muscular Caucasian hunk who didn't fit in with the Afrocentric vibe of the rest of the place. The dude in the artwork looked around my age and was somehow familiar, but because the face was unfinished I couldn't make a positive ID. Next to the desk was a wooden easel draped in a black sheet, and when I pulled it back, there was a canvas with a half-finished painting of yet another white person, this one a young blond woman, her legs long and lean, her naked breasts glistening like newly peeled fruit. The blonde in the painting had a mysterious half smile, eyes that followed you like a store detective, and her snowy cheeks were slightly pocked.

But the thing that hooked my eye was the mural. I had seen an extension of it in the hallway, and in here it spilled onto all four walls of the room. The art was in-the-works but it was already exploding with color—black, gold, and green—like hip-hop graffiti spray-painted across a subway car. Some of the art reminded me of WPA murals, celebrating brawny workers in heroic poses. Many of the images were of protests on campus, like marches around the Yard and sit-ins at Massachusetts Hall. One motif popped up repeatedly: block quotes proclaiming things like, *I know my soul*, and, *I love this cultured hell that tests my youth!* I knew all those quotes—they were from the same Jamaican poet I used to read in high school. I was on the right track.

A small shelf near the bed was stuffed with books, most of their pages dog-eared and tagged with Post-it notes. There were a couple of textbooks by radical legal scholar Geneva Crenshaw and a few plays, like Tremonisha Smarts's male-bashing musical *Wrongheaded Man*. The rest of the titles on the shelf were similarly eclectic, including Rutherford Calhoun's seafaring memoir *Rutherford's Travels*, Arkady Darell's sci-fi epic *Unkeyed Memories*, and some mystical texts, such as *The Garden of Forking Paths* by Ts'ui Pên, *The Key to All Mythologies* by Reverend Edward Casaubon, and *Of the Beginning of Time* by Quennar i Onótimo. On a nearby nightstand were paperbacks of Emmanuel Goldstein's *The Theory and*

Practice of Oligarchical Collectivism and E.G. Morris's *Around Harvard Square*, the latter open with this passage underlined: *The names people give themselves mean more than the ones they are given*. But I didn't see a book by the author I was looking for, the writer behind the quotes on the mural.

A pile of clothing lay on the bed, including T-shirts, leggings, and one of the white aprons of the dining hall staff, and all of it was warm to the touch, fresh from the laundry. When I was in high school, I used to have my uniform washed right before every game so I could slip on a hot-from-the-dryer jersey and pair of shorts just before tip-off. I held some of the laundry from the bed up to my nose and it had that clean toasty smell I recalled from game days, and something else too—what was that aroma exactly?—springtime, sweat, soap, and—that's interesting—a hint of mango? Whatever it was, it was beyond beautiful and I felt like I could breathe again.

Something—a huge mosquito or a tiny hovercraft—zipped by my ear.

I must have been lost in the madeleine cookie moment of it all because whatever buzzed my ear caused me to lose my balance and my elbow knocked into the easel, spilling a jar of green paint onto the front of my shirt and down to the crotch of my pants. This put me in a bit of a panic, because I only had a couple of decent T-shirts and a single pair of jeans and this shit was going to stain if I didn't wash it off soon. I looked around quickly, maybe too quickly, to make sure nobody was coming, and then stripped to rinse off my clothes in the washbasin.

When I was almost completely naked, that's when you walked in.

"Wah di rass?"

The music stopped, our eyes locked, and just like that I warped onto your event horizon. What can I say about what I saw? If I were to write about your looks, almost by definition I'd be reducing you to your appearance. If I were to describe the things about you that drew me in that other guys might not have noticed or appreciated, there's no way that's gonna seem anything but condescending. Maybe there's no way for me to get across what I saw when I saw you, your geyser of dreadlocks, the total eclipse of your cheeks, your brown skin glowing like rum in a bottle. See, I'm doing what men do: sexualizing and objectifying. We're always comparing black women's skin to food and drink, like coffee and chocolate and caramel, like we're about to consume it like dessert or an aperitif. Maybe we should talk about what *you* saw when you saw me. You would have seen a tall, skinny black kid butt naked except for my tighty-whities and tube socks. You might have noticed my almost concave chest, or my nearly hairless arms and legs, or the bad haircut I got from an upstate barber who actually used scissors to trim my fade. I pulled back on my sopping shirt and pants.

"This isn't what it looks like," I mumbled.

"What do you think it looks like?" you said.

"I think it looks like I'm a creep stealing your laundry."

"My panties are too big to fit you—you're tall but you got some small-ass hips."

I couldn't help noticing your lilting West Indian accent and I saw you were holding *The Cycle*—exactly the book I had been expecting to find.

"The quotes in your art—they're all from that poetry collection, right?"

"Well, ram pa pa pam!"

"*If we must die, let it not be like hogs / Hunted and penned in an inglorious spot . . .*"

"*While round us bark the mad and hungry dogs, / Making their mock at our accursèd lot.*" You gave me a brief look of admiration that quickly morphed back to admonition. "So what the hell are you doing in my room?" You spat those last words in flat American tones—your accent ebbed and flowed with your mood.

"Sorry, you must think I'm a stalker. I'm Tosh."

That seemed to relax you. "My favorite Wailer."

"My grandma is from Jamaica."

"I'm from West Omelas."

"Where's that?"

"Off the north coast, near Laputa."

"So what's your name?"

"Zipporah Windward," you said. "But you can call me Zippa."

"But you signed a different name in the *Harpoon* guest book, right? You used the pen name of the poet who wrote the book in your hands—Rhonda Hope."

Your eyes suddenly grew cold. I had crossed some sort of line in your head. A look passed over your face like wind across calm water, and I saw ripples of emotions I couldn't name, and then the surface stirred into a stormy sea. "A wah di rass clot yuh chat 'bout?" you cursed in patois.

"Sorry, I didn't mean . . ."

You were really angry now, in fact it was past anger and well into rage. You snatched some of your undergarments off the bed. "A fuckery dat. Did the Peerponts send you?"

"What? I don't . . ."

A hummingbird—petite as punctuation—flickered into the room and perched on your right shoulder. That explained the buzzing in my ears. The bird had a thin green beak and two black tail feathers that curved behind it like parentheses. You held up a small bottle of sugar water for it to suck but kept your hurricane eyes on me.

"Nuh ramp wid mi," you growled. "If we cross paths at the castle, stay away."

Your hummingbird flicked its tubular tongue at me like a tiny Bronx cheer.

CHAPTER FOURTEEN

CAR WHEELS ON A GRAVEL ROAD

Somebody was giggling on the seventh floor of North Peerpont Hall. It was a weird kind of giggle, somewhere on the laughter spectrum between a titter and a full-blown maniacal laugh, the kind of giggle that makes you wonder not so much what's so funny as what's wrong with the person who makes that kind of sound to express amusement. It was early afternoon and most of the other students from the dorm were at lunch or at class. I was still worked up after my encounter with you and I wanted to get to the bottom of what was up with the crazy laughter. I followed the sound to a door at the end of my hall, and since it was ajar, I let myself in.

Tilfer was there on the floor, surrounded by crumpled-up sheets of paper, yellow legal pads, an open canister of Planters Cheez Balls, two empty boxes of Jell-O Pudding Pops, and three different flavors of a bottled sports drink—one bright red (*Fierce Berry*), the other radioactive-green (*Frost Whitewater Splash*), with a third (*Midnight Thunder*) completely drained.

Tilfer stopped writing and burst into a new fit of giggles.

"You okay?" I asked.

"Busier than a one-legged possum with a b-b-bag full of farts!" Tilfer replied.

"What you just said is not a saying on either side of the Mason-Dixon Line."

Tilfer buried his face in his hands, laughing and snorting.

"Where are your roommates?" I asked.

He looked at me like he hadn't quite realized there was another person in the room, or on the planet, until that moment. "Barron and Dennison? They got p-p-punched and moved out." He shrugged and took a swig from one of his bottles (*Frost Whitewater Splash*), giggling and then sniffling and gagging as sports drink the color of Bruce Banner's alter ego spurted out his nose.

I had heard enough. "What's up with you? You're laughing like a supervillain."

"I'm d-d-doing my *Harpoon* piece."

He snorted and more green beverage bubbled up from his nostrils.

"I'm afraid to ask, but what's it about?"

"It's p-p-personal."

"Come on, all the *Harpoon* editors are gonna see it. Show it to me."

Tilfer handed me what he had been writing. The piece was about this kid who lands a summer job working for a family-owned hardware store in Paducah when a big-box retailer moves in across the street. The kid falls in love with the hardware store owner's daughter, but after she rejects him because he's a small-town kid with no prospects, he goes to work for the superstore and the family store goes under. The tone was more sad than funny and the piece ended with an elegy to mom-and-pop stores everywhere.

I handed Tilfer back his piece. "How do you know about any of this shit?"

"W-w-what do you mean?"

"I thought your family was rich."

"Spooner and I have different moms. My dad didn't bring me up to live with him until high school. I-I-I have family in Paducah."

"Where's that?"

"It's in Kentucky, where the Ohio and Tennessee rivers c-c-come together."

"So you have a mansion down there or something?"

"M-more like a trailer. You never saw broke like the broke I saw growing up."

Like I said, I have only two rules in life: 1) don't talk about race with white people, and 2) don't talk about race with white people. If they ain't down, fuck 'em, 'cause talking to them ain't gonna bring them around. But even if they are down, talking to a white person about race can still fuck with you because even the ones you like are gonna say some fucked-up shit that you can't un-hear. I didn't know if Tilfer was down or not, but I did know the shit he was saying was crazytown and I was gonna have to break both my rules. "What the fuck you know 'bout broke?" I asked.

"My m-m-mom packed me syrup sandwiches for lunch," Tilfer said.

"My mom thought condiments were a vegetable," I replied.

"My f-f-family couldn't afford No. 2 pencils. We had to settle for No. 3s."

"You had pencils? I had to use my index finger and dirt."

"Y-y-you had dirt?"

"Okay, fuck this. You're rich now."

"I w-w-wasn't then."

"But you're rich now."

"What's your p-p-point?"

"Poverty isn't a permanent condition for you folks. You get assimilated."

"Black people get assimilated too! H-h-half the black people at Harvard are half-white! Most of them went to better high schools than I did!"

"What the fuck you know about that?"

"N-n-nothing! I'm j-j-just trying to write about how I-I-I grew up."

"That's the point—that's how you grew up, but that's not where you're at. Now you're in the .0001 percent! You're a Peerpont!"

"You don't know what goes on in my family. Just because you come from money doesn't mean you belong there."

Tilfer went back to scribbling on his legal pad.

My argument with Tilfer had energized me, and when I got back to my room, I went to work. I popped one of Dorian and Davis's red pills and felt the world slip away and took a seat in the common room. Lao and I had agreed to work as a team and share credit on the pieces we submitted to the *Harpoon*; Meera had decided she wanted to do the business comp, so she was working her contacts in India, where it was daytime, trying to sell ads for the magazine.

"We should do something on theater concession stands," Lao suggested. "Everything comes in three sizes—too big, too large, and I'm gonna need a kidney."

"Are you serious?" I said. "Theater snack sizes are the biggest cliché in comedy. Jokes like that only come in one size: too much."

"We could focus on candy—like circus peanuts. The only thing that tastes worse than circus peanuts are packing peanuts. Something like that."

"I don't think most people give a fuck about circus peanuts or packing peanuts. Maybe just focus on peanuts. What about a cartoon where Mr. Peanut takes his family to the ballet—but things turn tragic because they see *The Nutcracker*?"

"Do you need a nutcracker to open a peanut? The Peanut family is in mortal danger pretty much anywhere. Things could take a bad turn for them at *Swan Lake*."

"Okay, what about a piece on candy corn? It's like they were trying to come up with something that tastes worse than vegetables but is still completely bad for you."

Lao plopped down on the couch. "I dunno, this all seems kinda useless. What's our comedic style? Silliness or social commentary?"

"Well, it's a comp, right? So let's be competitive. When I was playing ball, I was at my best when I was aggressive. Let's really go after someone with what we write. Comedy can be cruel. Maybe we should write something about that Morven guy."

"The *Magenta* editor with the alligator boat shoes?"

The pills were really kicking in and I was feeling loose and I started sketching out a concept. Lao looked it over and balked at first, but then he rolled with it and helped me rewrite it. I kept thinking about Morven trying to get me to turn into a whistleblower for the *Harpoon* and that made me think of basketball referees blowing whistles and that always gets me angry. The piece Lao and I ended up writing was ruthless, but I thought it was funny. It was a double-sized story, so we figured it would count as our first two submissions. After we were done, we showed it to Meera.

She was silent for a long time.

"Don't get shy on us now," I said. "What do you think?"

Meera shook her head. "You guys are . . ."

"Hilarious?" I said.

"Geniuses?" Lao said.

". . . better than this."

Lao shook his head. "We're really not."

"What don't you like?" I asked her.

"This piece reminds me of Bollywood," Meera explained. "Which reminds me of school when I was a fifteen-year-old. Which reminds me of hell."

"Why does everything in life seem to boil down to high school?" I asked.

"You don't have to hurt people to be funny," Meera said. "It's not a good look. I've had to deal with guys like that my whole life."

"I think you're making way too much—"

Meera held up a hand. "I've had guys cut me off, cut me down, and steal ideas I just said when I'm still in the room. Then they try and gaslight you, act like you're the one being sensitive when you call them out. In my experience, guys are the fragile ones—they lash out because they can't stand being hurt. It's so *ridiculous*."

"This is not that . . ."

"Your piece feels like you're mocking him for being short. That's like being racist against little people. Is that what you're doing?"

"Not at all."

"Well, it's kinda what we're doing," conceded Lao.

"No, it's not," I argued.

Meera pointed to a line in the piece. "So this part about Bashful, Doc, Dopey, Happy, Sleepy, Sneezy, and Grumpy has nothing to do with height?"

"You're reading too much into it," I said.

"You call Morven a *hairy-footed Hobbit motherfucker*. That's not an attack on how short he is?"

"Hobbits are cool. They invented second breakfast—and elevenses."

"Lao, how would you feel if someone made fun of your missing eye?"

He shrugged. "It's like they say—it's only funny after someone loses an eye."

"That's the *opposite* of what is said." Meera put her head in her hands. "You guys are mental. This is the locker room stuff I had to deal with back in Bollywood."

"This is a comp," I said. "That's not short for *compassion*."

"You guys are better than this." Meera handed me back the piece. "And if you're not, you should be."

CHAPTER FIFTEEN
PAPER CUTS

After our classes, Lao, Meera, and I went to the *Harpoon* to hand in our work. The time was early evening and there was already some sort of party happening on the upper floors where compers weren't allowed to go, and the sound of laughter and dancing feet and a song by that alt-rock band Novacain drifted down to our ears. The group's lead singer had taken his own life and now his songs, which had seemed so punky and petulant before, sounded like suicide notes and it made them that much more raging and real. Dying young is the ultimate amp; death takes you to eleven. As the song rocked on, rattling windows and shaking the walls, Meera registered her sales in a ledger in the castle anteroom. She looked upset.

"How's business?" I asked.

"Not good," she fretted. "There must be a hundred people comping for the business staff. How am I ever going to beat out so many candidates?"

Lao looked at the other names on the business ledger. "Half of these kids are children of CEOs, the other half are children of CFOs. I know this because I sell pot to most of them. They've got connections."

"Can't you tap your Bollywood network?" I asked Meera.

"Don't you think I've been trying?" Meera sighed. "The problem is, I have a lot of enemies in the Indian entertainment industry."

"Why would you have enemies?"

"I've been trying to tell you—"

A low wailing floated into the room that sounded like a dinosaur caught in a tar pit. The sound was mournful and undulating, and if there had been percussion, it might have been a track on a Novacain album. We all dropped what we were talking about to go investigate.

We walked into the library, where there were already maybe fifty other comp pieces scattered across the carpeted floor. In the middle of them sat a boy softly sobbing into a sheath of papers cradled against his face.

I dropped my piece onto the carpet. "Tilfer?"

He had come into the library to read the early comments on his submission. Through the crumple of papers, I could see that his face was even puffier and redder than usual and his chipmunk cheeks were streaked with tears.

Meera rubbed his shoulder. "You're Tilfer Peerpont, right? I'm sure it's not that bad."

Tilfer held out a piece of paper and Lao took it from him and flipped it over, and we all read the comments on the back.

> *What do you know about suffering, summer jobs, and small towns, Mr. White Privilege? Being a legacy doesn't make you funny, and being a Peerpont won't get you on staff. I've had funnier things come out of my vagina, including the time I got a urinary tract infection in San Carlos. Next time you file a story this unfunny you better include a fucking bottle of cranberry juice, you trustfund baby lardass cheesesteak-eating motherfucker. —VLH*

"This is pretty bad," Lao said.

"It's meaner than cattywampus on a d-d-dill pickle," Tilfer sobbed.

"Stop that!" I said. "What you said is not a thing!"

"Just leave him alone," Meera cooed, rubbing Tilfer's back.

As Meera tried to console him, I started reading through some of the other submissions. There were pieces about some stale subjects: ex-girlfriends, ex-boyfriends, and—Lao and I dodged a bullet—one about Mr. Peanut fucking someone with a peanut allergy. There were a couple submissions that were fresh and funny, including a great one about whether or not Pluto was a real planet, although it ended with a cheap joke involving Uranus, and an even dirtier one about the Virgo Cluster. I got worried that my thunder had been stolen when I read a story by someone making fun of *Magenta* editors, since that was what we were doing, but the rival piece was toothless and I decided it wasn't a threat. Most of the pieces had comments from *Harpoon* staff members scrawled on the back, each editor identifying him- or herself by their initials. The *Harpoon* editors were brutally honest when it came to critiquing the submissions and most of the comments were sharper and funnier than the pieces that had been turned in.

I picked up a packet of cartoons, which turned out to be your submission. I could see at first glance there was a level of craft that went beyond anything in the room. Your artwork was striking, with bright colors and bold lines, and the humor was cutting, making strong points about race, inequality, and everyday life. You had a fully developed style and point of view and your color palette made me think of tropical waters, anime, and hip-hop graffiti all at once.

"This is pretty special," I said.

"Brilliant!" Meera agreed, peeking over my shoulder.

"The real question is, what kind of feedback did she get?" Lao said.

I flipped the piece over. There was a comment from Vecky: *This piece is so brilliant it reminds me that Tilfer Peerpont's was a piece of shit. —VLH*

Tilfer began to sob even louder.

Meera patted his shoulder. "Don't let Vecky get to you."

"Yeah," I added, "maybe I'll write my next piece about her."

Meera suddenly motioned for me to quiet down, Lao mouthed the word *Stop*, and Tilfer looked petrified, but I had just popped one of Davis and Dorian's little red pills and I was feeling that uninhibited, unhinged, unstoppable feeling that had earned me my goddamn nickname back when I used to play. That imaginary ref was right in front of me making that T sign with his imaginary hands and blowing his imaginary whistle, but like I always do, I just kept on charging ahead. There's something about official unfairness that rings me like a bell. I could hear the imaginary crowd chanting, *Tech! Tech! Tech!* and I just kept on going.

"That's exactly what I'll do—I'll write a piece about Vecky," I boasted. "Remember that stupid speech she gave in the dining hall? Nobody laughed because she's frigid as a fish!" I then launched into an impression of Vecky's New Orleans accent, an imitation of her green-hair flip, and a pantomime of her stumbling in her Rollerblades. "I've got a great title for my piece: 'The Icewoman Cometh!'"

Behind me, I heard the bright jangle of a ring of keys.

CHAPTER SIXTEEN

MYSTERIOUS WAYS

Tilfer was quivering like a dashboard bobblehead, Lao was covering his face with his hands, Meera was looking at me with withering disapproval, and my knees were shaking like I was a bad free-throw shooter stepping to the line. I felt Rorschach tests of sweat spreading around my armpits. "I-I-I don't know why I just said all that," I stammered. "That wasn't me."

Vecky had skated up behind me on her damn Rollerblades. "I hate when people talk shit behind my back." I started to reply but she lifted one finger. "I want to show you something."

Holding my just-submitted double-sized piece in one hand, she used her other hand to pull out a silver skeleton key from the ring on her belt. "The *Harpoon* is about safeguarding traditions," she said. "That's why we have the great Vault of Time on the thirteenth floor where only members can go. Down here, for the compers, we have two other lockboxes you should know about."

She motioned for us to follow her into the next room, a huge chamber with arched ceilings and a Sistine Chapel–ish mural showing angels fluttering in a heavenly light on one side and sinners suffering in the fires of hell on the other. Vecky used her key to open a gilded lockbox, pulled out a folder of manuscripts, and flipped her green hair out of her eyes. "This is the Golden Cabinet. Inside are the greatest pieces ever submitted for the comp, by writers like Killy Trout and Heinz Beck. They were once where you are, but now they're legends."

She held out the comp pieces so we could see—they were all wrinkled and yellowed to varying degrees and they dated from decades past to just a few years ago. There was a funny poem about getting blackballed by the Frog Club ("The Toad Not Taken"), a fantasy send-up set in modern-day Sweden ("Fjord of the Rings"), another set in an Upper East Side apartment building ("Landlord of the Rings"), and a cartoon about a presidential assassination in which it turns out the actual target was Bugs Bunny and the accidental assassin was Elmer Fudd. There were humorous takes on Prohibition, on Desert Storm, on domestic robots. Some of the articles were instantly amusing, others quietly droll, and a few laugh-out-loud funny. I got a little sick of the sword-and-sorcery parodies, but I had to laugh at the one about a Middle-earth-themed buffet ("Smorgasbord of the Rings"). All the pieces were signed with initials—*VCP, CP, CB, VLH, KKT, NZ*, and so on.

"VCP—th-th-that's my dad," Tilfer stuttered.

"HB is probably Heinz Beck," Lao speculated. "I'm guessing KKT is Killy Trout even though I'm not certain about his middle name."

"NZ has to be Natty Zuckerman," I said.

"Who is CB?" Meera asked.

"CB was on the staff about two decades ago," Vecky said. "Some of these are so old we don't even know who wrote them, we only know the initials."

Lao peeked over her shoulder. "That's you—*VLH*."

"You have good eyes—or eye." Vecky pulled out one thick submission and flipped through it wistfully. "I spent two semesters writing this 20,000-word comp piece and my proudest moment was when it made the Golden Cabinet."

Lao took the piece out of Vecky's hand. "This is a book-length manuscript about the benefits of a probiotic diet."

Vecky smiled. "Exactly."

Lao skimmed through the booklet. "Sauerkraut . . . kombucha . . . kimchi. Where are the jokes?"

"Humor is more than funny ha-ha," Vecky replied. "It's about making people feel good about themselves. What makes people feel better than a probiotic diet?"

Lao scowled. "There's twenty pages about you taking a shit."

"I wouldn't expect a man to understand it," Vecky sniffed, and returned the manuscripts to the Golden Cabinet. "You want to know why I'm tough on compers? These pieces are why. It takes talent to make this staff and I intend to keep it that way. I'm diversifying the *Harpoon* but I'm going to make it deeper, not thinner."

Vecky turned to a gray safe mounted in the wall, entered the combination, and pulled out another stack of papers. "Welcome to our Legion of Dishonor. These are the worst *Harpoon* comp articles ever. Most of these were submitted by people you've never heard of, and probably never will."

She showed us some of the submissions—a number of them were wildly inappropriate riffs about deadly diseases, like polio and AIDS, others were bigoted screeds that targeted racial and LGBT groups, and all of them were horribly, howlingly, blindingly unfunny, so much so that reading them made one's face hurt and eyes water, and left the reader feeling deeply ashamed for the human species.

"But shouldn't comedy take chances, like Spooner said?" I asked.

Vecky shook her head. "Comedy isn't a gun, it's a bulletproof vest."

"Meaning?"

"Jokes should help, not hurt. You use them to tackle taboos or as safety valves for aggression or to get a Neanderthal to laugh instead of clubbing you to death. Easy targets aren't funny targets. When Lemuel Gulliver wrote about his travels among the Lilliputians, he was satirizing Britain, not fucking with actual dwarves."

At the word *dwarves*, Meera shot me an I-told-you-so look. I thought about my piece and my forehead got red hot.

Vecky thumbed through the Legion of Dishonor and pulled out a sheet of paper. "I know this guy, he had some talent. I used to tell him, *You're getting laughs, but not the laughs you need to get.* He didn't listen, so he ended up in the Legion of Dishonor. But we can only keep ten pieces in the lockbox at a time, and this guy's offensive shit is finally being bumped for some new offensive shit."

I scanned the article. It was an icky piece mocking gay and transgender kids and it was signed MSM. "Morven S. Morlington? Editor of the *Magenta*? He wrote this?"

"Why do you think he hates us?" Vecky replied. "Why do you think he had my alligator turned into his *goddamn boat shoes*? That gator was my *pet*, she was the unofficial mascot of this place, she was loved . . ." She stopped short, composed herself, and flicked away a tear. "Anyhoo, before all of that, back when he was comping for the *Harpoon*, Morven thought shock humor would get him over. But we cut his ass instead and he crawled over to the *Magenta*."

"What's taking his place?" Meera asked.

"Funny you should ask," Vecky said. "But not funny ha-ha."

She pulled out the story that Lao and I had submitted about Morven, and added it to the stack of Legion of Dishonor pieces. When she closed the safe, the sound seemed to echo.

"We're holding a vote soon to decide who is going to be *Harpoon* president," Vecky declared. "Ever since I was a little girl, I wanted to write for a late-night comedy program. I got an internship on a show my sophomore year, and I thought I was killing it—until I overheard the male writers talking shit about me. Literally they were talking shit, because I hid out in a stall in the men's room to find out what they were saying. My point is that comedy is a boys club and I need to be president of the *Harpoon*—not just interim—if any of the head writers are gonna take me seriously. I have to beat Spooner in this election."

"Why are you telling us this?" Meera asked. "We're just compers."

"All editors get to vote, including new ones, and I get the feeling that you're more like Spooner than you are like me. I can't have you adding to his voter base."

I started to speak but she put her finger to her lips again.

"I'm going to keep your piece locked up in the Legion of Dishonor, and I'm gonna make sure every other editor reads it," she said. "You done fucked up. Once everyone sees the shit you wrote about our undersized brothers and sisters, you're never gonna make it onto the *Harpoon* staff."

I put my head in my hands. "We're finished before we even started."

Vecky winked. "That's what she said!"

CHAPTER SEVENTEEN

COMING CLEAN

"She's a *beeeeetch* on wheels, am I right?"

Her keys jangling, Vecky had Rollerbladed out of the castle. It was getting late, and I had to study for my economics class, and we were all going to leave, but we heard a voice coming from the shadows of the stairwell. His golden goblet in hand, Spooner strolled into the light.

"Yeah, I know she's president—acting president—but she's still a *beeeeetch*!" Spooner continued. "Go ahead, you can agree with me, I won't tell her."

"Uh . . ." I said.

Spooner clapped me on the shoulder. "I thought your piece was hilarious."

"Wait—what?" Meera said.

Spooner grinned. "Comedy means never having to say you're sorry."

"Did you even read our submission?" I asked.

"I didn't have to. You're taking the piss out of midgets, and that's good enough for me. Humor is making fun of our fears. What do people fear the most?"

"Humiliation?" Meera said.

"Robots?" Lao said.

"Being completely forgotten as the universe expands endlessly?" I said.

"Wrong, wrong, wrong," Spooner said. "People fear other races, other cultures, other others. They're afraid they'll say something racist or sexist or homophobic or, worst of all, some phobic that they haven't come up with yet so there's no way to guard against it."

"It's not funny if someone gets hurt . . ." Meera started to say.

"It's only funny *when* it hurts! Funny is when someone slips on a banana peel—*not funny* is when someone falls on a padded mat. Pain is what makes the joke. If you have safe spaces and political correctness, you can't have pain, and you can't have humor. I don't want to live in a world like that, I don't want to go to a college like that, and I don't want the *Harpoon* to become like that."

Meera shook her head. "Making fun of people who are in pain isn't being a comic, it's being a bully."

"We fuck around with everyone here," Spooner said. "Like that one fat girl who's comping—if she makes it on, she better be prepared to get roasted."

"Who are you talking about?" I asked.

"That big-boned Jamaican girl, mon," Spooner replied in a fake island accent.

"Don't talk about her like that—that's not funny."

Spooner laughed. "You know who doesn't have a sense of humor? Dictators. The Third Reich was a bunch of thin-skinned motherfuckers."

"Really?" Meera scoffed. "Straight to the Nazi analogy?"

"Let me try another approach. How many times does Jesus smile or joke in the New Testament?"

"Don't know, don't care—I'm Hindu."

"Well, *namaste* to you," Spooner said, bowing, his hands pressed together over the stem of his golden goblet. "The answer to my question is zero. Jesus does laugh in the Apocrypha—the books the Church cut from the Bible. What does that tell you?"

"Again, the Bhagavad Gita is more my thing."

"The answer is sanctimonious prigs don't have a sense of humor. The Church has such a fucking rod up its own ass it couldn't imagine a God that smiles. Fuck that—my God has a sense of humor and the Bible is *hilarious*. Mary tells Joseph that

God knocked her up and he still believes she's a virgin? That's funny as shit."

Meera shook her head. "I don't know about Jesus and virgins. I just think comedy should be a place everyone feels comfortable. Is that too much to ask?"

"Yes, it is. Wasn't the whole point of feminism to make it inside the boys club? Well, guess what's inside? A bunch of boys with their clubs hanging out. You may not like it, but that's what you wanted."

"You're missing the point of feminism."

"You're missing the point of comedy. A punch line is supposed to surprise you, to wake you up, to make you uncomfortable. The release comes afterward, after you've said and heard the naughtiest, nastiest things in the world and the world doesn't come to an end after you've said and heard it. It's like an orgasm—if you're not willing to get naked, it's not going to work. You have had an orgasm, haven't you?"

Meera crossed her arms. "You sound like an overprivileged white male who's never had to deal with being the butt of a joke."

"Where have you been for the last century? Rich white guys are the last people it's okay to mock, am I right? I would give my ball sack not to be a white man. We're about to be a demographic minority and we get no support. I had to earn my spot at this college with zero special privileges—or I could have ended up like *that* one."

Spooner pointed at Tilfer, who began to stammer, "W-w-w-w-w—"

"Come on, fat boy, use your words!" Spooner mocked.

"W-w-w-w-w-w . . ."

Spooner sneered. "You never would have gotten into Harvard if Dad and I hadn't legacied your fat ass in the door, and you sure as hell don't deserve to be on the *Harpoon*!"

Tilfer shrank away and Spooner kicked him in his butt as he slipped out.

"Here's the difference between me and Vecky," Spooner continued, sipping his goblet. "Vecky wants to diversify this place, I want to make it stronger. She wants to make jokes off-limits, I say the only limit is your tolerance for pain. She wants to be a late-night comedy god and I'm like, *Not with those tits, you're not*. One of us is gonna be president. You guys can decide who you want to get behind."

Spooner reached into his pocket and pulled out a key. "Here's the deal: I made a copy of Vecky's key and I can unlock the Legion of Dishonor and tear up your piece so you'll still have a shot at making it on the staff. If I do that, you'll have to do something for me."

I swallowed hard. "What's the something?"

CHAPTER EIGHTEEN

THE MASK

Somehow I ended up at some stupid party at Kirkland House and I was being talked at by some Goth from Adams House with black eye-makeup and black lipstick and black fingernails and knee-high black boots. I had had too much to drink and so had she and I couldn't quite catch her words and they seemed to flutter out of her mouth with piercing little cries and leather wings like black bats from a cave.

Sue? Was that this white girl's name? She was taking a long drag on a thin white cigarette and the tip was bloodred from her lipstick. She was saying something else in her screeching bat language but I wasn't really listening because as soon as she said something about interning at a hedge fund, followed hard by something about liquidity and dead-cat bounces, somewhere along the line she got impossible to follow, like trying to unfold a map while driving at night on a twisty road in the Adirondacks. I looked around the party and it was full of Final Club androids and new pledge robots, and one of the pledges—as some sort of hazing thing—was collecting spit in a cup which he said he was going to do shots with later. If you want to be beaten, join 'em. Screech screech. I was trying to escape it, but the *Harpoon* was on my mind and it was hard to focus on anything else. I had to get away from this party, this Goth from Adams House, these Final Club phonies, these spit-drinking pledges.

I tried to turn away, but the Goth from Adams House kept talking. A bunch of jocks wandered into the room and they were still wearing their jerseys and I thought how sad it is that those numbers on their backs really don't add up to anything. Then I thought, *Hey, that's a good one, I should write that down somewhere*. Then I thought, *That's so good it's easy, and someone at some point probably said it already*. The jocks were forming huddles around the room and laughing loudly and getting drunker.

There were people on the dance floor and I thought about asking the Goth from Adams House to dance just so I wouldn't have to keep talking about what she was talking about, which was all derivatives and arbitrage and subprime loans. I was surprised people were dancing at this party because people don't always dance at Harvard. I only had a small sample set, but Harvard students seemed to have lost that critical connection between their souls and the soles of their feet. When they did dance, it was this twitchy gallop that wasn't entirely dissimilar to the jerky little jig people do when they have to urinate really bad. The whole party was getting into it now, wiggling their hips and hopping all at the same time.

I realized then that people at the party were doing the Macarena. Not in an ironic way, they were really doing it.

The lights at the party strobed with the music, but I couldn't tell if it was real or in my head, and I saw one of the Final Club phonies lean over to give a girl a kiss and I could see the slick flash of tongue, and when they pulled apart there was a long line of saliva stretching between their lips for a shimmering second, and then it was gone.

The girl was gone too and I noticed Lao and Meera were next to me.

"What are you doing here?" I asked.

Meera smiled. "The Macarena, of course."

"So you saw the dancing."

"I can't un-see it."

"Maybe you should show them how dancing is really done."

"And do a dance from one of my Bollywood movies? They can buy a ticket. I don't do private dances and I'm not available for parties."

Lao scanned the room. "It's cultural appropriation, but at least it's cultural. There's worse kinds of dancing than the Macarena."

"Like what?" I asked. "The Lambada?"

"Square dancing."

"How do you know anything about square dancing?"

"Square dancing is the official dance for like half the states in the US."

"Okay, I'll bite," Meera said. "What's the backstory?"

"Racist, antisemitic industrialists bent on keeping the culture pure funded a campaign to make square dancing a thing to compete with the spread of dancing to black music. Look it up, it's true. Why else would square dancing be the official state dance of Connecticut?"

Meera's eyes opened wide. "That *is* worse than the Macarena."

Lao sipped suds from a plastic cup. "So we gonna drop out of the *Harpoon* comp? Seems pointless to go where we're not wanted."

"I don't know about that. When my parents moved to Knockport in the 1970s, nobody would sell them a house, because the town was all white and we were all black. Finally, one family that was taking a long vacation let them rent out their basement. My parents loved the area—great schools, lots of land, job opportunities. My mom and dad ended up building their own house and settling there permanently."

"So you're saying we need to stay with this?"

"They wouldn't be fighting so hard to keep us off the staff unless getting on the staff was worth it."

"Did you think about Spooner's offer?" Meera asked.

I nodded.

"And?"

"I think we need to get out of here before anyone starts doing the dosey-do."

We bought a couple cases of this Zima shit from a convenience store in the Square and began drinking it out of paper bags as we stumbled past the homeless people sleeping on the sidewalks on Mass Ave., and then we wobbled through the Yard but never made it past the John Harvard statue. Zima's like this clear sugary alcoholic beverage aimed at younger drinkers—kind of the first step before you need eleven steps more. Almost every other freshman was asleep, and the lateness of the hour, the shadows of the night, and too many Zimae began to play tricks on my body and pranks on my head. The Zima had been Lao's idea and I don't know what's in it, but it made me feel warm and dirty at the same time, like when you piss in a public pool.

I shook my head. "Zima tastes like what a pedophile would give a seventh grader."

Meera nodded. "It's like a wine cooler and a urine sample had a baby."

Lao stuck out his tongue. "It's like if the Kool-Aid Man came in my mouth."

I blinked and the world blurred and inanimate objects began to mutate. "I'm a monster," I blurted out.

Meera rubbed my shoulder. "Why are you saying that?"

"*What you laugh at is who you are.* You were right, I never should have handed in that piece. I want to get on the *Harpoon*, but maybe I don't deserve it after that. I'm like a Sith Lord now, and the dark side blows. I mean it's cool you can shoot lightning out of your fingers, and Darth is a badass honorific, but every time you build a Death Star it gets blown up. I should have trusted the Force."

"I hate those movies," Lao grumbled.

"What? Why? Let me guess—robots."

"The robots in the series are slaves! They have to put restraining bolts on them to stop them from running away."

"So? I thought you hated robots."

"I do, but that doesn't mean I want to see sentient creatures in chains, doing the bidding of their masters. Someone would have to be a sick mother—*shut your mouth*—to enjoy the films in that franchise. After Y2K, when the robots take over, anyone with a *Star Wars* ticket stub is gonna face a fucking truth-and-reconciliation commission."

That's when you passed by. You were with what seemed to be a group of tourists in cargo shorts and polo shirts. When you spotted me you said your goodbyes to them and came over to where we were. Perched on your shoulder, your hummingbird flicked its tongue out at me.

"Well, ram pa pa pam! We meet again," you said.

"Wait—you're talking to me now?"

"Hey, everything is everything. I heard you made the Legion of Dishonor. If people in power hate you that much, you must be doing something right."

"Thanks, I guess," I said.

"Don't thank me too much, because I think your piece was fucked up."

"You read it?"

"Picking on little people doesn't seem your speed."

"How do you know my speed?"

"First day of school, I saw you get your ass kicked helping an overweight kid. I have a soft spot for people who help people with soft spots."

I looked down at my sneakers. "I didn't help much."

"At least you did something. For every inaction there is an unequal and opposite oppression. Truth."

Meera cleared her throat. "I'm pretty certain that's not Newton's Third Law of Motion. How do you two know each other?"

I made the introductions and you sat down with us next to John Harvard as the bird on your shoulder fluttered his wings.

"Cute bird," Meera said.

You smiled. "I had to smuggle him past customs—green-billed swallow-tailed hummingbirds are an endangered species. They're nearly impossible to catch, but assholes slow them down by grinding up drugs and sprinkling them on flowers. My grandma found lil' Festus after poachers took his parents—now where I go, he goes."

"Are you afraid it'll fly away?" I asked. "Or natural predators?"

"*Unnatural* predators are the threat," you said. "Cats are evil motherfuckers."

"I saw you at the dining hall strike," Lao slurred.

"The richest university on earth won't pay us a living wage," you said. "Workers have to shower at the YMCA because they don't have hot water at home. I go home every night with doggie bags full of food other students don't finish. It's fuckery."

"You can drink with us for free," Lao said, handing you a bottle.

You laughed. "It's not Red Stripe, but it'll do."

"So how do you do it?" I asked. "People at the *Harpoon* love your stuff. What are we doing wrong?"'

You took a sip. "History."

"How is history gonna help us with the present?" I asked.

"Invisible things have visible effects," you said.

"Wait—what?' Lao said.

"I get it," Meera said. "It's like dark matter—the space between the stars seems empty but it has its own gravitational pull, whether we see it or not."

"Exactly, mon." You pointed beyond Straus Hall. "Just past Straus Gate, in 1755, Cambridge executed two runaway slaves, Mark and Phillis, by hanging him and burning her alive. Students in the Yard could smell roasting flesh."

Meera gasped. "Oh my god, that's terrible!"

"*The women thronged to look, but never a one / Showed sorrow in her eyes of steely blue . . .*" you began.

"*. . . And little lads, lynchers that were to be / Danced round the dreadful thing in fiendish glee,*" I finished. "The artist formerly known as Rhonda Hope."

"Very good," you said.

"I try."

"Get a room," Lao growled.

You pointed at John Harvard. "You know why that's the statue of three lies?"

I shook my head.

"Look at the inscription," you commanded.

"*John Harvard, Founder, 1638,*" I read aloud.

"Lie number one: Harvard was founded in 1636, not 1638," you said.

"Maybe that's just a mistake, not a lie," Meera said.

"A mistake can be a liar's way of covering their tracks," you responded. "Lie number two, John Harvard didn't found Harvard."

"Wait a second," I said. "John *Harvard* didn't found Harvard?"

You took a long draw from the bottle. "He was just a guy who donated books and cash to the school, which had been established two years before. So right from the start Harvard was giving big donors more credit than they deserved."

"What's lie number three?" Meera asked.

"Number three, that's not John Harvard."

"Are you serious?" I asked.

"There are no known images of him. The sculptor had no idea what he looked like, so he got a pal to pose for the head and he pulled the rest out of his ass."

I looked up at the statue. "He looks kinda like the Great Emancipator."

"The sculptor also did the Lincoln Memorial—he specialized in great men in chairs. I'm sure if the artist had lived long enough, FDR would have been next."

"You should be a tour guide," Meera said.

"I used to lead tours back in Jamaica. I would show people my part of the island, sell them my artwork, paint their portraits next to local sites. I've been leading tours around Harvard Square for extra cash."

"But you're a freshman!" I said. "How do you know anything about this area?"

"I pick things up," you answered. "Cambridge is full of stories about all sorts of things—secret slave graveyards, hidden butterfly preserves. Did you know square dancing is the offical state dance of Massachusetts?"

"Somehow that doesn't surprise me," Lao said dryly.

You pointed at the John Harvard statue. "How about this—look at Johnny's left boot."

"It's shinier than the one on the right," I observed.

"That's because guides tells tourists that if they rub it, their kids will go to Harvard—and students here, late at night, just to be jerks, piss on the boot."

"What does any of this have to do with the *Harpoon*?" I asked.

You sipped your beer. "Sometimes you need a guide."

"Like a mentor?"

"That's a great idea!" Meera clapped. "Tosh, it's like that story you told us about your hometown—your parents needed an insider to establish themselves. They do the same kind of thing in Bollywood—veterans will take newcomers under their wing!"

"How are we going to find someone like that at the *Harpoon*?" Lao asked.

"There's Spooner," I said. "But I don't trust him and don't want to owe him."

"What's the something he wanted us to do?" Lao asked.

"I'm sure nothing good," I said.

Meera punched me in the shoulder. "Remember? Vecky showed us the best pieces ever written for the *Harpoon*. If we could get one of those authors to help . . ."

"Heinz Beck is a Hollywood producer now—we'll never reach him," Lao said. "Killy Trout is a recluse, and Jack Reed died seventy years ago."

"Well, whatever you decide, get yourself a tour guide," you advised. "The white boys act like they're doing it by themselves, but they have guides behind the scenes helping them every step of the way. Family money fuels their rugged individualism. Truth."

"Who is *your* tour guide?" Meera asked.

You shrugged. "I have someone who helps out."

"None of this even matters," I said. "I'm in the Legion of Dishonor, remember? Once all the other editors see that piece we wrote, they're never gonna let me on the staff. I fucked myself, but good."

You smiled. "That's where you're wrong." You pulled out my work that had been in the Legion of Dishonor, ripped it in two, and handed the pieces to me.

I stared at you wide-eyed. "How did you get this?"

You winked. "I told you, I pick things up."

"You saved my comp," I said. "You saved my life!"

Lao looked like he was going to say thanks—then he threw up right at your feet. Festus, startled, rocketed off your shoulder and hovered above all our heads.

"Wah di rass!" you shouted.

"I'm drunk, I'm sorry," Lao croaked.

You left to clean off, and after that our vigil turned into a celebration of our new lease on life at the *Harpoon*, and we all kept drinking at the base of the statue—even Lao, who'd had too much already. I lost count of how many bottles I had downed when I ran out of fingers to count them on, or maybe it was after all my fingers blurred into a single paw and then the entire Yard turned like a kaleidoscope. John Harvard appeared to have three heads, the cloak around his shoulder spread out like a bat's wings, and his bronze skin glittered like he was frozen in ice.

I woke up in an unfamiliar bed.

CHAPTER NINETEEN

DIVORCE SONG

As the morning slanted through the venetian blinds, I woke to Meera standing over me, and the only evidence that I wasn't dead was her smile. Meera's smile was as sweet as cereal milk. I was dizzy from the night before but I figured out I had to be in her room. The walls were plastered with posters from her movies, laminated photos of her in character, and framed costumes that she had worn during the film shoots. Judging from the photos, Meera had made an adorable little boy. But my eye was drawn to one memento in particular, captured behind glass in a large silver frame—a purple midriff-baring sari with an emerald sash embroidered with flowers. Low cut at the top, and with a thigh-high split on the side, the gauzy outfit looked like a *Kama Sutra* position waiting to happen and was more sexualized than anything I had seen on Meera.

"What's the story with that dress?"

"I wore it in my final film," Meera said. "The role was supposed to take me from child star to sex symbol. The movie was a big hit, but I decided I didn't want make a living having people ogling my cleavage."

"It's very . . . fashionable."

"Maybe, but I have no interest in sexiness, sex, or anything like that."

"Seriously?"

"I'm not closeted or repressed or anything. I just don't care. Intercourse holds as much interest to me as Greco-Roman wrestling, maybe less because at least that's an Olympic sport. I keep the dress to remind me why I left Mumbai."

"So you're really okay with the no-sex thing?"

"Are you *not* okay with me being okay with it?"

I needed a joke to get me out of this. "I just liked the dress. I guess Bollywood is never having to say you're sari."

She punched my shoulder. "I'll blame that pun on your hang-over."

I stumbled out of bed and into the common room. I couldn't resist doing some snooping. Near the TV there was a video game console and a dozen game cartridges, all of them labeled in Hindi. "I thought you hated video games," I said.

"I don't hate them—I hate what they've become," Meera replied.

The cover of one of the cartridges featured a woman in an elegant golden sari next to a man with blue skin. "Is this how you got so good at playing them?"

"Give that back!" Meera said, snatching the video game out of my hand. She stuffed it into her aquamarine backpack. "I've been meaning to throw that out."

There was a tremendous groan from the bathroom.

"That sounds like Lao," I said.

"He's in there throwing up everything from last night," Meera said. "Speaking of last night, you were talking in your sleep."

"Oh no."

"You kept calling out, *Tech! Tech!* That's what your old roommates called you outside the Frog Club. What's that mean?"

"*Tech* was my nickname when I played basketball."

"Why would they call you that?"

"It's complicated."

"Whenever people say something's complicated, it's usually pretty simple."

"Do you know anything about basketball?"

"Of course I do! But I much prefer cricket or *kabaddi*."

"What's *kabaddi*?"

"It's a wonderful Indian pastime! Two teams of seven players face off in a square field. Each team sends raiders across the field and the raider has to keep yelling, *Kabaddi!* without inhaling and cannot stop repeating—"

"That sounds . . . ridiculous."

"Big men dunking orange balls into tiny holes sounds serious?"

"Basketball's the only court where you can get judged fairly—at least I used to think that." I glanced around the room. "This is a double—where's your roommate?"

"Miss Angela Sabina? She has a boyfriend at the Frog Club. After three days she grabbed her things, flipped her blond curls, and hasn't been back here since. I slept in her room last night."

"The Final Clubs are like the Rapture for rich people."

Meera's phone rang and I instinctively picked it up. "Hello?" I said.

"Ehhff . . . seee . . ." I heard heavy breathing. "I was wondering if you might be interested in a little . . . action."

I hung up.

"Who was it?" Meera asked.

"Some perv," I said.

Lao tottered into the room, hands on his head. "What's all that ringing?"

My head was pounding too and my knee felt terrible, so I sat down on a couch in the common room.

"You okay?" Meera asked.

"I'm just thinking about the *Harpoon*," I said. "Vecky *and* Spooner are our enemies—we're in the DMZ and both sides are shooting at us. We need help."

"So what about Zippa's tour-guide idea?"

"We already covered that. I don't know any *Harpoon* alums, do you?"

"There's one we didn't consider: CB from the Golden Cabinet."

"CB would be terrific if we knew CB's actual name and had some way of reaching out. We don't have either."

"I had an idea this morning," Meera said. "We just need the Red Book."

"Mao's Little Red Book?" I asked.

"Why did you look at me when you said that, you racist?" Lao said.

"*Harvard's* little Red Book," Meera said. "You really don't know about this?"

"I have no idea what you're talking about," I said.

"You've lost me too," Lao said.

Meera rolled her eyes. "You guys need to get to the library more. Follow me!"

We left the room and headed over to Widener Library, going up the wide stone steps at the entrance two at time and rushing past the ivory columns. It was still early in the morning and Widener wasn't open yet, but one of the librarians recognized Meera as a frequent visitor and let us all slip inside.

"You have to be a real nerd when Harvard librarians recognize you," I said.

Meera laughed. "Do you know the story behind Widener?"

"I know sometimes people come down to the stacks to get it on," Lao said.

"That would be in the fiction section," Meera said. "The story I was thinking about has to do with the *Titanic*."

"I hate that movie," Lao said. "Why couldn't they both squeeze on the door?"

"Jack lets go of the door so Rose can live," I said. "That's fucking poetic."

"They *both* should have survived!" Meera said. "It's not about the size of the door—it's about *buoyancy*. I did the math—it's basic fluid mechanics, with an adjustment for how saltwater would affect the door's ability to float. But this isn't about the movie—I'm talking about the *real Titanic*."

"What does that have to do with Harvard?" Lao asked.

"In 1912, one of the Widener kids drowned when the ship sank," Meera explained. "Legend has it he was big bibliophile and he died going back to his stateroom for a rare book. The mom wanted a memorial, so she donated money to build this library."

"That's got to be an urban myth," I said.

"It gets more interesting. The story goes that the Widener money came with three conditions. One—not a single brick could be changed, ever. Two—every Harvard student would have to pass a swim test to graduate. And three, the Red Room."

"What's the Red Room?" I asked.

"You're about to find out," Meera said.

We followed Meera deep into the stacks until we came to a small red door. She opened it and motioned for us to follow her. I had to bend down to squeeze through. Inside the room, every shelf was lined with red books and every table was bursting with red flowers. "The boy who died on the *Titanic*, red flowers were his favorite. His mother's final condition was for this room to be filled with fresh red flowers every day, forever. Only the librarians know where they get them all from."

"Why are all the books in here red?" I asked.

Meera ran her hand along the shelves. "There's another part to this story. When you graduate, you get a 'Red Book' with the contact information for everyone in your class, and you get an updated edition every five years. They've been publishing them since 1642, even before the Wideners built this place."

"How many people did they have in the class back then?" Lao asked.

"Nine—but they still wanted to network," Meera said. "A hundred years before America was even invented, Harvard grads were building a good old boys club."

"It's crazy that you know all this," I said.

"You spend time in the library, you learn stuff—funny how that works!" Meera pulled a Red Book off the shelf. "Vecky said CB graduated twenty-five years ago, right? This is the most recent edition for that class."

We started flipping through the book. Beneath each name

there was a brief bio about what the person had been up to for the last five years. A lot of the folks in this class had gone on to do big things—there were a couple college professors, a few CEOs, a bunch of published authors.

"I count six people with the initials *CB* in this class," Meera said.

"Three of them don't list e-mail addresses or phone numbers," I said. "We don't have time to write letters."

"One of them has to be our guy," Lao said. "Are we missing something?"

"Why do you keep saying *guys*?" Meera complained. "CB could be a woman. Maybe she changed her name or something."

I thought about that for a few moments, and I started to laugh.

"What's so funny?" Meera asked.

"You were right," I smiled. "Sometimes complicated things are pretty simple."

CHAPTER TWENTY

LOSER

Professor Hyacinth Bell was writing questions on the blackboard faster than any of us could copy them down in our notebooks. The time was 8:15 a.m. and everyone except the Chair was still in a state of REM sleep. Meera was still wearing the sweats she slept in, Lao was still nibbling on a bagel he had snagged back at breakfast, and my sneakers were still slick from the morning dew on the grass I had to slide across to get to class before I was late. Maybe there's no ideal time to confront the eternal questions of the universe, but before the morning's caffeine has kicked in definitely isn't the right moment. None of this deterred the Chair from continuing to scribble out philosophical queries in a cloud of chalk dust.

Why is there something instead of nothing? she scrawled.

Does free will exist?
Can you justify happiness in a world of suffering?
Is love just a chemical reaction?
Why are you yourself instead of somebody else?
Is the world random or predetermined and aren't both conditions disturbing?
Is reality real?
Is reality a computer program?
Is reality a video game?
What is free will?
What is consciousness?
Does God exist?

Does the Devil exist?
Why the hell would God create the Devil?
Where is the soul?
Do you even have a soul?
Is there a difference between humans and animals?
Is meat murder?
Can a computer think?
Can humans think?
Are humans computers that think they're human?
Why should we be moral?
In a vast universe with billions of stars, why does anything a single person does matter?
Does it matter if our lives don't matter?
Is this life all there is?

The stream of eternal questions flowed on endlessly like a river of chalk, and after she filled the blackboard she erased what she had written and began to scrawl another set of philosophical questions in the same black blank space.

I had jotted down some of what was on the board but there were more questions than I could handle. My mind wandered and so did my eyes. The muted TV next to the blackboard showed a man gently removing a strand of hair from the rim of a soda can. I plopped down my pen in defeat even as the Chair plowed on.

Is the death penalty wrong or right?
What do we owe to each other?
Is any war justified?
How do you know that anyone else is thinking?
How do you know that anything besides your thought exists?
If people from the future haven't visited us yet, does that mean that time travel will never be invented?
If I ignore the rule "ignore all the rules," am I obeying the rule or ignoring it?
If scientists built a dream machine that would allow you to program

your fantasies, would you hook up to it forever?
Is love real?
Is hate inevitable?
What is art?
What is music?
What is justice?
What is reality?
Can something be immoral in one culture and moral in another?
Can something be moral in one time period and immoral in another?
Is the universe infinite?
If the universe is finite, what's beyond the edge?
If it's infinite, does every possibility exist including that of a finite universe?
What happens after death?
What happened before birth?
When does life begin?
When does it end?
What is life anyway?
If you split my brain in two, which half is me?
If I die and go to heaven, do I go as old me or young me?
If I'm reborn as someone else, am I still myself?

As the chalk dust settled, the Chair paused. Then she sneezed.

"Bless you," I said.

The Chair put down the chalk and looked at the class. "That's your lesson for today." Then she walked out of the room, letting the door slam shut behind her.

Lao, Meera, and I went to see Professor Bell after class. "Before we talk to her, I should tell you this other story I heard about why they call her the Chair," Meera said.

"It's not because she lost the vote to chair the department?" Lao asked.

"That's the start of it. After that battle, she barricaded herself in Dean Kinney's office to protest the lack of women on the faculty, until they dragged her out screaming, *There's crimson on your hands!* They were gonna fire her but she got a network of female alumni to endow her chair—hence the nickname." We had reached the Chair's office and Meera tapped a silver nameplate on the door reading, *Hyacinth Bell, Harriet Seldon Chair of Philosophy.*

I knocked lightly on the door, which was half open, and we all entered. Inside, the Chair's office was cramped, windowless, and undecorated except for framed maps of Afrolantica, New Zanzibar, and Birnin Zana that filled up most of her back wall. The only light was a blinking, buzzing fluorescent tube on the ceiling that hung over the room perpendicularly like the lightsaber of Damocles. The sides of her office were dominated by large cardboard boxes that were stuffed with manila files. I noticed a fat, furry caterpillar slowly crawling on the top of one of the boxes, and from a nearby garbage can I caught a whiff of the remains of takeout food, probably Indian. The Chair was at her desk, tapping out a note on her bulky computer and cursing under her breath in French, German, and, judging by the clicks, Xhosa. "Office hours are between 10:15 and 10:30 a.m.," she grumbled without looking up.

Meera glanced at her watch. "It's 10:29 a.m.," she whispered to Lao and me.

"This isn't gonna work," Lao muttered.

"Just be ready when I give you the signal," I said.

The Chair held a finger to her lips. "I'll be with you presently—the university is trying to rescind the admissions of two prospective freshmen for participating in a SLAM protest and I'm trying to make sure that does not happen."

We waited silently for a few moments until she hit the return key and turned to us. "Office hours are ending momentarily. Are you here for anything specific?"

I cleared my throat. "You went to Harvard as an undergraduate, right?"

The Chair looked up from her computer. "Correct."

"Your name was in the Red Book. Did you go by Cindy? Short for Hyacinth?"

The Chair drummed her fingers on the table—she didn't do it in ordinary 4/4 time, but tapped out her impatience in some jazzy time signature, maybe 5/7. "Why are you asking this?"

"There was a CB on the staff of the *Harpoon*, and a Cindy Bell in the Red Book. CB, Cindy Bell—those are both you, right?"

The Chair's eyes narrowed and her flying fingers were drumming in 15/8. "That's what you want to talk about? The school humor magazine?"

"I didn't mean to be—"

"You have ten seconds before the end of office hours. Nine . . . eight . . . seven . . ."

"Are you serious?"

"Six . . . five . . . four . . ."

I shot Lao a look for him to do his thing.

"We have weed," Lao offered, holding up a plastic baggie of the stuff.

The Chair turned off her computer and motioned for us to step completely into her office and close the door. "Office hours have just been extended."

I was missing EC-107, and Meera was freaking out about some homework she had due for physics and a quiz she had coming up in computer science, but Lao told us all to relax as he and the Chair sampled his supply. Pretty soon the small office had filled with smoke, the morning had morphed into the afternoon, and except for Meera, who still looked worried about her work, we all forgot about our other commitments, or were at least too buzzed to be that bothered about them.

"I needed this," the Chair said, lighting a fresh joint. "I've been suffering this unrelenting state of dysphoria. Some days, I don't know what's worse—hemiplegic migraines or reading student applications."

"I'm so sorry about your . . ." Meera began.

"Out with it," the Chair demanded.

". . . situation," Meera concluded.

"Serving on the admissions committee may be aggravating, but at least it's not permanently debilitating," the Chair replied.

"I was talking about . . ."

"I know you were," the Chair said, blowing smoke and turning to Lao. "My head hasn't felt this good in weeks! What do you call this strain again?"

"It's straight outta Compton," Lao said. "They call it the Chronic."

"So many names! Back in my day, we called it grass, herb, wisdom weed . . ."

"Now we call it 420, Mary Jane, kush, sticky icky icky . . ." Lao said.

The Chair kept going: ". . . pot, reefer, ganja, sweet leaf, muggles . . ."

"Muggles?" Lao asked.

"That's what jazz performers called it in the twenties," the Chair said. "Satchmo had a song called 'Muggles.' King Louis was a big-time muggle smoker."

"Why so many names for cannabis?" Lao asked.

"Two reasons," the Chair explained. "Smokers coin terms to stay ahead of the cops. It's hard to arrest someone if you don't know what they're talking about."

"What's the other reason?" I asked.

"Xenophobia. Pot wasn't even really against the law in the US until the early 1900s. The FBI pushed the term *marijuana* to describe it because it had a Spanish sound and they wanted to use drug laws as an excuse to prosecute people from black and Latino communities. The drug war was just a front of the larger war against immigration and black music and culture . . ."

Meera cleared her throat. "We should tell you why we're here . . ."

The Chair took a long draw on her spliff. "You're comping for the *Harpoon*, and you're looking for a tour guide."

Meera, Lao, and I looked at each other in surprise.

The Chair exhaled smoke. "There's a reason my full name isn't in the Red Book. I trust you all are familiar with *sous rature*?"

"That's like sauce you put on escovitch fish, right?" I answered.

"Close. It's a philosophical stratagem in which text is crossed out but left legible to get the point across that the language available is inadequate but necessary. For me it's about the bigger message, the larger mission."

"Is that why you don't talk about the *Harpoon*, like, ever?" I asked.

The Chair seemed to choose her words carefully. "A number of years ago, I left something very precious there. So no, I don't talk about it much."

"But can you help us?"

The Chair extinguished her spliff. "I've given you the information you need."

"Why do you say that?"

"Weren't you in class today?"

"All you did is write questions that nobody can answer on the board, and then you erased them. Was that *sous chef tour* or whatever?"

"What do you think?"

"Can I be honest?"

"Please."

"I thought it was bullshit."

The Chair laughed. "The questions weren't the lesson."

"The only other thing you did the whole class was sneeze."

"If I told you that was the lesson," the Chair said, "what would you say?"

"I'd say that was bullshit too," Lao broke in.

"Maybe it was—but I do have allergies. Philosophy's like jazz—sometimes you improvise. When I sneezed I realized that said everything I needed to say."

"Wait, I think I get it . . ." Meera said, before trailing off again, as usual.

The Chair drummed her fingers on her desk and fixed Meera

with a glare that was a bit like if Jupiter had two red eyes instead of one.

Meera was shaken, and started talking again. "I-I-I was saying that philosophy is about big questions, things that never get answered."

"Go on," the Chair said, drumming her fingers on her desk.

"I think what you did in class was your way of suggesting that maybe we should be focusing on things that are part of our daily lives and why we do them. In Bollywood we would kick off every movie with a ritual and it helped focus us."

"You got all that from a sneeze?" Lao said. "Imagine what you'd learn from a fart!"

The Chair lit a new spliff and took a long draw. "Do you know why there are buttons on your sleeve? They were to keep a man's lace cuffs out of his soup. Or why brides carry bouquets? The flowers used to be bundles of garlic and herbs to ward off evil spirits. We carry the relics, but the meaning has become nostalgia."

"So saying *bless you* after a sneeze is the same sort of thing?" I asked.

"People have been saying that for centuries, but it became formalized in Europe around 590 AD when the bubonic plague swept across the continent and Pope Gregory I ordained that all the members of his flock should say *God bless you* when any Christian sneezed in an attempt to bring about divine intercession to stop the spread of the disease. Today, everyone says it out of custom—but the *why* is lost. An appendix of the past, like shirt cuffs or bridal bouquets."

Lao cleared his throat. "So you're saying we should question the things we do in our everyday life to see if they're meaningful or just a habit—"

Meera interrupted: "I think she's saying that rituals have power and that we should create our own and not just follow the ones that have been handed down."

"I have no idea what she's saying," I broke in. "Professor, can you give us some concrete advice?"

The Chair blew out smoke. "A student once asked a great poet the same question, and I'll give you the reply that he did. My advice is stop asking for advice."

"Isn't that basically no advice?"

"You're looking outside yourself for answers, but real answers come from inside. Draw from what you know and use what you have."

"If you tell us to use the Force I'm gonna lose it," Lao fumed.

"Lao, calm down . . ." I cautioned.

"No, let him speak," the Chair said.

"You're hiding behind a bunch of words," Lao said. "We know which droids we're looking for. Can you give us anything that could help on the *Harpoon* comp?"

The Chair paused in thought. "No, I don't think I will."

"Why not?"

"Can I be honest?"

"Please."

The Chair blew smoke straight into Lao's face. "Because you're losers."

Lao coughed. "Why . . . why would you say that?"

The Chair didn't blink. "Look around—there are families sleeping in the streets, there are workers protesting on the steps, and a generation of students with transcripts inflated by their family's wealth and status are sweeping into this university and acting like they deserve it. And you want to spend your time cracking jokes? Your friend Meera may be on the right track. Start your own traditions. Create your own rituals. You're losers because you're fighting for a lost cause."

Lao's faced turned red. He started to speak but instead he just sputtered, and after a few seconds of this he turned and left the office.

Meera snorted toward the Chair in anger. "Why did you . . ."

The Chair held up her hand. "I get what you're doing with this little hesitation move you pull when you talk. You start a thought and you force us to stroke your ego to finish it. I don't know what kind of shit went down in your life back in India where you now require positive reinforcement to express an opinion, but don't pull that passive-aggressive crap in my office. Stop stopping and start starting. Launch your own ritual, do your own thing. Now get out of my office."

Meera folded her arms tightly against her chest and left.

I was alone in the cramped, smoky office with the Chair.

"So that's it?" I asked her. "You're really not going to help us?"

The Chair walked around her desk to offer what I thought would be a handshake. As she leaned in my direction and I leaned in hers, it seemed like this was turning into a cosmopolitan air kiss, so I made a kind of course correction, but then it seemed we were doing Euro-style cheek kisses, but by the time I adjusted, her mouth ended up smack on mine. Her lips were as dry as chalk, and her hands fumbled around my waist before I pulled away. A silver line of saliva stretched between our lips for a second like the bridge of San Luis Rey. Clearly I had fucked up the handshake in a major way. Did she think I was making a pass at her? What was going on here? I didn't know what to say or do, so I said nothing and stood rigid.

The Chair looked at me, took a draw on her spliff, and when she spoke a puff of smoke followed her every word like punctuation. "Office hours are over."

CHAPTER TWENTY-ONE

ROMPECABEZAS

I had a sex dream, but it wasn't about you. I was alone in a classroom with the Chair and she was writing words and phrases on the blackboard in red chalk.

Veil of ignorance
Utilitarianism
Turing machine
Reductio ad absurdum
Egalitarianism

I raised my hand, but she ignored it and put down the chalk. "Cursive is a dying art," she said. "I'm going to give you a lesson on writing each and every one of these words—with your tongue."

She clapped and a cloud of red dust rose from her hands.

I looked down and I was naked except for a pair of purple-and-teal Air Jordan Vs.

She pushed me roughly to my knees.

I woke up to a pounding above my mattress.

"What are you doing down there?" Lao was saying from the top bunk. "Some of us are trying to sleep!"

It was eleven a.m. and I was in the phone booth in the North Peerpont anteroom talking to my buddy Ben at the bank. He had been three years ahead of me at Knockport High, and although we hadn't chatted in a while, I figured he could help me get to the bottom of whatever was going on with my dad.

"So there's nothing in savings?" I asked.

"Unless your father has another account," Ben replied.

"He used to work for the town. He got a big disability judgment."

"Yes, five years ago. The account is overdrawn—he's been bouncing checks like you used to bounce basketballs."

"What? Are you kidding me?"

"I wouldn't joke about this. Can you wire his account any money?"

"I'm a student—my ass is broke. What the hell happened to his savings?"

"Tosh, I could get fired for telling you what I've told you so far. Why don't you just come in here with your dad and we can clear everything up?"

"I got stuff to do here. Maybe I could have my sister come in."

"I dated your sister. She is not the right person to handle your dad's business."

"You dated her for three weeks."

"We dated for twenty-one nonconsecutive days stretched over three years. Saying it was an up-and-down relationship doesn't begin to cover it. Being with her was like dating the stock market."

"Let's focus on my dad. How the hell could he be broke?"

"Tosh—we have rules about disclosures like that."

"C'mon, man."

"I just graduated from community college—I need this job."

"Who convinced Coach not to cut you from the team back in the day?"

"Really? You're going to play that card?"

"From the bottom of the deck."

"Tosh, have you thought of putting him in a home or something?"

"Or something?"

"That sounded harsh, but that's what people do. Don't blame yourself."

"Who said—"

"Your sister told me. I know your dad went downhill when she was away from home and you were still in high school . . ."

"I wasn't really home. I had to be at practice or a game like seven days a—"

"Don't get defensive. Your sister just said that if you had been spending more time with your dad and watching his meds, maybe none of this would have happened."

"That is such bullshit! Is she a fucking doctor now?"

"Forget I said anything."

"She's always been jealous of my basketball so she's trying to make it an issue."

"Are you even playing ball anymore?"

"C'mon, man, I don't want to talk about ball."

"You brought it up, man. When I was a senior and you were in ninth grade, you were already so good you could tell coaches who to cut and not cut. You were the chosen one, everyone knew you were gonna do something worth remembering. How can you not be burning up the Ivy League?"

"I just need to know the three biggest checks my dad bounced."

"That's the problem. The three biggest checks he wrote all cleared."

"Do you remember who he wrote them to?"

At fifteen minutes to midnight, Lao, Meera, and I were standing in front of the John Harvard statue finishing off another case of Zima. No other customers were buying the stuff, so we were getting it at a discount, and without being carded. Most of our fellow freshmen were asleep, and just about the only other person awake was John Harvard himself, immense, immobile, and unblinking in his chair.

Lao passed me the bottle. I took a swig and looked up at the stars. "Do they have the same constellation names in China?"

Lao grunted. "Fuck if I know."

"What do you call Orion's Belt over there?"

"In India we call it Mriga, the deer," Meera broke in. "Did you know that in the West, Harvard women discovered it?"

"That's not right," Lao said. "Orion's Belt has been talked about for centuries."

"Harvard women didn't discover the whole thing, just a really important part," Meera said. "Have you heard of Pickering's Harem? This guy ran the Harvard Observatory in the 1880s and he was trying to catalog all the stars. He realized getting smart women to do it cost less than smart men, so he hired a bunch of women—including his own maid."

"Pickering's Harem?"

"That's what the male astronomers called them. They were also known as the Harvard Computers. I learned all this in one of my classes, Stellar Astrophysics and General Relativity. The women cataloged ten thousand stars, helped develop a new system for mapping the cosmos, and Pickering's ex-maid discovered the Horsehead Nebula. Getting reduced to a harem is what it took for these women to reach the stars."

Lao grabbed the bottle from me. "Is that why you brought us down here?"

Meera turned away. "What I really wanted to say is kind of personal."

Lao handed her the bottle. "You have the floor."

She wiped the lip of the bottle with the flap of her shirt, took a small sip, and cleared her throat. "I was thirteen . . ."

"I'm regretting this already," Lao said. "Is this gonna be your life story?"

Meera plowed ahead: ". . . I was in Mumbai for my first film, and I was so homesick I thought the condition was fatal. Then, my first day on set, the cast and crew performed the *mahurat*."

"Is that like a dance?" Lao asked. "Like the Macarena?"

"Please stop. The *mahurat* is a ritual every Bollywood film does to kick off shooting. It's like baptizing a baby, only the baby is a movie."

"So that's why I have this coconut?" I asked.

"And that's why I have this." Meera pulled out a silver candleholder with engravings of a guy with an elephant head. "Lao, do you have the flowers?"

Lao held up a bouquet of white roses. "I feel ridiculous."

"Think about Pickering's Harem," Meera said. "They were domestic servants and students and they created a new system of seeing the stars. The Chair was so right—we have to start our own rituals, establish our own thing."

I flashed back to the Chair's dry lips and her hands fumbling at my waist. Had I imagined the whole thing? The memory made me feel turned on and then dirty, and the dirtiness made me turned on, and on it went in a feedback loop. "I don't know if following the Chair's advice is the best thing to do."

Meera folded her arms. "She's the only *Harpoon* alum we actually know."

Lao put down the roses. "I'm sorry, I can't."

Meera frowned. "Why not?"

"Because Professor Bell is right."

"I don't understand. Why won't you just do this?"

"I don't know shit about the whole ritual stuff, but she's right that we're losers, and we're playing the wrong game. How does it help the world if we get on the staff of a goddamn humor magazine? Is that gonna prevent the Cyberpocalypse?"

"Comedy isn't some useless thing," Meera said. "Some of the most political films I ever worked on were comedies."

"How so?" Lao asked.

"Because when you put something political in a joke, it's less threatening. But in a way it's more threatening because jokes can spread like diseases. Most people won't share political pamphlets, but they'll share a joke. That's kind of the purpose of art—you slip in messages that say what you can't say."

"If we're gonna do this, I want to know something first," Lao declared. "Meera, why did you leave Bollywood?"

"Why do you need to get up in her business?" I asked Lao.

"The Chair said we were all losers, and it was like she knew something. I just want to know why Meera gave up on fame and fortune to come here."

Meera sighed. "It's complicated." She looked at me and then at Lao, and something small and fragile inside of her seemed to sputter out like the filament in a lightbulb, and she started to cry. Lao sat down next to her and put an arm around her shoulders.

She was full-on sobbing now. "The Chair was right—I am a loser."

"What's the matter?" I asked.

"What if I told you something about myself . . . something awful . . . would you still try to get to know me or would this thing be impossible for you to get past?" She looked up at us, her cheeks wet with tears.

"Hold that thought." Lao stood up. "I'm ready for the *mahurat.*"

Meera blew her nose into a tissue. "Really?" Wiping her eyes, she stood up, her mood brightening. Holding the candle with both hands, she walked around the John Harvard statue three times.

Lao and I followed and she began to sing something in Hindi. I had no idea what her song was about, but Meera had a high, clear voice that I could have listened to all night and the Zima was still flowing through my brain and it all made me think of how great it would be to be on a Bollywood film set with costumed dancers and chorus girls and tea breaks between scenes. After a few minutes of circling and singing, I split open the coconut by slamming it against the base of the statue, and we took turns drinking the sweet silver-gray water before it all drained out. Then Lao took a piss on John Harvard, and I followed, and Meera insisted on taking her turn, but she made Lao and me turn around as she handled her business, and Lao and I did what she said and looked away and snickered at the sound of the statue's midnight baptism.

"You know what?" Meera asked.

"What?" Lao replied.

"I don't feel better," she said, "but I feel closer to you guys."

"Please, no group hugs," I said.

"We should share an intimate story," Meera said. "Something from childhood."

"Why?"

"In quantum physics, just the act of observing an electron changes it. The more we know about each other, the more we change each other. That's a good thing!"

"I'm not good at sharing."

"One story," Meera said. "Something personal. Something embarrassing! Like when you were young, where'd you hide your porn?"

"Are you serious?" I said.

"Every girl knows that every guy has a stash of girlie videos somewhere. Tell me! You know I'm fascinated by the secret lives of men."

"I don't know about—" I began.

"I used to hide mine in plain sight," Lao cut in. "I'd rip the labels off and stack them with the other videos."

"You don't think your dad got curious about all the videos with ripped-off labels?" Meera laughed.

"I never thought about that."

"You and your dad were probably masturbating to the same porn!"

"My dad was too busy running a multinational corporation to masturbate."

"I thought your dad was a farmer," I said.

"We had a big farm."

Meera put her head against Lao's shoulder and then against mine. "What I love about being friends with you guys is you know all we are is friends and nothing ever will come of it in a million, billion years."

"Thanks, I guess," Lao said.

"Okay, enough sharing," I said. "So what do we do now?"

Meera blew out her candle. "We get to work."

CHAPTER TWENTY-TWO

MY HEART, MY LIFE

Lao and I were pacing around our dorm room, which was filling up with the debris of attempted creativity—crumpled paper, broken pencils, empty beer bottles, discarded mini cereal boxes, pizza crusts, crushed soda cans. Meera was on the phone making calls to Mumbai and trying to sell more advertisements. Lao had let me borrow one of his Mee Corp. computers and the blank screen mocked me. There was less than an hour before the final *Harpoon* deadline at midnight.

Meera walked over to our part of the room. "How's it going?"

"I'm trying to crank out funny stuff and Lao is looking for some sort of cosmic comedic epiphany," I said. "We don't have time for art-house shit."

"Just don't do any nasty personal jokes," Meera advised.

Lao snorted. "Like about how Tosh is so broke he can't afford a phone?"

"Or something about Lao's pot-growing parents?" I shot back.

Lao frowned. "Very funny. My birth parents were killed by an automated thresher when I was a kid. I was sent to an orphanage, got an eye infection, and nearly went blind. It was pretty fucking horrible."

"Are you serious?"

Meera covered her mouth with her hands. "I'm so, so sorry!"

Lao laughed. "I'm fucking with you."

Meera shook her head. "You guys are mental." The phone rang and she left.

"I think we could be overthinking this," I sighed.

"What does that even mean, *overthinking*? How can you think too much? I think whoever came up with that word was overthinking things."

"You're overthinking overthinking."

"We need to get out of this room, get some inspiration somewhere. I got this new shit from a farming collective in the Yunnan Province . . ."

"Will you shut up about weed?" I said. "Comedy is not some mystical thing we're gonna find on a vision quest."

"That's exactly what it is," Lao replied, lighting up. "Comedy is an art."

"No, comedy is a craft," I said. "You can't even stutter when you tell a joke or the timing will be off and nobody will laugh. Creating a joke is like putting pieces of wood together. Comedy is basically carpentry, but funnier."

"I disagree. I'm a Taoist so I know even in the shallow end of the pool there's deeper stuff going on."

"You're Taoist?"

"A nonpracticing Taoist who doesn't actually believe in Taoism."

"Doesn't that basically make you not a Taoist?"

"Or the best Taoist ever. There's a line in *The Book of the Tao* that goes, *When smart people hear about the Tao, they start to follow it. When stupid people hear about the Tao, they laugh. If they didn't laugh, it wouldn't be the Tao.*"

"That actually makes sense to me."

"Really? Because I have no idea what I just said. This Yunnan Province shit I smoked is really messing with me."

"In eighth grade, I had this Mandarin teacher named Ms. Finney. I got straight A's in every class except that one. I used to study four hours a night for that single course. I used to go to all her after-school help sessions. Nothing helped."

"How will this anecdote get us on the *Harpoon*?"

"I'm getting there. Ms. Finney totally got in my head. I began to neglect all my other courses to focus on hers, and pretty soon all the teachers began to think I was a fuck-up when it was really only this one class. I started reading a lot of Mandarin poems and books and philosophy just to practice. Then I came across this one passage in *The Book of the Tao* that really stuck with me: *Chase your ambition and your heart will never unclench. Care about approval and you will be a prisoner.*"

Lao exhaled smoke. "So what happened with the Mandarin teacher?"

"She flunked me. It was the best thing that could have happened."

"What? Why?"

"I dropped the course, got the grade wiped from my transcript, and started up with Mandarin again in high school, but this time it was because I loved it, not because I was trying to suck up to some teacher. Last time I ran into Ms. Finney, I spoke the language better than she did. When she realized that, she started laughing."

"*If they didn't laugh, it wouldn't be the Tao*," Lao said. "So your point is that we're trying too hard to write what we think they want to hear."

"Let's just write what we think is funny, and if they don't like it, fuck 'em."

I can't remember the details of that final piece, I only recall that Lao and I wrote it together and it was good. We tried to tap everything we knew about comedy and make it as ironic, irreverent, and self-deprecating as we could. We read it out loud to each other and we kept laughing at our own jokes, which was a sign we were geniuses, narcissists, or a bit of both. Periodically Meera would put down the phone and complain about how poorly things were going for her ad sales and how business was so much tougher than comedy. At one point, Lao said he was sick of her complaining and walked out of the room for a bit to clear his head and maybe smoke some pot, but when he came back everything was cool again.

We were just putting on the finishing touches when Meera interrupted us again, but this time she had a triumphant smile on her face. "I landed a big sale!"

"Congrats!" I said. "Who did you sell the ad space to?"

Meera looked embarrassed by her luck. "Mee Corp."

"They're the biggest tech firm around!" I exclaimed. "They're even bigger than Yoyodyne Technologies! Pretty much all of Lao's electronic equipment is from Mee Corp. Now that I think about it, why is that?"

Lao shrugged. "I just like the brand."

"The weird thing is, they came to me," Meera said.

"Don't question it, just go with it," Lao said. "Let's head to the castle."

Midnight was approaching. At the *Harpoon*, a dozen other compers were circling the circular library, scoping out the competition, and nervously paging through the other submissions. The room was warm and there was no ventilation and the place was starting to smell of sweat and anxiety and lattes. That kid in the army jacket and surgical mask slid up to me.

"Another knock-knock joke?" I asked.

The kid stared at me. "Can you think of a funnier utensil than a spork?"

I considered this. "Snail tongs maybe. Grapefruit spoons. Chorks."

"Is a chork chopsticks crossed with a fork?"

"Uh-huh. And it's not at all weird that you asked."

"Once again, *you* made it weird."

The kid melted back into the crowd of compers, and I kept wandering around by myself. I spied Tilfer's latest piece as I was dropping mine on the carpet. It was a twenty-page parody of *The Kingdom by the Sea*, that literary novel by Vladimir Sirin about a teacher who obsesses over an underage pupil.

Lao peered over my shoulder. "Looks like your boy Tilfer's trying to fit in."

"You think this is funny?"

"Not in the least—and you know I love me some Sirin. Tilfer's just trying to show he can write about more than superstores and trailer parks. Sirin was a real Harvard insider—did you know he had a side career on campus as curator of lepidoptera at the Museum of Comparative Zoology?"

"He was a butterfly collector?"

"The story is he had a butterfly preserve off campus, but nobody's seen it. Tilfer's playing politics writing about him. The brainy comedy faction will go for it."

I dropped Tilfer's piece back on the floor.

Then I saw your piece.

You had left your artwork propped up against the library's wall at an insolent angle, like a pimp leaning against a lamppost. It was covering that tapestry of the inkblot, the bird, and the jester in the tentacled hat, and was impossible to miss—a massive cartoon mural mounted on cardboard that was taller than me and broader than Lao and me standing shoulder to shoulder. Lao came over to gawk at it too, then we were joined by Meera, and the surgical mask weirdo and a couple other compers crowded behind us.

"This is really great," I said.

"It's better than that," Lao said.

"What's better than great?" Meera asked.

"You and I may never know," Lao replied.

Your piece was a sprawling cartoon map of Harvard Yard, a grand symphony of bold lines and bright colors, a sharp skewering of college life. In the artwork, there were deft caricatures of well-known professors, other freshmen, and various characters known to hang out around Harvard Square. Speech bubbles and caption boxes deconstructed various campus rituals, traditions, and fads. Your artwork read like a graphic novel and looked like it should be hanging in a gallery. You commanded your canvas like I had once ruled the basketball court.

I heard a familiar jangle behind me—Vecky. "Some people

are just born funny," she said. "But nobody dies funny, so it all evens out in the end."

"Are you gonna hold my first piece against me?" I asked.

"Do you want to admit that you stole it from the Legion of Dishonor?"

"Not really."

"You know what guys like Heinz Beck, Killy Trout, Hank Chinaski, Jack Reed, and Natty Zuckerman have in common?"

"They're *Harpoon* alums?"

"They're unrepentant chauvinists. I used to think the misogyny in their writing was daring because they were willing to bare their souls. But I was giving these assholes too much credit—the golden words I thought I saw were just them writing cursive by pissing in the snow. They don't write about abusing women because they regret it, they do it because they want to relive it! E.G. Morris is the only one of those motherfuckers who doesn't write prose that makes me want to swab my vagina with a police rape kit after I've read it. Confession without reconciliation is just hate speech."

With another jangle of her ring of keys, Vecky disappeared up the stairs.

"We are so fucked," Lao said.

I put your piece back down and we headed out the door. It was a cool night and most of the stars were hidden behind clouds. A few homeless people ambled down the street, mixing with wobbly students heading home from late-night parties.

"So what happens next?" Meera asked.

"The *Harpoon* editors go through the submissions," Lao answered. "Then, when we least expect it, we're going to get a knock on the door. They're going to recite the *Harpoon* credo and tell us whether we're on the staff or not."

"How do you know all this?" I said.

"I told you, my dad went to Harvard."

"If your dad knows so much, why can't he help us?"

"If you knew my dad, you'd know why," Lao said. "Just drop it."

"What do we do until we get the knock on the door?" Meera asked.

"Two things." Lao pulled out a bottle of Zima and a baggie of weed.

"I'm doing two other things," Meera said. "Study and study. Exams are coming."

I waved off Lao and Meera. "I'll catch you guys back in the Yard."

We had been heading down Bow Street, but I doubled back and slipped inside the castle. I wanted to take another look at your artwork, try to figure out what made it so terrific and suss out what I could maybe do better.

When I stepped into the library I saw you. The deadline for submission was about to pass and the other compers had dropped off their work and cleared out. You stood there alone in the center of the library looking at your artwork.

Then you struck a match and lit it on fire.

CHAPTER TWENTY-THREE

EVERYTHING I DO SEEMS TO COST ME $20

I rushed into the library, snatched your artwork away from you, and beat the flames out with my bare hands. But the match had done its work and the middle of the cartoon had completely burned away, leaving only embers and ash to float up to the ceiling. "W-w-why did you do this?" I asked.

Your eyes were distant. "I have my reasons."

"Such as?"

"SAMO."

"The graffiti artist?"

"You say *graffiti* like it's a put-down. His art hangs in museums."

"What does any of this have to do with you burning your cartoon?"

"You ever heard of *sous rature*?"

"The philosophical stratagem where you cross out a word in the text but leave it visible to get the point across that the language available is inadequate but necessary? Of course, I'm not a barbarian."

You raised an eyebrow but continued: "SAMO was all about *sous rature*. He used to remix words like a deejay, scratching out some, painting over others. He even kind of pulled a *sous rature* on his whole identity because people didn't even know his real name for years. It's not about credit or the individual work—it's about . . ."

". . . the larger mission. I see where you're going with this, but your piece is due *right now*. You're not crossing out your work, you're destroying it."

"I've changed my mind about what's funny. Fuck irony and all his friends."

"What are you talking about?"

"A couple late-night comics came up with irony, and then irony became a fad, and then a Top 40 song. Have you read any of the other comp pieces?"

"Only all of them."

"They all use the same ironic tricks—self-deprecation, irreverence, cynicism, meta-references. Every word in every piece felt like it should have air quotes."

"What's wrong with any of those things?"

"Well, I was wondering why all these rich Ivy League assholes are all so irreverent and cynical and ironic. Then I realized irony blocks you from believing in anything—including change. That's just the way the motherfuckers in power want it."

"But if you burn your work, what are you gonna do?"

From a leather pouch, you pulled out a one-page cartoon. Your first piece had been cynical, but this was sincere. Where the bigger one had been sprawling, the smaller cartoon was focused. One of the hardest things to learn in art is what to cut, and you had clearly mastered that lesson. The result was a piece that allowed your talent to shine through. This art felt real, and the laughs felt earned.

I rubbed my chin. "This one is even better than the first one."

"Thanks," you said.

"So what's your larger mission?"

You turned to leave.

"Oh come on. Are you gonna leave me hanging?"

You were almost out the door.

"You want to grab something to eat?" I called out to you. "It's on me!"

I screwed up. I didn't have a credit card or a bank account or a work-study job and the only cash I had left was one of the crumpled twenty-dollar bills my dad had given me when I left for school. As we exited the castle into the cool starless night, I tried to think of a place that was 1) open, 2) cheap, and 3) wouldn't give us food poisoning.

I stalled for time.

"So where's Festus?" I asked.

"I haven't seen him in a minute. I have to let him spread his wings now and again. One time I saw him fight an albatross to a standstill. Truth. It may have been a stork or a crane, it was some sort of long-legged bird. He followed the bigger bird back to its nest and trashed it. Cooping that energy in a basement is hard on Festus."

"So why are you living beneath a trapdoor?"

"You didn't know?" you replied. "Harvard was on the Underground Railroad."

"Are you serious?"

"Truth. Back in the day, they hid runaways in the North Peerpont basement."

"I didn't know that."

"The Ivy League was all up in the slave trade—some administrators were abolitionists, some were profiteers. Harvard, Yale, and a bunch of colonial colleges were started with slave-trade money. The very first instructor at Harvard was also the owner of the very first slave in New England. Ever heard of the Royalls?"

"Like a Royale with cheese?"

"What?"

"That's what they call Quarter Pounders in France."

"Because of the metric system. Yeah, I saw that movie, and it has nothing to do with what I'm talking about. The Royalls were a slave-trading family and they donated the land for Harvard Law School. The HLS seal is based on their family crest."

I finally had an idea on where to go, so we wandered over to the Chinese place which was almost empty and we slipped into a booth and got drinks, but while we were waiting to order you spotted some spring rolls headed for another table lying flaccid in their own grease, and I decided we could do better.

We drained our drinks and left the restaurant, and after the tip I was down to $11.25 and we still hadn't eaten. We stood on the sidewalk and tried to think of restaurants, but I couldn't come up with a place where I could get a meal for two people with the money I had left. Plus, it was after midnight now and places were starting to shut down so our options were dwindling.

"We could go to the Mexican place on Brattle," you suggested.

So we headed off down the cleared-out streets. A light breeze blew through the nearby trees, scattering stray leaves across the sidewalk. When we got to the Mexican place, it was crowded but we got seats near the window, and our waitress, a brown-haired white girl in a sombrero, brought us the menus as well as complimentary chips and salsa.

"Can I get you any appetizers?" she asked.

"If we get more chips are they also complimentary?" I responded.

"Yes, but guacamole is extra."

"We'll just take chips for now. In fact, we'll take two bowls, one for each of us."

We kept flipping through the menu and I tried to take my time on each page like I was carefully considering my options when I was really hoping for you to fill up on chips and decide to skip the appetizers and the entrées and maybe finish the ordering with a nice cheap glass of ice water. I was like a team that's barely ahead on the scoreboard and is passing the ball around waiting for the clock to run out.

Our waitress came back with more chips. "You ready to order?"

"Yes," you said.

"I need a moment," I said. "And we need more chips."

The waitress looked skeptical. "Do you at least want an appetizer?"

I was about to say no when you said, "I'll take the mini chimichangas."

That was the first time in my life the word *chimichanga* sent a chill through my bones. I scanned the menu—the chimichangas were mini, but the price was maxi. After buying them, I'd be down to $3.95. I needed to really work the clock now. I put down my menu. "So why are you comping the *Harpoon*?"

"Why do you ask?"

"You're like this campus radical. Why do you give a fuck about making the staff of an elitist institution?"

"See, I fucking hate that."

"What?"

"Elitists always think that if you're not one of them, you couldn't possibly have any interests in the things they care about, and they usually take it a step further and act like it's a contradiction if not complete hypocrisy for someone like me to want something that they want. It's how they keep us down—like we can't have nice things."

"I didn't mean . . . I just wanted to know where you're coming from."

"You know about Jester, Ibis, and Blot?"

"Wait—I saw something like that on a tapestry in the *Harpoon* library."

"The clown, the bird, and the inkblot are the symbols of the *Harpoon*. They're in every issue and their images are all over the castle. Only if you look at the old issues, the original blot was a pickaninny with baby dreads."

"Like a minstrel thing?'

"Exactly a minstrel thing. The *Harpoon* is founded on racism—like Harvard."

"This is why I keep going back and forth. Maybe I shouldn't be trying to join."

"Have you ever been to Faleesá?"

"Are you changing the subject?"

"I'm trying to explain why I'm comping, mon."

"I thought you said you were from West Omelas."

"West Omelas is where I'm from, but Faleesá is where I worked. It's a private beach, only rich tourists go there. My grandma and I had a booth on the sand. We'd sell cartoon caricatures I'd do while you wait, watercolors of seascapes, souvenir shit."

"I guess that's where you learned to be an artist."

"Nobody learns to be an artist. If you look in the mirror and see an artist, you're an artist. But that beach is where I learned to appreciate art, and I used some of the money I made to buy art books, to study the greats, like . . ."

Our waitress was back. "You ready to order?"

"Still choosing," I said. "Can you bring us more chips?"

"So you're just gonna fill up on chips?" the waitress asked.

"Um, yes," I admitted.

"As long as you leave a tip," she said, walking away.

The manager came out next. His face was engorged and veiny like an erect penis. "You guys have ordered a lot of chips. You're gonna have to order some entrées. Understand? I'll be back in five." He said this loud enough for the tables nearby to hear and then he walked back to the kitchen or to hell or wherever he had come from.

You leaned forward at the table, took my hand, and squeezed it three times. "How much money do you have on you?"

"More than nothing," I said. "But less than enough."

"I have a $500 bill, but it's Jamaican money." You stood up. "Just leave a tip. We're going somewhere else."

"After the tip, I'm not going to have enough for someplace else."

"Trust me, mon."

You took me behind J.D. Hall to an entrance I had never seen. "You know why they call the place J.D., don't you?" you asked.

I shook my head.

"Jonathan David. He was a Jamaican-American math major,

won the prize for the highest average his freshman year. He had the highest GPA of any student in his class who completed all four years. Summa cum laude."

"How come I never heard of him?"

"They gave the valedictorian honor to a white kid who had completed three years, but graduated early. But those of us who know call this place J.D.—just to remember."

We walked down some steps. It looked liked the place was closed for the night because all the lights were off and the curtains were drawn, but you knocked three times in a distinct pattern on the door and a guy in a *SLAM* T-shirt opened up.

"Is Miguel here?" you asked.

The man just looked at you.

"Get Miguel—he knows me."

"这个地方是封闭的女士," the man said.

"I have no clue what you just said," you said. "Can you just get Miguel?"

"I got this," I broke in. "我的朋友是一个疯狂的女人, 所以你应该让我们在她在这里造成一个场景之前."

The man laughed. "Your pronunciation sucks."

But he let us in.

"Well, ram pa pa pam! You've got skills," you whispered to me.

You led me down a long hallway deep inside the building, and as we walked the sound of partying was getting louder and the smell of roasted meats and simmering spices was growing stronger.

"Where are we going?" I asked.

You just kept walking and the hallway opened up into a backroom kitchen where a feast was being prepared. Actually, that's not exactly right—there were multiple meals in the works, with a United Nations level of variety. In one corner, some men were frying up beer-battered halibut to a golden crisp and topping it with shredded cabbage and salsa; nearby, some women were stirring up a pot of chicken curry; just a few feet away, discs of golden bread were being stacked up in a basket.

Finally, we stopped in front of an oven where a man and a woman were pulling out a tray of something. I could smell it before I saw it—a bready aroma shot through with spices, warm and pungent, and my stomach immediately began to growl.

"How did you know beef patties were my favorite food?" I asked.

We sat down on a bench in the corner. "Do you mind?" you said, and unbuttoned the top of your jeans. "Ahhhh, that's better."

You handed me a beef patty and took another for yourself. The filling was hot enough to burn my tongue but too good for me to stop eating.

"Okay, tell me what's going on here," I said, my mouth full.

"You ever been in a restaurant after closing time?"

"I live upstate. The only restaurant in my town is a twenty-four-hour Mickey D's."

"Well, if you live in a real city and go into a real restaurant after hours, the staff is always making themselves food that's better than anything on the menu."

"So these are all dining hall workers? I thought you guys were locked out."

"Fuck management—this is our house."

I took another bite of the patty. "So you never finished your story."

"What?"

"The beach at Faleesá."

"Oh yeah. So I start getting into art and some shit happens that makes me think I should apply to Harvard. But I get totally cock-blocked. It's like the fastest rejection ever—I get the letter rejecting me two weeks after I apply."

"What happened? Why?"

"Harvard is always moving students around from class to class. Sometimes they want kids to take a gap year so they can mature, other times they want them to take a calculus refresher course so they don't fuck up when they get here. Applicants will do what they're told and hold off on offers from Yale or Berkeley or wherever because Harvard has the whole higher-ed game on lock."

"So what did they want you to do?"

"Well, I got this crazy call from someone in the admissions department. They said I could join the next Harvard class—if I promised to do one thing."

CHAPTER TWENTY-FOUR

LET DOWN

As usual, Professor Hyacinth Bell's lecture that day was unusual. The Chair stood in front of the class and pretended to slowly grind open a large, heavy door. "The philosopher Lefty Parfit poses this question: Imagine I've opened the gateway to a teleporter. Just like the teleporters you see in sci-fi movies and TV shows. This teleporter records the exact state of every cell in your brain and body, and in doing so, destroys it. The information is then transported at the speed of light to Mars, where your body is reconstructed like something issued from a 3-D printer. Would you step into this machine?"

"Hell no!" Lao called out.

"Is that the depth of your insight? Give us more. Why?"

"Because it wouldn't be me. It's new matter shaped to look like me."

"Let's adjust the parameters. What if the machine was able to deconstruct your body, cell by cell, and reconstruct it on Mars using those exact same cells?"

"Still no. Because I'd be dead during the time I was being transmitted—and I'm not sure I'd still be alive when my body was reconstituted on Mars."

"So we have isolated a few important principles that could well be key to personal identity," the Chair concluded. "One: matter matters. If we're not in our own bodies, it's not really us. Two: stream of consciousness matters. If there are interruptions in our consciousness, it calls into question our continuity—and identity."

"That sounds about right," Lao said.

"What if I told you that everything we discussed already happens to you every hour, every day, every year? Cells in your body, memories in your head, are continually replaced by new ones. There is not one cell in your body today that is the same as the ones that you were born with. Every time you sleep, there is a break in your stream of consciousness. You will have different atoms in your body, and different thoughts in your head, and many interruptions in your consciousness, from dreams or drunkenness or drugs, from the start of this semester to the end. Perhaps by senior year you will still consider yourself the same person you were as a freshman—but maybe you will be someone else entirely. This same shift can happen to communities and companies and countries. We are never who we were."

"So are you saying that there's no such thing as identity?" Meera asked.

"I'm saying that we're all riding on a beam of light," the Chair replied. "It's an open question who we'll be when we land on Mars."

The Chair's office was dark when I arrived after class. I peeked through the glass windows and the only light inside was the greenish gleam of a computer screen and the orange glow from the embers of a spliff in the ashtray. There were stacks of boxes on her desk and the floor. One of them read, *Archives*. Office hours had ended just five minutes earlier but the Chair was already long gone.

I left Emerson Hall and headed out into the Square. I didn't feel like eating or studying or doing much of anything. It was a clear fall day, and there was a steady wind brisk enough to reach under my clothes and give me a chill. Homeless families floated up and down the streets, unable to find anywhere warm to stop and rest, still thwarted by the university's spikes on all the grates. I approached a small group of street women challenging Harvard's defenses, lying defiantly on some of the spiked grates like gurus on beds of nails. I fished around my pockets for change to give them and instead pulled out that baggie of red pills.

"I'll go down on you for that shit," one of the street women rasped.

I considered the pills in my hand. They were little red reminders of Dorian and Davis in pharmaceutical form. A couple of the capsules had broken open, leaking tiny crimson spheroids around the bag like the sprinkles on a cupcake. I thought about throwing all of it out because this shit had caused me nothing but trouble. I wasn't the kind of person who did the kind of things that Dorian and Davis and those Final Club fuckers did. But I didn't cast the pills into Mount Doom like I should have; instead, I returned them to my pocket and felt around for some change. This time I pulled out a quarter, two nickels, and a wad of something that unrolled and uncrumbled into a slip of paper.

There was an address written on it: *550 Arouet Avenue.*

Where had this note come from? I started to make connections in my brain. Had the Chair slipped it into my jeans when we shared that awkward goodbye in her office? The scrap of paper was so small I hadn't noticed it before.

I knew I was heading toward trouble even before I starting walking.

CHAPTER TWENTY-FIVE

PARANOID ANDROID

The address wasn't far away. I pulled up my collar and walked about a mile until I came to a modest brownstone on a residential street. I knocked on the door and a teenage girl wearing an oversize Boston Bruins jersey opened it up. She had uncombed hair and snaggled teeth and I got the sense she was homeless, which was weird because she was in the doorway of a house.

She looked me over. "You here for the thing?"

"Um . . . I don't . . . Yeah, I'm here for the thing," I replied.

The girl flashed her snaggled smile. "I didn't know there were so many of us!"

In a cozy living room, about a dozen teens and twentysomethings, some of whom I had seen on previous days and nights sleeping on sidewalks around the Square, were sipping wine, smoking ganja, and vegging out on couches, ottomans, and throw rugs. Some of the guests looked raggedy, with tattered clothes and worn-out sneakers, others were as neatly groomed as summer interns. The room was decorated with framed watercolors of Cambridge life: Bradstreet Gate in the sunlight, Mass Ave. in the rain, a crew team on the Charles. Professor Bell was in the center of the action, reclining on a love seat and sucking on a large bong. Spotting me, she got up, gave me a kiss on the lips that was almost as unexpected as the first one, and then patted the love seat for me to sit down next to her.

"How did you find me?" she asked.

"You gave me the address. What's going on?"

"Just listen." The Chair addressed the group: "Let's get back to what we were talking about. Athena, what do you think are the essential qualities of a just society?"

Athena, a morose girl in a hoodie, swirled her glass of wine. "I don't think any place is fair if there are people sleeping in the streets. These assholes have billions and there are kids in shelters—I don't know how they live with themselves."

"But what about people who argue that by entering into a society, you agree to a social contract, and that whatever happens after that is your fault? Oliver?"

A boy with a buzz cut and a green collared shirt rubbed his pink nose and answered, "That's some stupid shit, excuse my language. I never agreed to nothing. I was just born and bad things have been happening ever since."

The Chair exhaled smoke. "Okay, we can agree that the world is a messed-up place. If you were going to start again from scratch, what would be some of the founding principles you would use to create a just society? Grace, any ideas?"

The girl in the hockey jersey who had met me at the door spoke up: "Kant would say that there are universal principles—but he died a virgin so I don't know how much we can really learn from him, you know?"

The entire group laughed, including the Chair. "So how do we come up with foundational principles? A colleague of mine wrote a big green monster of a book that poses an intriguing thought experiment. He argues that if we could step behind a veil of ignorance, and not know our own individual characteristics, we could imagine the ideas that could make up a fair social order. What do you think?"

"That's some ignorant shit," Oliver said.

"Why do you say that?" the Chair asked.

"I'm not me unless I know who I am. How can I come up with laws to rule a country if I don't have any memories?"

"That's an interesting answer. What makes you say that?"

"I was in the 128th Infantry Regiment of the 32nd Infantry

Brigade. They called us the Red Arrow, and we were tight. Me and this buddy of mine, Deacon, he was the best—if he only had a sandwich, he would give you half. We went to donate blood at a field hospital and he took off his helmet and he was shot by a sniper." Oliver snapped his fingers. "Just like that."

"I'm sorry for your loss."

"Deacon was only eighteen. That shit has stayed with me, made me who I am. If I can't take that memory behind that veil of stupidity you talked about, what's the point? Whoever came up with that shit never lived a life."

"Maybe morality isn't a set of rigid principles, and it's not something we can conjure in isolation," the Chair concluded. "We have to know each other before we can figure out how we can all live together—and that starts with knowing ourselves."

After the session most of the guests filed out, but Athena milled around near the door holding her empty wineglass.

"Did you forget something?" I asked.

"Just tired is all," she sighed. "I'd like to wake up one morning and have a stack of pancakes. Wouldn't that be something?" She handed me her glass and headed out into the cold.

I moved into the kitchen to help clean up—but first I took a detour into the Chair's study and closed the door behind me. Time for a little snooping. Her legendary book wasn't hard to find—I spotted a manuscript next to her computer titled *My Legendary Book*. I took a peek at the first page and saw it was blank except for in the right-hand corner there was a stick-figure drawing of a person on a roof. The next page had the same thing—it was one of those cartoons that becomes animated if you flip through the images. I flicked at the pages with my thumb and the stick figure on the roof seemed to be waving for help. Was this some sort of joke? I glanced around the room but didn't see any other original writings by the Chair. It looked like the only work she had done on her book in twenty-five years was this stupid cartoon. I did see a padded bra draped over the back of a chair—a bit of vanity I wouldn't have expected from the Chair, and discovering it made me feel I had crossed all sorts of personal boundaries. I exited to the kitchen.

The Chair came up behind me as I dried the dishes. "What did you think?"

"Um . . . of what?"

"Of my gathering."

"Oh, *that*. I don't know. What was this exactly?"

"A philosophy discussion for homeless youth. I've been doing it for a decade."

"Do they need philosophy or do they really need food and a place to sleep?"

"Cambridge nourishes the bodies of the indigent, but people appreciate sustenance for their minds. Some of them are just here for the wine and weed, but that's okay. I usually meet the kids individually, but this time I thought I'd throw a party for my current mentees and my alums. Grace used to sleep on the T—but she just finished her GED. Oliver did two years in the army and one more on opioids—now he's getting a professional certificate in water management at Tufts."

"Wow—have you gotten any of them into Harvard?"

"Why do you ask?"

"You work on the admissions committee."

"You've already made it to the promised land."

"I'm curious about the process."

"A hundred years ago, the main requirement for admission was a student's score on subject-based exams Harvard made up. You could take them until you got the score you wanted, and if you messed up and you came from the right family, you could get admitted with 'conditions'—about half of every class got in like that."

"The rich white ones, I bet."

"Back then, pretty much all the students at Harvard were rich white Protestants—then Jews started dominating the tests, and in 1918 all the top college deans held an emergency meeting in Princeton to answer the question, *What can be done to limit the number of Jews at the top schools?*"

"God!"

"In the 1920s, so they could screen out Jews, Harvard started making students provide not-at-all-subtle information like: maiden name of mother, religious preference, race and color, and my favorite question, *What change, if any, has been made since birth in your own name or that of your father? Explain*."

"That's fucked up."

"So the number of Jews went down, the number of Christian whites went up, and everyone pretended that Harvard's admissions policies were about focusing on character, not just grades. That's basically the state of play—every few years, the top colleges make tweaks in what *meritocracy* means to make sure there are never too many Jews, Asians, blacks, or lower-class people of any color. They don't even try to hide some of this. You know what the final line is in Harvard's official song?"

"I don't know the first line, or any of the lines."

"Well, the last one is, *Fair Harvard . . . Be the herald of Light, and the bearer of Love, Till the stock of the Puritans die*." The Chair shook her head. "There's so much I love about Harvard, but there's so much to fight for. Real diversity in admissions, a living wage for campus workers, getting more women and minorities on the faculty . . ."

She poured me a glass of wine.

"I'm not old enough to drink," I said.

"I'm still young enough not to care," the Chair replied.

I sipped the wine. "So how do you know Zippa?"

"How do you know that I know Zippa?"

"Because I know her too."

The Chair motioned for me to follow her out of the kitchen and into the living room, where she relaxed on the love seat, and I sat next to her. If she was surprised by my question, she wasn't showing it.

"Zippa is an interesting case. She was homeless for a period and she wrote about it in her essay, even included some artwork. But it's really not for me to talk about individual applicants."

"Why did you tell Zippa that if she wanted to get into Harvard she had to promise to join the *Harpoon*?"

The Chair refilled her glass and mine. "Did Zippa tell you that?"

"Doesn't matter where I heard it. You told me and my friends that the *Harpoon* is a waste of time. What's going on?"

"The *Harpoon* *is* a waste of time—for you."

"Why?"

"Your first piece was fucked up."

"You've been reading my comp pieces?"

"Tell me, why do you want to get on the staff?"

"I like jokes, I guess. Isn't laughter what makes us human?"

"Actually, it isn't. Lots of animals laugh—chimpanzees, gorillas, orangutans, bonobos—pretty much every primate does."

"What would make a bonobo laugh?"

"I assume penis jokes. Primates have evolved, but not much."

"Why didn't you help me and Lao and Meera from the start?"

"Great comics play a hundred clubs to come up with one good joke—it's a grind, it's what it takes. I can't teach you to be funny, I can only fan the flame that you have inside of you and hope you use it to set everything you touch on fire."

"You called us losers."

"Real losers are the ones who haven't lost anything. That pain you feel, that humiliation, that rage—that's not a deficit, it's a gift."

"Getting fucked by the world is some sort of present?"

"Every year I get told I-was-born-a-poor-black-child stories by people trying to get into Harvard on the strength of what they've suffered. What really counts is the quality of your response. We females have had a foot in our face for forever—men get a little kick in the shin and their default settings switch to indignation or victimization. Both reactions are inadequate. You and your friends Meera and Lao—you've been through some shit and I think you're ready now. At least I hope you are."

"Ready for what?"

The Chair smiled. "You really are an innocent. Are you a virgin?"

"No. I mean, I've done everything but . . . Why am I telling you this?"

"There's this term in French—*esprit de l'escalier*—which loosely translates to *staircase wit*. It's when you come up with the perfect comeback after you've already left the party. Diderot, the eighteenth-century French philosopher, came up with the idea. French apartment buildings in his time were often on high floors, which required walking down long staircases after a get-together. You'd have a lot of time, as you made your way to the street, to think about what you could have said better. I don't like that feeling. I want to say what needs to be said before I leave the party."

"Well, it's time for me to leave this party. I still don't get why I was invited."

"You don't give yourself enough credit—you're more special than you realize. I was impressed that you had the guts to swing by my office, to challenge what I had to say. I've seen your admission files, and I have a sense of what you've gone through."

"You went through my files?"

"I don't have any family, I don't have any kids—I don't even have a parakeet. I just wanted to gather around me people to whom I feel some sort of connection."

"Why now?"

"I'm finished," the Chair said. "This will be my last semester at Harvard."

CHAPTER TWENTY-SIX

KARMA POLICE

At eight o'clock Professor Bell, a *SLAM!* pin on her lapel, burst into room 237. She was holding an armful of books by Victoria Lucas, Mary Ann Evans, and Chloe Wofford, and she plopped the whole stack on her desk.

"A man is trapped on the roof of his house in a flood," she began. "He prays to God to save him. While he is praying a man with a rowboat comes by and says, *Jump in, I can save you*. But the man on the roof says, *No, I'm waiting for God to save me*. Then a woman in a speedboat comes by and says, *Get in, I can save you*. But the man says, *No, I'm praying to God to save me.* Then a helicopter flies by and the pilot calls down, *Climb up, I can save you*. But the man refuses, saying, *No, I'm praying to God to help me*. So a few minutes later the rising floodwaters overwhelm the man and he dies. When he gets to heaven he's angry with God and says, *I prayed to You. Why didn't You save me from drowning?* And God says, *What, you didn't get the rowboat, the speedboat, and the helicopter I sent?*"

The class laughed politely, but I was silent as I thought back to the Chair's flip book. She had labored twenty-five years on a book and the result was a tired joke?

She continued: "I see this as more than just an old joke—it's a challenge for us to reconsider reality. People from different religious faiths, political parties, economic groups, racial backgrounds, or gender identifications can look at the same set of facts and draw radically different conclusions about what it all means. The man on the roof, trapped in his point of view as much as he is held prisoner by the flood, is unable to see his potential rescuers for what they are because he is too focused on divine intervention. That begs the question for all of us: What signs are we missing? Is our certainty keeping us from seeing reality?" The Chair headed to the door. "We're going on a field trip to find out."

We walked out of Emerson Hall into a bright, cloudless morning. Harvard Yard was pretty much an empty green carpet since most students were either still sleeping, still at breakfast, or still inside a lecture hall for their early classes. A few pigeons fluttered through the sky, and I heard the muffled swoosh and rumble of traffic beyond the redbrick walls cocooning the campus. The Yard was a world unto itself, as calm and comforting as an amniotic sac. A golden retriever chased a squirrel in front of Thayer Hall as a toddler pursued them both, two women nuzzled beneath an old elm tree next to Memorial Church, and a gray-haired professor gripped the railing as he edged down the steps of Widener Library. The Chair strode through the Yard and then paused in front of the John Harvard statue and waited for all of us to catch up.

"There's not a whole lot of grinning when it comes to statues," the Chair said, looking at the unblinking, unsmiling bronze figure. "You certainly don't see it in Roman sculpture. But there's a good reason for that. Do you know what it is?"

The dozen members of the class looked at each other without an answer.

"There's not really a good word for smile in Latin," the Chair said. "*Ridere*, their word for laughter, comes the closest. We know Romans loved satire—anyone who's read Naso or Iuvenalis knows that—we just don't know for certain what they did with their faces when they were feeling what we'd call happiness."

"How does this connect to the joke you told?" Lao asked.

The Chair coughed, and cleared her throat. "We take for granted humans all share certain emotional states like amusement and anger and jealousy, but these are learned behaviors. Even newborns have to learn to smile. There are many emotional states some cultures don't have, and others that would be unfamiliar to many Americans. Babies aren't born with a sense of *schadenfreude*, except maybe in Berlin or on the Upper West Side of Manhattan. There's a phrase in French, *avoir le cafard*, which translates *to have the cockroach*, but unless you've spent time in Paris, the melancholy the words are trying to get across might lack a little *je ne sais quoi*."

"Everyone has to ground the way they see the world in something," one student said. "Race, sex, class . . ."

"Race is an illusion. There's not a single genetic trait that blacks have or whites have or Asians have that isn't also found in other races. There are Asians with dark skin, whites with curly hair, blacks who get sunburned in winter. Sex is fluid—my bet is that many of you will find that out by your sophomore year, probably during spring break. I won't even get into the illusion of money. We've all heard stories of people who felt economically comfortable growing up, only to find as adults that their circumstances were considered abject poverty by most. So many of the things we think are the building blocks of reality are actually the products of our interpretations of it. If you and I are constructing different realities based on flawed foundations, how can we effectively communicate with each other?"

"Let's go back to the emotional piece," Meera said. "Aren't there some basic feelings that everyone has, like love? That's universal, right?"

"Is it really? I was married for ten years and my partner and I never agreed on the meaning of love, on furniture, or even the proper method to load the dishwasher. Do you really think the definition of love, the experience of love, is a constant across cultures and centuries? If that were true, we'd have a lot fewer divorce attorneys and my ex wouldn't be living with some bitch in the Hamptons."

The class laughed.

"We all know about the color-blind who can't see green or blue or whatever, but did you know that there are people who see more colors than you do? The average person has in their eyes three kinds of cones, structures that absorb different wavelengths of light and send the data to the brain. Tetrachromats, because of a rare genetic mutation, have four cones, allowing them to see 100 million varieties of color that people like us can't. Try to imagine how different the world would look to someone like that. Just think of all the things we are likely missing with our limited senses of sight, smell, taste, touch, and hearing." She paused and closed her eyes.

I rested my hand against the cold, smooth boot of the John Harvard statue. The smell of just-cut grass wafted through the breeze. Ants marched down a tiny section of the concrete walking path that led through the Yard. Beyond Johnston Gate, an ambulance sounded its siren. In my mind, I could still taste the wine from the Chair's party. I opened my eyes and moved my hand when I remembered I was touching the John Harvard foot students pee on.

The Chair opened her eyes. "The way out is in. I want you to keep walking, keep talking. Pay attention to things around you and how your take differs from what your companions may be seeing. What are you missing that other people are getting? What are you getting that they may not see? Discuss how your experiences color what you perceive. The only way you can know the world is by knowing yourself and trying to know others. We'll meet up at the Weeks Footbridge in thirty minutes."

The Chair began to walk ahead but paused beneath Bradstreet Gate. She ran a hand along one of the wrought-iron side columns and then motioned for me to come alongside her. "Tosh, you're with me."

As we walked down Mass Ave. toward the Charles, after we were out of earshot of the others, the Chair broke the silence:

"You haven't told anyone, right? I need you to keep what I said the other night as a secret between us."

"People are going to be hurt. You're a real leader on campus."

"I've been planning to leave my teaching position for some time. It's publish or perish and I haven't been doing the former, so I'll be doing the latter."

"But doesn't quitting give them exactly what they want?"

"I've been pushing for more women and people of color in the department for years without moving the needle. The administration has ignored my pleas about workers' rights, diversity, homelessness. Everyone sees me as an old joke, a cliché, a creature of the Cretaceous. Leaving my position will call attention to things I've been trying to highlight. It's worked before—the law school didn't have a tenured black female professor until my mentor Derrick quit his tenured position as an act of conscience."

"So they hired someone after that?"

"The wheels are in motion."

"That doesn't sound like a revolution—it sounds like career suicide."

"It's a spark. You're young, you don't understand. Colleges, corporations, elite institutions—they're isolating and brutal and their moral inertia is incredible. It takes a spectacular act of resistance to move them. I have an opportunity to do just that."

"Can I say something?"

"Of course. You can always speak freely with me."

"I saw your manuscript."

She went silent.

"I don't get it," I said. "You haven't done any work on your book at all?"

"Writing that book is killing me. If you ever see the completed manuscript, you'll know one or both of us is dead."

"I don't under—"

"My life hasn't been particularly happy, and my career hasn't been as productive as it might have been. There was an early setback, and I've never recovered. There have been opportunities denied, appointments thwarted, a parade of tiny indignities, like termites. The university owns my house, my health insurance is through my teaching position. The department's been waging war against me for years, threatening to take it all away. I'm a little scared and I have been for some time."

We had reached the Charles, but the bridge was still half a mile off. A group of girls dressed in white food-service uniforms walked along the grassy bank. Seagulls cawed overhead and I could smell fresh-baked pastries from a café. Far away I heard someone practicing a cello, drawing the bow low and slow over the strings.

A dead bird lay on the sidewalk in front of us. It was hard to tell what kind of bird it had been; a cat, or another bird, had mutilated it almost beyond recognition.

"That's a pretty bad way to go," I said.

"There are good ways to go?"

"Drowning, maybe. Old age."

"I used to be terrified of aging and becoming a burden."

"What changed?"

"I've begun to think of reality as a reel of film—there's the illusion of movement, but each moment exists as a separate still. A bird flying is one still, the bird dying is another. Perhaps there's no personal identity at all, only an infinite series of moments, and therefore no suffering over time. Or maybe there's no reel, and all that exists is one moment, a single frame, and the illusion of time passing."

"Life as a still life?"

"Life as art."

"I don't know if that's comforting or terrifying. Maybe you could explore all this at the next class."

The Chair's dark eyes filled with tears and she took my hand in hers and kissed it. Then she abruptly turned around and headed back toward the Yard.

"Where are you going?" I asked. "I thought we were meeting everyone!"

At the corner of Plympton and Mill, a homeless man was digging through the trash. SLAM protesters were streaming down sidewalks along DeWolfe and their chants were carrying in the wind. An ambulance was speeding down JFK followed by a line of police cars, sirens blaring. I could smell something burning but couldn't see the flames.

The Chair kept walking, fading into the distance like the trapezoidal crawl at the start of a *Star Wars* movie, and I turned toward the Charles. A priest was strolling across the Weeks Footbridge as three women in a crew boat skimmed the water.

That was the last time I would ever see the Chair.

CHAPTER TWENTY-SEVEN

KISS OF LIFE

At ten to midnight no one had heard anything. Lao, Meera, and I were waiting around the dorm room hoping there would be a knock on the door, a phone call, a slipped note, something. Lao was hitting the Zima hard and Meera was studying for her physics exam and I was flipping through the channels on Lao's mini Mee Corp. TV, trying to pass the time.

"Why is every sitcom about young urban white people?" I asked.

Lao belched. "Because all the sitcom writers are young urban white people. The only thing brown on these shows is the coffee."

"This is why we need to get on the *Harpoon*."

"It's also why we're not gonna get on the *Harpoon*."

Meera flipped a page of her book without looking up. "They're gonna come."

I peeked at the clock as it ticked ahead to 11:51 p.m. "We have until midnight. That's when the last notes are delivered."

"This is bullshit," Lao spat.

"They're gonna come," Meera said. "This is just a test—I've never failed a test."

I shook my head. "The Chair said we were losers because we hadn't lost."

Lao laughed bitterly. "More bullshit. She was absolutely no help."

Meera looked at me suspiciously. "It was weird she asked you to walk with her during the field trip. What were you talking about?"

"Nothing much," I mumbled.

"But why did she want to talk to you?" Meera pressed.

The clock ticked forward to 11:53 p.m.

"Let's play one of your games while we wait," I said to Meera.

She smiled and clapped her hands. "Fantastic! Okay, here's today's question: would you rather listen to your favorite song on repeat for all of eternity or listen to a constantly changing mixtape of the worst songs ever recorded for the rest of forever?"

"That's a tough one," I said. "How bad are the bad songs?"

"We're talking boy-band bad."

"What would you do?" I asked.

"I'd listen to the same great song for eternity," Meera said. "If something is great, it's endlessly interesting."

"No way," Lao said. "Give me the worst songs forever. If the playlist is always changing, at least I wouldn't get bored."

Soon, the clock struck midnight.

I exhaled hard. "We're out of time."

There was a knock and we all looked at each other before Meera got up and opened the door. Spooner, goblet in hand, and Ruggles, his left arm in a cast, were standing there.

"Is now good?" Spooner said as they sauntered into the room. "We've reached a decision on the comp and we wanted to let you all know. Can you all take a seat?"

This was it, the decision that was going to determine my semester, my college career, maybe my life. Lao and Meera sat down on the couch with me in the middle. Lao grabbed my left hand and I noticed right away his palms were sweaty, and Meera clutched my right hand to her chest and I could feel her heart beating, which made me freak out a bit and my stomach began to rumble so loudly I was sure the whole room could hear it. I had a bad feeling about what was going to happen. I was just a hick from Knockport, New York, which was so far upstate it was practically Canada. There was no way the *Harpoon*, with all its sophistication and history, was going to let someone like me in. What the hell was I thinking?

Spooner faced us. "It's been a tradition since 1902 that the Ibis of the *Harpoon* personally stops by to tell compers the results of their comp. I know you've been waiting for some time, so I'm not going to draw this out, it wouldn't be fair."

Ruggles nodded and tightened his bandanna. "We hate making compers wait."

"You're only freshmen, after all," Spooner went on. "This is the biggest thing that's happened to you at college, maybe in your lives . . ."

"So we plan to tell you whether you made it onto the staff of the *Harvard Harpoon*—without further ado," Ruggles added.

Spooner raised an eyebrow. "What does that even mean, *without further ado*?"

Ruggles considered the question. "It means without any more delay or ceremony or fuss. You know, like *Much Ado About Nothing*."

"I know what it *means* means," Spooner replied. "But why even say it? Saying you don't want any further ado is in and of itself contributing to the ado. Does anybody ever request more ado? *Please, sir, may I have more ado*? Not bloody likely! *Without further ado* is one of those things that should go without saying."

"I think *it goes without saying* should go without saying."

"Don't forget *the exception that proves the rule*. That's just someone trying to cover their ass, am I right?"

"Or *less is more*. Is it really? Or do motherfuckers just not understand math?"

I cleared my throat and spoke up: "So are you gonna tell us whether we made it on the *Harpoon*? I think it goes without saying we are dying to find out."

Ruggles cracked his knuckles and Spooner smiled.

"This whole comp has been a pain in the ass, am I right?" Spooner said. "Tosh, I know some people were against you for the wrong reasons, because they think some things are too sacred to joke about. My feeling is those are exactly the things we need to take the piss out of. The piece you wrote about short people took real guts."

"*Harpoon* one, political correctness zero," Ruggles said.

Spooner pressed on: "But as Ibis, I have to make the final call. You may not understand this decision now, but trust me, you'll get it later. Am I right?"

"It will definitely hit them later," Ruggles agreed.

I couldn't wait anymore. "So did we make it?"

CHAPTER TWENTY-EIGHT

CIEGA, SORDOMUDA

They howled as they gathered on Harvard Yard.

They poured out of Widener Library with borrowed books in their hands.

They ran across the darkened Yard, shoeless, shirtless, pantless, braless.

They streaked naked except for top hats and tuxedo jackets. They climbed on John Harvard and gave the stars the finger.

They climbed atop Johnston Gate and Holworthy Gate and Bradstreet Gate.

They danced on the grass and the sidewalks and the rooftops.

They ran down the steps of Apley Court and Hollis Hall, Canaday and Hurlbut, Pennypacker and North Peerpont, heads back, throats open, and howled at the moon.

They howled until their throats were raw and their ears were ringing.

They howled until the buses on Massachusetts Avenue honked back.

They howled until dogs on Cambridge Street barked along.

They howled until cats on Linden Street yowled in protest.

They howled until homeowners on Peabody Street screamed for those fucking Harvard assholes to shut the fuck up already.

They howled and they howled and they howled some more until every student was howling and every dorm was howling and the whole Yard was howling and all of Harvard was one enormous howl and that howl was never going to end.

They had been howling for as long as anyone could remember. The howl marked the official start of the horror of exams. The howl was an exercise in exorcising demons, a way of letting students let loose, a chance to see fellow students naked. The howl was an opportunity to take everything that had been building inside every building from all the studying and the worrying and the classes and the review sessions and let it all erupt all at once all over Harvard Yard.

Then the howl was over. Then every student, every freshman and freshwoman, buttoned up their shirts and blouses, snapped their bras back on, slipped back inside their jeans and pants and skirts, jumped off the iron lap of John Harvard, descended from Johnston Gate and Holworthy Gate and Bradstreet Gate, walked up the steps of Holworthy Hall and Thayer Hall and Wigglesworth Hall, moved back into the stacks of Widener Library and Lamont Library, and braced for what was about to hit them.

I woke up in my bottom bunk at five a.m. with a pounding headache that turned out to be Meera pounding on our door.

She rushed in cradling a stack of textbooks. "Why are you still sleeping?"

"Because I'm a human being and that's the way biology works," I said.

"There's no time to be human. We've got exams. Get up!"

It hadn't been that long since we'd heard from Spooner and Ruggles, but I needed to push the *Harpoon* out of my head and focus. I took a quick shower and I got down to breakfast just when they started serving so I was able to grab the best mini cereal boxes—Sprinkle Sprangles, Strawberry Freakies, and Breakfast Bears—before they ran out. Meera didn't even stay to eat, she had tests in physics *and* computer science, so she just scarfed down an English muffin while she was in line, sucked down a cup of steaming hot coffee, and went running off. I sat down at one of the small tables so people wouldn't think I wanted company and start talking at me about parties or sports or geopolitics or whatever, and I drank five cups of coffee, ate a corn muffin, and read through the entire source book for my EC-107 class, highlighting important sections in yellow, very important sections in pink.

After breakfast, I moved into Hilles Library, lugging in two paper shopping bags stuffed with books and notes. I took a seat on the third floor and opened up the reading list for the class. I went book by book, taking notes on possible questions the professor might ask based on what was stressed in the reading. I highlighted important sections in yellow, very important sections in pink, and parts I really needed to memorize I underlined in red.

At noon, I left my books at the table in Hilles so I wouldn't lose my seat and I went over to Cabot House for lunch, taking along my lecture notes. I went to Cabot because I didn't know too many people there so I figured I'd get to eat in peace. I drank four more cups of coffee and went through my lecture notes again, underlining in red the points that the instructor seemed to stress. Sections that seemed unclear, where I had missed something the instructor had said, I circled in blue pen so I could go back to the recording I had made of the lecture and transcribe exactly what had been said. I caught a glimpse of Lao shuffling through the cafeteria with a spliff in his mouth.

"Are you serious?" I asked.

"What?"

"It's exams!"

"Exactly." Lao and his spliff shuffled off.

After lunch, I went back to Hilles to check out all the nonrequired reading. I had read it all before and taken notes, so this was just for review. I skimmed through the six optional texts for interesting passages or ideas that I could apply to any potential essay questions. After I had gone through the optional reading, I went online to where they kept old tests on file and I downloaded ones for the class going back five years. As I went through the older tests, I picked out questions and then I went through my notes looking for material that could be referenced in possible answers. For the most recent tests, I outlined answers for each one of the questions, without looking at my notes, and afterward referred back to my notes to check my accuracy. After I had worked my way through all the old tests, I went through the online catalog and printed out chapters from two of the books the professor had written that weren't on the assigned or nonrequired reading list and also got links to six articles he had written on related subjects.

I packed up all my study materials and headed for dinner. On the way out of the library, the old man who guarded the door went through my stuff and did everything but give me a body-cavity search. When I got over to the dining hall at Cabot I decided to not even look for a seat because dinner was too crowded, and with that many people around someone was sure to join me and start talking and knock me out of my zone. I poured myself a cup of coffee and drank it standing, then poured another and took it with me out of the dining hall. Then I headed back to my dorm room, went into my bedroom, and rolled onto my bed in the bottom bunk with all my books.

I skimmed through all the EC-107 instructor's books and articles, taking general notes in blue pen, important notes in red pen. After I was done, I clicked on my lecture recordings, borrowed Lao's Princess Leia headphones, and listened to the professor's most informative lectures and his most confusing ones, following along with my class notes. It was getting late and I was getting tired and the test was in the morning. Midnight had come and gone and I went over to a crappy café in the Square and got a cup of coffee and drank it and also bought a Coke and drank that too and went back to my room where Lao was already asleep on the top bunk, the smell of spliff smoke in the air. I got into my bed, woozy from all the caffeine and the studying and the fact that I hadn't had anything solid to eat since breakfast. It was so late it was almost early and I couldn't even focus on what I was reading anymore. Light was beginning to filter through the sides of the closed shades and I had the queasy feeling you get after staying up all night. They were going to start serving breakfast pretty soon so I went down to the dining hall and got a cup of coffee and took one those red pills to calm my nerves and it all hit my empty stomach like a bag full of hammers and I began to heave but I didn't throw up, which maybe made it even worse.

Meera sat down and slung her aquamarine backpack, stuffed with books, over the back of a chair. She had a fierce look to her today, like the way a panther's eyes appear all scary and reflective when they are caught on night-vision cameras in nature documentaries. Exams were her natural habitat.

"Are you okay?" she asked.

I didn't want to be rude and it was nice of her to come over because I knew she had a test that afternoon, but I had to keep in my zone so I was kind of a dick and just left without saying much. I could feel the sugar and caffeine and my pill rushing through my veins like Niagara Falls, and not the clean Canadian side, but the crass, tourist-trap American side, with its pay-per-view binoculars, and motels with vibrating waterbeds, and gift shops with T-shirts that boast *Niagara Falls USA* on the front and *Made in China* on the tags. But I felt pumped up, I felt ready, I was definitely in my zone. I went back to my room, sharpened two No. 2 pencils, checked the ink levels in my blue pen, my black pen, and my red pen, and marched down to Memorial Hall.

Mem Hall is kind of an intimidating place, so of course that's where professors tend to give students their most intimidating exams. It's a Gothic affair, complete with gargoyles on the rooftops, that was built in the 1870s as a tribute to Union soldiers—half of the stained-glass windows in the place show Civil War battles in which Harvard alums fought and died. Antietam. Chickamauga. Gettysburg. A Harvard alum commanded the first all-black regiment in the Union Army. The one thing I tried to keep in mind whenever I went there is that I'd never take a test in Mem Hall that was tougher than the tests those Harvard students faced on the battlefield.

The exam was a shitshow from the start. Across the top of the test it said you could draw from any one source to back up all your answers. *One* source! I had totally overstudied. All the ass-wipe jocks in the room who had maybe flipped through a single book on the reading list would be able to sail through the test, no problem. There was a multiple choice section that was a giveaway, multiple choice always was, and there was even a fucking crossword puzzle for extra credit that had nothing to do with anything I had read or reviewed, or anything even remotely linked to the course. The test was a joke, and the joke was on me. As I filled out the crossword, struggling to come up with a nine-letter compound word that rhymes with orange, I was getting angrier and more upset and all the sugar and caffeine and whatever was in those pills were playing a number on my guts. Blue, pink, red—all my highlighting colors were spinning in my head. I felt like the room was rocking back and forth and I grabbed onto the side of my desk to steady myself. I could hear things cracking in my head like when you pour milk on Rice Krispies. I didn't even know if what I was writing was making any sense, I just wanted to finish the test and go throw up somewhere. But even in the depths of my nausea and despair I thought: *At least I didn't die at Chickamauga*.

I went back to my room, which was a whirlwind of crumpled notepaper, empty snack food packages, and discarded bottles of Zima. Towers of textbooks leaned against the walls, and three-ring binders and folders were scattered all about. Lao was sprawled on the floor in a pile of unwashed laundry and Meera was resting on the couch watching TV. I plopped down beside her.

Tears were streaming down Meera's face. "Liquid exerts a force on any object floating on it, and if that door was made of pine, it would have been enough for Rose *and* Jack. It's Archimedes' principle! This is basic stuff!"

"The door could have held them both," I agreed.

"No question the door could have held them both!"

"Not if the door was a metaphor for capitalism," Lao said.

Meera wiped her eyes and turned off the TV. "So how did everyone do?"

"I totally fucked up," I said.

"So did I," Meera sighed. "I overstudied—for both my tests."

"I fucked up too," groaned Lao. "But at least I was high."

"Did you really take your exams high?" Meera asked.

Lao lit a spliff. "You heard what the Chair said—we're losers."

I began to reply, but the words stuck in my throat like a fat rat in a sewer pipe. That's when it hit me. I had tried to push it out of my mind and now it was back and it just crushed me, like recycling in a compactor, like the fuck who charged into me in the state finals and fucked up my knee, like the asteroid that fell from space and wiped out the dinosaurs. I had always wanted to get out of upstate New York, but I had always been secretly concerned that upstate didn't want to get out of me. I didn't want to be another Knockport loser, delivering pizzas and curly bread, making keys at the local superstore, talking about could've-beens and would've-beens and the glory days of high school. I saw all the brilliant students at Harvard, and there was always this sneaking sense that I was an impostor, that I didn't have the smarts or the talent to be here and it was all a terrible mistake. I didn't want to admit it but this comp had become important to me, humor had become my new contact sport. I was no longer a basketball player so my brain was all I had left, and making the *Harpoon* was an important part of making the new me.

But the new me wasn't going to happen.

I was a loser, my friends were all losers, and our loserdom had been confirmed.

The *Harpoon* had cut every motherfucking one of us.

CHAPTER TWENTY-NINE

EXIT MUSIC (FOR A FILM)

Professor Bell always arrived for class exactly on time, but today, at thirteen minutes past eight o'clock, she was nowhere in sight. If an instructor is fifteen minutes late, you're allowed to leave and she's not allowed to mark you absent. In most classes, students longed for this to happen, even prayed for it, and counted down the seconds when they could bolt and leave some tardy boring professor's ass and class behind. The Chair's eccentricities, however, had grown on every student, and when the clock hit fifteen minutes after the hour, not a single person left their seat.

"I hope she didn't get into a fender bender," Meera fretted.

"We're still technically in exam week, so maybe this is some kind of test," Lao speculated. "Something about how time is an illusion."

"Quiet down," Meera scolded. "I have a bad feeling about this. I saw some other professors in the philosophy department talking and they looked concerned."

I cleared my throat. "She kind of hinted to me something was up."

Meera's eyes narrowed. "I knew it! What did she tell you on that walk?"

"She said she was quitting teaching."

"You're just telling us this now?"

"She told me to keep it secret!"

Twenty minutes later, with the entire class still in their seats and hoping the Chair would make an appearance, Ms. Pallas, the office manager for the philosophy department, trudged into the room. All the students stirred in their seats, anxious to find out what had happened. My stomach started to rumble, but I had a bag of Swedish Fish on me, so I scarfed down a couple and handed one to Lao and one to Meera. The office manager stood at the podium and bowed her head and we sat there chewing our candy as we waited. On the blackboard behind her someone had written, *Silent, upon a peak in Darien*. Finally, Ms. Pallas announced, "I have an important message for you all about Professor Bell."

"So she *is* quitting!" Lao said to Meera and me.

Meera socked me in the shoulder five times. "You! Should! Have! Told! Us!"

"Maybe we can change her mind," I said. "I have her home address."

"Why the hell do you have her home address?" Lao asked.

The office manager took a deep breath. "I'm sorry to inform you all that Hyacinth Bell, this university's first Harriet Seldon Chair of Philosophy, was pronounced dead at Mass General Hospital earlier this morning."

The class was silent, then a few students snickered, a couple more laughed.

I smiled. "This is clearly a test of some sort."

"Maybe she's not quitting after all," Meera said.

Lao pointed to the Swedish Fish. "Can you pass me another one?"

Then I noticed a still image of the Chair on the muted TV at the front of the classroom, an old photo of her smiling. A breaking news headline scrolled across the screen: *HARVARD PROF FOUND DEAD.*

Now everyone saw what I was seeing. A gasp went up from the class and stayed there, just above our heads.

Ms. Pallas clicked off the TV. "I'm sorry you had to find out this way. I know Professor Bell gave you all failing grades at the start of the course, and that was a cause of concern for many of you. That will now be changed, of course, and you will all receive an incomplete for the class . . ."

Meera leaped up from her seat. "Do you think we care about our damn grades?" Sobbing, she buried her face into my shoulder, and Lao pounded the arm of his seat.

I didn't know what to do with my hands or what expression to have on my face. The only other person in my life who had ever died that I had been close to was my mom. I felt like I had left my body and was watching the scene from above.

"How did she die?" Lao asked. "Was it an illness? An accident?"

The class turned to Ms. Pallas, waiting for a response.

"Out of respect for her privacy—"

"Goddamnit, just tell us!" I shouted.

Ms. Pallas took a step back, and her calm administrative air dissolved. There were tears in her eyes. "She was walking along the Charles," she said, lips quivering. "And she threw herself off the Weeks Footbridge. She didn't leave a note."

I ran out of the class and into the bathroom down the hall. I had a few of those red pills in my pocket and I dove into a stall and took them out and held them in my palm. They were the same crimson color as the ones I used to take for my knee; the red made me think of apples. Back in Knockport, every so often my mom would make us attend Sunday-morning service at the Free Methodist Church, and I'd read the Bible instead of listening to the sermon, puzzling over Genesis. I always thought Eve got shafted. God told Adam not to eat the forbidden fruit, He never said shit to her.

I flushed the toilet and watched as the pills swirled down the drain.

I felt this rage but I didn't know where to direct it—the Chair? God? Myself? Maybe the Chair saw herself as a martyr by doing what she did, but to me it felt like a surrender, even childish. Every teen or twentysomething, at one point or another, from Romeo and Juliet up to that lead singer for Novacain, has thought about ending it all, but I always felt there was something deeply narcissistic about the act, which left others to clean up the messes the dead left behind. I could hear Novacain's raging guitars in my head, a siren song for suicides, followed by feedback, then silence. I kept thinking of all the music the lead singer could have made if he had lived. Death wasn't an amp, it was a mute button; it didn't take you to eleven, it dialed everyone back to zero.

Maybe I was angry because I saw myself reflected in the water she drowned herself in. When I first wrecked my knee, I felt discarded and useless, like an empty, nonrecyclable container. I wanted an answer to the question: does anybody love me? I imagined myself at my own passing, and maybe this is what suicides do, watching my own funeral from on high, reveling in all the grief as posthumous proof that I was loved. But the joke is on the dead because I don't think they get answers. I don't think they get to see what happens next. If there's no God, then they're just dead, and they wasted the one chance the universe will give them at life. If there is a Creator, then it's even worse: God's going to want answers from them.

Those were my first thoughts, then my anger receded. I didn't know what the Chair was really feeling and now I would never know. I knew I had to somehow channel the pain flooding through my brain or it would drown me too. I don't know why people do what the Chair did—maybe it's about mental illness, opportunity, bad circumstances, or a million other variables. People study these things, but nobody can be sure about specific cases. Suicide is like bad weather—we should prepare for it, at times we can forecast it, but sometimes, despite everything, lightning strikes.

Meera, Lao, and I rolled back to the dorm room in a fog. I felt like I was trapped in a nightmare, fighting to wake up. Meera went into a corner to cry while Lao went into a fury, turning over a desk, dragging his mattress off the frame, throwing his

Mee Corp. headphones across the room, and shredding a few of his philosophy books before he fell on the floor completely spent. We sat in silence until Lao broke it.

"Tosh, what the fuck was going on between you and the Chair?" he asked.

Meera wiped the tears from her cheeks and sat up to hear my reply.

"I don't know . . . She's got some larger game going . . . I think she thinks I'll play some special role . . ."

"*You've got mail,*" my borrowed computer interrupted.

I scanned the first message in my inbox and turned off my computer.

"Um, can I borrow some cash?" I said to Lao. "I've got to go home."

CHAPTER THIRTY

NY STATE OF MIND

Hometowns are like the clothes you wore as a kid—when you grow up, you wonder how you ever fit in them. I had only been away from Knockport for a few months and the whole place already felt like sneakers that pinched at the toes. Knockport was my entire world when I was growing up, and like some pre-Galilean cosmology, the whole solar system seemed to revolve around it. After just a short time in Cambridge, it was now clear to me that the village where I was raised in upstate New York was a meteoroid in a minor corner of a vast universe. The fact that the place had ever seemed big to me made me feel immensely small.

Like the dusty stuff on the shelf at a convenience store, everything in town was pretty much the same and was likely to remain pretty much the same every time I visited. Kids in cargo pants spilled aimlessly out of the pizzeria on Main Street like they always had, a herd of deer darted dangerously near the cars on Redman Road like deer had been doing for decades, and a cluster of cross-country runners from Knockport High ran through the forest across from the Free Methodist Church, following the same dirt pathways teams had been following for years. Same shit, new generation. Nothing changed in Knockport except the seasons.

The bus dropped me off half a mile from my destination, and I started to walk the rest of the way to my parents' house. I guess it was just my dad's house now, but it was weird to even think that. The house seemed smaller than it had when I left, and I noticed the roof needed new shingles, and the lawn, dotted with dandelions, looked like it hadn't been mowed in weeks. But everything else was the same. The same car my dad had been driving when he taught me to drive when I was fourteen was still parked in the same gravel driveway with the same bumper sticker—*Proud Parents of a Knockport Student*—that he had stuck on four years ago.

"Tosh?"

A balding, potbellied man came jogging over to me from across the street.

"Mr. McGunter?"

My old math teacher looked the same, maybe a little balder, maybe a little more potbellied, as he had the last time I'd seen him a year or so earlier. He wiped some sweat from his forehead with the bottom front of his shirt, briefly exposing his pink paunch. "Your sister said you might be coming home today."

"Um . . . Hello, Mr. McGunter. I didn't expect to see you here."

"I wanted to talk to you about your dad. Can we go somewhere?"

"I'm actually here to see him now and I only have a few hours. Can I call you like tomorrow or something?"

"Yes, I imagine you must be busy with your studies at Hah-vard. We're all so impressed and proud that you're there."

"Thanks."

"I imagine that Hah-vard must be very expensive."

"I have some scholarships . . ."

Mr. McGunter wiped his forehead. "I've been a friend of your family for, what, ten years or more? I went to all of your home games and most of your away games too. I was there for the state championship—that was unfortunate, wasn't it? A tough break. You were so close to doing something memorable."

"Mr. McGunter, what do you want?"

"I'd like you to come down to the bank with me—and your dad too, of course. If you could give me power of attorney, I could help put your father's affairs in order and you could focus on your studies."

"Thanks, Mr. McGunter, but I think—"

"Your father is not well. He needs someone like me to help him handle his affairs. People are talking, Tosh. There's been more than one bounced check . . ."

"Do you live in this neighborhood now? Were you waiting for me?"

"Listen, Tosh, this is important. If we find an additional savings account, or a safe-deposit box, it could be beneficial for both of us. I'm sure Hah-vard is very expensive, and you have needs as a student. Your father is an old man now, and has fixed expenses, and if he has money socked away, as young man it makes sense for you to put it to good use, and I can help you. Do you understand what I'm saying? *Damnit, we could both use this money!*"

I looked at him and he looked at me, and he realized he had gone *way* too far.

He wiped his forehead again and cleared his throat. "Maybe we could talk tomorrow."

"Yeah, let's do that." The stones crunched under my feet as I walked up the gravel driveway to my father's house.

My sister was at the kitchen table feeding Cap'n Crunch to a puppy. The kitchen was a mess, with stacks of bills piled on the counter and piles of dishes stacked in the sink. There were wilted flowers in a vase on the windowsill and the kitchen garbage was overflowing and it smelled like someone had missed pickup day a couple weeks in a row.

"Hey," I said.

"Hey," my sister replied without looking up from feeding her puppy.

"I don't think they're supposed to eat that."

"So just because you go to Hah-vard you think you know dogs?"

"I know they shouldn't eat sugar cereal."

"Cereal is the only food Dad keeps in the house."

"Is that a greyhound?"

"Yup."

"What the fuck?"

"I'm gonna race it when it grows up. I'm done with betting on the dogs—breeding them is where the money is."

"You killed every pet you ever had growing up."

"Bullshit."

"What about that golden retriever you had, King?"

"He died of natural causes."

"Not feeding him for two months is not natural."

"That was a vegan diet; some dogs love edamame."

"What about Terry the Turtle? You straight-up murdered him."

"He was dying anyway."

"You fucking took his shell off with pliers. After that he was praying for death."

"Then it was assisted suicide," my sister replied. "He hadn't come out of his shell in days and was clearly clinically depressed. I was doing him a favor."

I heard barking from the backyard.

"How many more greyhounds do you have?"

"I dunno. More than a few, less than too many."

"You don't know the exact number?"

"Greyhounds are fast, it's hard to keep track."

My sister put the puppy down and it plodded away.

"It looks like it has a limp," I commented.

"They all do, that's why I got a discount."

"You're breeding greyhounds with a congenital asymmetric abnormality?"

"I don't know what the fuck Hah-vard language you just said, but this is a business."

"So what, are you putting the money you make in a 401(k)?"

She pulled back her hair and pointed to her neck. "I got this."

"A neck tattoo? You realize the only job you can get once you have a neck tattoo is giving other people neck tattoos. A tramp stamp is smarter—the only people who see that are already having sex with you."

"This neck tat has meaning. It's the Chinese symbol for *bravery*."

"Sissy, I hate to tell you but that's the Chinese character for *penis*."

"So because you go to Hah-vard you think you know Chinese?"

"我知道普通话, 因为我学习了五年的语言."

"Show-off. When my dogs really start paying off, you ain't getting a dollar."

"Where's Dad?"

"He went out to get some Chicken McNuggets or some shit."

"Fast food? What about his blood sugar? We talked about—"

Just then the screen door swung open and my dad was in the doorway holding two greasy bags. "I forgot what you wanted so I just got double of what I—" His eyes met mine and he looked at me like I was a stranger. "What are you doing in my house?" he barked.

"Dad, it's me," I replied.

My image connected to something deep in his brain and a smile spread across his face. "Tosh!" he said, then placed the bags on the kitchen table.

We hugged. "Good to see you, Dad."

"Does your mother know you're home?"

"Mom passed, Dad. Three years ago this January."

A look of confusion swept across his face and, seemingly unable to find a way to process what I had just said, he moved on: "You hungry? I only got enough for two. I would have gotten you some if I'd known you were home."

I gave my sister a look. "So sissy not only knew you were getting this poisonous shit, she asked you to bring back some for her too?"

My sister shrugged. "There's nowhere else to eat in this shit town."

My dad pulled McNugget boxes and tiny cartons of dipping sauce out of the twin bags. "How was practice?"

"Practice?"

"Yeah, weren't you at practice? At the high school?"

"Dad, I'm at college."

He looked up from the bags of fast food. "What?"

"He's at Hah-vard." My sister took some fries out of the bag. "I've been telling you, Dad's not right."

I shook my head. "You're not helping. You should know better than to let him eat at a place whose mascot is a blackface clown."

"Ronald McDonald is not wearing blackface. If anything, he's in whiteface."

"That whole big red clown mouth has its roots in minstrelsy."

"I am so tired of your Hah-vard shit." My sister popped a McNugget in her mouth. "What are you gonna tell me next, that Colonel Sanders is some sort of segregationist?"

"Just get out. I need to talk to Dad. And yes, Colonel Sanders is."

"I'm not going anywhere. What can't you talk about with me here?"

"Just go out and come back in an hour. I'll be gone by then."

"Dad?"

He looked at my sister and for a second he had the knowing eyes of the dad I grew up with. "Just go for a few minutes. Tosh and I need to talk."

My sister turned from him and glared at me. "You know, when we were kids, Mom took us to a shrink to have us tested—do you remember that?"

"No, not really."

She laughed bitterly. "Sometimes I don't know whose memory is worse, yours or his. Mom got us IQ-tested, remember? I scored higher than you. But you still got all the attention because you were Mr. Basketball."

"This isn't about you and me."

"I could have gone to Hah-vard. I could have gotten out of this shit town. People forgot about me from the beginning."

"Nobody forgot about you."

"I'm as smart as you. Smarter."

"What's a nine-letter compound word that rhymes with orange? Can't answer that, can you? 'Cause nothing rhymes with orange."

"Door-hinge."

"That's cheating—and there's a hyphen."

"Was that some Hah-vard test?"

"Screw you. Nobody forgot about you."

My sister's greyhound puppies began to limp into the room, drawn by the smell of food. Some of them weren't puppies at all and had reached almost adult size. A couple of them rose up on their hind legs to sniff at the bags of fries and Chicken McNuggets on the kitchen table. Their frantic paws scattered some of my father's letters and unpaid bills across the kitchen floor.

My sister grabbed one of the bags of fast food and whirled away. "Whatever. I got shit to do."

My sister was gone and the greyhound puppies had been put outside and I picked my father's bills off the floor and stacked them back on the kitchen table. With my dad, I starting searching the house for some of his financial records, but he kept getting distracted by other things.

"I can't get this phone to work."

"Dad, that's the TV remote."

"Oh, that's right." He slipped the remote into his shirt pocket. "Why are you moving everything around? I need to leave things be or I can't find anything."

"You e-mailed me and said you needed me to take a look at your checkbooks because something didn't add up."

"I said that? I don't even remember my e-mail password."

"You said it was urgent and you really needed my help."

"I been thinking about going back to school, maybe getting

my degree. I always wanted to study art history. I only started doing my job because—"

"Where's your blood-sugar monitor?"

"Is this it?"

"Again, that's the TV remote. Where do you keep your meds?"

"I stopped taking them. I've been having these problems with my memory."

"Dad, the medication helps with that."

"What medication?"

"I'm going to come back and take you to a specialist."

"I don't need a specialist. I've been thinking about a trip to Rome. I always wanted to see the Colosseum. Wouldn't it be something to see a gladiator match?"

"I don't think they have those anymore—and you can't travel by yourself."

"I'm thinking about getting my degree. Maybe art history or business."

"Do you have any idea where this checkbook is? You wouldn't have e-mailed me unless it was important."

My dad closed his eyes. "I think it's in the trophy room."

I went into the sunroom off of the den. My dad had turned it into a shrine for the sports achievements of my sister and me, but it was mostly filled with my stuff—ribbons and medals and plaques and prizes from my basketball-playing days.

My dad picked up a large golden trophy. "You won MVP after the state final, do you remember that? First time they gave it to a player from the losing team."

"Dad, your bank account is completely drained. I need to find out what happened so I have to find that checkbook. Are you sure it's in here?"

"You hurt your knee real bad but you played anyway. Gutsiest performance I ever saw. You had a triple-double in the first half."

A row of my trophies was placed on a small wooden stand with a single drawer. It was jammed, but when I managed to yank it out I saw it was stuffed with old checkbooks. I pulled them out and found the most recent year.

"Knockport was up one point with eleven seconds left and Fairport had a fast break. They had a big man on their team, Siddy Finch, must have been 250 pounds, and he was barreling down and you were the only man between him and the basket."

I found the checkbook for the most recent calendar year and flipped to the back to see who my father had been sending his money to.

"You couldn't elevate with that bum knee to block the shot and I thought you'd step out of the way to protect your injury. Hell, everyone in the stands thought that and everybody would have understood it. But you stood and took the charge."

In the memo section, I found receipts for the three big checks that had cleared out my father's bank accounts. "Dad, you paid Mr. McGunter all this money just to go over your finances?"

"That was the most memorable play I ever saw on a basketball court. You sacrificed yourself to win a game."

"Holy shit! You wrote a check to buy her all those damn dogs?"

". . . What happened after you took that charge was a damn shame . . ."

"Dad, please stop talking."

". . . I don't think anyone will ever forget what they did to you after . . ."

"Dad, stop fucking talking!"

He sat down in a brown easy chair in the corner of the room and fell silent for a moment. Then: "I'd like to go to Rome. Maybe see the Colosseum."

"Yes, you said that. Now, according to this checkbook, you spent almost half your money paying Mr. McGunter and investing in Sissy's damn dogs. What happened to the other half?"

My dad didn't say anything.

"There's a checkbook missing from this year. Do you know where it is?"

"I don't remember."

"C'mon—think. Where's the checkbook?"

My dad paused for a second and then pulled a checkbook out of his pocket.

I grabbed it out of his hand and flipped to the back. "You spent half your savings . . . on my tuition and room and board at Harvard?"

My dad just looked at the ground.

"You never let me see the bill. You said you worked it out with financial aid."

"I did work it out. They said if I had the money, I had to pay."

"So the reason you're broke is you've been paying my Harvard tuition?"

My dad got up from his seat. "I think I'm going to go to sleep."

"Dad, we have to talk about this."

"Could we say a prayer? You and your mom used to say a prayer at your bedside every night when you were a toddler. You remember?"

"Dad . . ."

"*The Lord is my shepherd; I shall not want. He maketh me to lie down in green pastures—He leadeth me beside the still waters. He restoreth my soul—He leadeth me in the paths of righteousness for His name's sake. Yea, though I walk through the valley of the shadow of death, I will fear no evil: for Thou art with me; Thy rod and Thy staff they comfort me. Thou preparest a table before me in the presence of mine enemies: Thou anointest my head with oil; my cup runneth over—*" My dad's voice broke and there were tears in his eyes. "*My cup runneth over . . . My cup runneth over* . . . I can't . . ."

I finished up: "*Surely goodness and mercy shall follow me all the days of my life—and I will dwell in the house of the Lord forever.*"

My dad wiped his eyes. "Amen." He left the room.

The dogs began to bark. I realized I only had a few minutes to catch my bus. I headed out of the house, across the gravel driveway, and down the street to the bus stop. Damn. I'd left the checkbook in the sunroom. I needed the numbers on the check so I could call the bank in the morning and put a lock on his account, talk to financial aid about getting a better deal. I ran back to the house and knocked on the door.

My dad opened up and looked momentarily confused. He was sweating and I got a little hint, a small reminder of how he used to smell when he was working, because that unholy trinity never completely washes off—the stink of decay, disinfectant, defeat.

"Where are my children?" he asked, his voice quivering with anguish.

"Dad, it's me—I'm right here."

His grimace became a grin. "Tosh, you're back home!"

"Dad, I was just here."

"Did practice end early? Let me get your mom."

Before he could turn away, I hugged him and buried my face in his shoulder, but it didn't muffle the sound of those goddamn greyhounds.

CHAPTER THIRTY-ONE

KICK IN THE DOOR

The sun had set, there was no moon, and the evening air was cold. North Peerpont was quiet as I trudged up the stairs. Someone had written *Ubersectionality Lives!* on the stairwell walls on the seventh floor and I had to choke back a sob when I thought about the Chair. Meera and Lao were up waiting and munching on snacks when I got back to my dorm room.

"*Dhokla?*" I asked.

"*Dhokla!*" Meera answered. "Or the best I could do with a microwave."

"So what the hell have you been doing for the last twenty-four hours?" Lao asked.

"That's the first thing you say?" Meera scolded.

"I had to see my dad." I shrugged. "Lao, I'm good for the money you loaned me."

"Fuck the money," Lao said. "Is your dad okay?"

"He's having some issues."

"You don't have to talk about it if you don't want to," Meera said.

"No, it's okay. He's having some memory issues and some money problems and it's not a great combination."

"I'm sorry," Meera said. "It's hard leaving home."

"You guys have it tougher," I said. "Home is farther away for you."

"The distance doesn't matter to me. I've got my *dhokla*. I'm never going back."

"What? Why?"

She sighed. "Video games."

"You hate video games," Lao said. "You're good at them, but you hate them."

"I never said I hate video games. I just hate what video games have become."

"What do video games have to do with you leaving Bollywood?" I asked.

Meera reached into her aquamarine backpack and pulled out that video game with an ornate cover featuring a woman in a golden sari and a man with blue skin. "I haven't been able to throw it out."

"That's the game I saw in your room," I said. "So what's the big deal?"

"I designed it," she said.

"You designed a video game?"

"I'm a physics *and* computer science major, so yes, I can design a video game. You know what a physics engine is? Basically, it's the program every game uses to simulate how objects move on screen so it looks real—bouncing balls, crashing cars, falling water. I was the best video game physics engine coder in Mumbai!"

"I'd love to play your game sometime."

Meera pushed the cartridge into the console. "Now's your chance!" The game, she explained, was inspired by *The Ramayana*, the Indian epic poem about the legendary prince Rama, but with his wife Sita as the only playable character. The graphics were basic, but the story line was fun and the face-off with the ten-headed demon king Ravana—in this version Sita saves Rama and not vice versa—was epic.

"How did you make the leap from movies to video games?" I asked.

"I did voice work for a video game when I was between roles. Women's parts in Bollywood can be very formulaic, but with games they're still making up the rules, so I figured I'd have a chance to stretch. I thought I'd get to set the foundations for a whole new world, build my own tree house. That was my thinking going in, anyway."

"This is the greatest game I've ever played," Lao gushed. "I wish I could put this game in a bong and smoke it."

"Why aren't you still making games like this?" I asked.

"I was working on one called Arjuna's Dilemma, but . . ."

There was a knock at the door and I got up to answer it.

The kid with the surgical mask from the *Harpoon* comp was at the door. He plunged his hands into the pockets of his army jacket, looked at his boots.

"Did you make the *Harpoon*?" I asked. "We all got cut."

The kid looked up. "Nothing revolutionary comes in argyle."

"You're acting weird again."

"You made it weird." The kid hurtled down the stairs out of sight.

I closed the door.

"Who was it?" Meera asked.

"That weird kid from the *Harpoon*."

"You're going to have to be more specific," Lao said.

There was another knock on the door. I got up to get it again.

"What do you want?" I started to say even before I had the door open. "I've had a shit week and I'm not in the mood—"

But it wasn't the surgical-mask kid—Spooner and Ruggles were at the door. Spooner was wearing shell-toed mustard-colored suede vintage sneakers, and Ruggles had on a patent-leather limited-edition pair, with blackout netting and glossy heel guards, that hadn't even been released to the general public yet.

Something was going on.

"Tragedy is comedy," Spooner said.

"Madness is genius," Ruggles added.

"Life is a joke," they said together.

I didn't notice the hood until they had it over my head.

Thirty minutes later, when the hood came off, I was still in the dark. I had been marched, pushed, driven, bum-rushed, and finally carried down a flight of stairs. The air was dank and smelled of cotton candy, marijuana, and red wine. I couldn't see anything but I could hear the mumbling and stumbling of other people around me.

I called out in the dark: "Lao? Meera?"

Meera answered: "We're both here."

"Great! Um, where is *here*?"

"W-we're in the basement of the *Harpoon* c-c-castle," stuttered a voice that could only have been Tilfer. "Th-th-the rejection was a p-p-p-p-prank—we all passed the first stage of the c-c-comp."

I hadn't been cut! I had been abused, bruised, and manhandled, but now I didn't care—I hadn't been cut, I wasn't a loser, I had made it onto the *Harvard Harpoon*!

But then I realized something. "You said we passed the first stage—there are more stages?"

Tilfer didn't speak for a bit before he answered, "I d-don't know."

My eyes were beginning to adjust to the low light and I got the sense that we were in a dungeon below the castle, how far underground I couldn't tell. We were ankle-deep in water that was slowly drizzling from the ceiling and we were all chilly and miserable. I could feel the cold rocky floor beneath my feet, dimly make out a stone spiral staircase leading up, and I spied a bolted iron door at the top. Nobody had any idea when the *Harpoon* editors would be coming back to check on us, but I was praying it would be very soon. The ventilation was pretty much nonexistent, and Tilfer kept passing gas, so things were getting desperate.

"I-I-I'm a nervous farter," Tilfer apologized.

"Could things get any worse?" Lao complained.

"Well, at least the water is starting to warm up," I said.

"Th-th-that's not warm water," Tilfer said.

"Ew," Meera said.

With a clank, the iron door at the top of the stone stairs swung open, a flash of angled light beamed into the dungeon, and a voice addressed us from above.

"Welcome to Phoolz Week, y'all," purred the voice of Vecky Higginbottom.

We all looked up from the floor of the dungeon but the light was too bright to see much of anything. We could only hear Vecky's voice floating down from above us. She had stopped talking—she was laughing.

Her laughter, at first, was more of a titter, and then it built into a giggle, and momentarily it was a kind of guffaw. At that point, some of the Phoolz on the dungeon floor began to join in, nervously, but soon wholeheartedly, and it wasn't long before the whole dungeon was echoing with full-throated, gut-busting, stop-it-you're-killing-me laughter. Lao and Meera were doubled over, and some of the other Phoolz were on their knees or lying on the wet stone floor. I laughed so hard I couldn't breathe and my sides hurt.

Vecky stopped laughing; following her lead, we did too.

"Did you know laughter is one of the few physical states that's contagious?" she asked. "Did you know you're 30 percent more likely to laugh if you're with someone than if you're alone? I saw it on the Internet so it must be true! Laughter is the opposite of masturbation—you want to be around other people when you do it."

The Phoolz looked at each other and I looked at Meera and Lao.

"Who did you look at after you laughed? When you laugh in a group, the people you look to first are the people to whom you feel the closest. People laugh to show they get it, that they're part of the group. There's nothing more frustrating than everyone around you being part of an inside joke that you're outside of. And you know what? The *whole world* is a cruel inside joke that we're not a part of."

Vecky laughed again, and this time her laughter was bright

and clear and unreservedly happy. My eyes had adjusted to the light a bit, and now I could see a smile spreading over Vecky's face. "All of you are on your way to becoming a part of the *Harvard Harpoon*. The long, cruel joke is over—we're going to get the last laugh."

The light from above went out and the door slammed and we were suddenly in the dark again and the water had risen to above my knees. The entire chamber was suddenly filled with another voice—Spooner's—amplified to an enormous volume. "You're not in the *Harpoon* yet," he barked. "You're in a world of hurt."

A liquidy substance began to fall on us from above that had the stink, warmth, and viscosity of human vomit. The horrid stuff kept falling until it covered our hair, our faces, our entire bodies. Some of the shorter compers started doggy-paddling in place just to stay on the surface of the sewage-like slush flooding the room. I felt as if I had been dunked into the clogged toilet of a giant suffering from diarrhea. The smell was so overwhelming I couldn't breathe.

That's when the flushing began—a single, humongous *whoosh*. We were spun around the room like we were circling a drain and the floor gave way and the dungeon vanished and we were falling and sliding, sucked downward and sideways, and suddenly we all found ourselves in a tangle of limbs on the sidewalk in front of the castle, dazed, shivering, and covered in thick, foul-smelling muck.

I saw you getting to your feet on the sidewalk. "Zippa?"

You wiped muck from your bare arms. "Looks like we both made it this far."

It was dark but there was a little starlight between the clouds. Spooner and Ruggles, each dressed in a tux and tails and each riding a donkey, trotted up to the soggy, smelly group of Phoolz as we tried to stand up.

"I've been right where you guys are now," Spooner laughed, as he looked over the group. "You've always been the smartest kids in the room, you've always done everything your parents told you. Time to flush all that, because geniuses break shit—that's the only way anything gets done. You know one thing your mom told you that's spot-on? Sticks and stones, motherfuckers. That's what we're about, that's what these final steps are about. Fuck 'em if they can't take a joke."

Spooner held up a long sword that glinted in the moonlight. "Rise, each of you," he declared. "Rise and be given your Phoolz name."

"Rise, Phool Muffin Top," Spooner said to Tilfer, bringing the sword down and lightly tapping him on the shoulder.

"Rise, Phool Odin," he said to Lao.

"Rise, Phool Big Sister Pink Passion," he said to you.

"Rise, Phool Bollywood," he said to Meera.

The sword came down three more times as he dubbed a brown-haired girl with big eyes as Phool Emoticon, and anointed that weird kid in the army jacket Phool Spectrum. All the names were mean, but Spooner took his time before coming up with an especially nasty one for me: Phool Tech. I had no idea how he found out. That damn nickname was sticking with me like an STD.

"You gotta pass three tests," Spooner announced as he sheathed his sword. "The first is a mission, the second is a prank, and the third . . . well, you'll find out when it happens, if you even make it that far. Go back to your dorms, clean up, and return to the castle by sundown. The ride is about to begin."

CHAPTER THIRTY-TWO

THE KING OF CARROT FLOWERS PTS. TWO & THREE

Time crawled along like an inchworm on a leaf and I couldn't sleep that night and neither could you. After we had cleaned up back at the dorm, I tried to go to bed, but Lao was louder than usual in the top bunk, and even putting my pillow over my head wasn't enough to keep out his moans. I kept seeing the Chair's dark eyes and her storm-cloud eyebrows so I got up and left the room and ran into you in the stairwell. You said there was someplace we could go to get away from everything.

"I just got back from seeing my dad, I don't know if I can get away again."

"Is your dad okay?"

"He's having some memory issues."

"I'm sorry to hear that. We're not gonna go too far."

"What about the *Harpoon* tests?"

"There's something I need to show you first."

We followed a walking trail through Cambridge into a public park that led to an open expanse filled with pine, sugar maple, and oak trees. The air was cool in the shadow of the trees and smelled like freshly fallen leaves. As we walked, you whistled.

"Festus sometimes comes when I whistle," you explained.

"You still haven't found your bird?"

"No, and I hope he's okay—he's one of the last green-billed hummingbirds around."

"Maybe he'll come back when he gets hungry."

"Food may be why he left. He needs to eat live bugs and things he can only find in the wild. Hummingbirds don't do captivity—he's airborne constantly. But he's good about sticking close. If you see me, he's usually close behind, and vice versa."

The rising sun was peeking over the horizon as you led me to a stand of evergreens, and inside the grove was a field dotted with red flowers. I hadn't been expecting it, but you wrapped your arms around me like a cocoon. "I want to read you something." Your hands felt good against my chest. "But take a closer look first."

I leaned forward and I saw some of the blossoms were fluttering and I realized the entire field of flowers was covered with thousands of resting red butterflies.

You smiled. "*And we will build a cottage there / Beside an open glade / With black-ribbed blue-bells blowing near . . .*"

"*And ferns that never fade*. I love that poem. Is that what you wanted to read me?"

"I'll get to that. The Chair told me about this place. Have you ever been to the Red Room in Widener Library? This is where they get the flowers."

"Lao said this place was a myth!"

"You can see it's for real."

"Was Vladimir Sirin behind this whole area somehow? He was into butterflies."

"The author of *The Kingdom by the Sea*? Yeah, but for me the interesting thing is Willie DuBois used to visit here."

"The philosopher?"

"He was the first black man to get a PhD from Harvard, and he needed a place to get away. Can you imagine being a person of color on this campus in the nineteenth century?"

"It must have been hell."

"The Chair gave me his books. His ideas about the Talented Tenth—that there's this vanguard of the black bourgeoisie who have to save the race—are really elitist. But the stuff he wrote about double consciousness, that shit is amazing—we're always being forced to look at ourselves as we really are and as white society sees us."

"It's all about white privilege."

"Is it though? I hate that term—it feels Jack-and-Jill genteel, like *noblesse oblige* and *prima nocta*. Or *white supremacy*—that almost sounds like a good thing, when it's one of the worst things in the world. Those words don't convey the brutality."

"You have a better term?"

"I've always thought a lot of white people suffer from *double unconsciousness*."

"You gotta explain that one."

"It's this perverse racial chiaroscuro—they see us, and only see race, but when they look at themselves, they never see race at all. They're unaware about the truth of our lives even as they sleepwalk through their own."

"If we get into Harvard, it's affirmative action, but if they do, it's hard work."

"Exactly! It's Big Brother doublethink, with a side of racism. It's like when deluded folks say shit like, *I don't see color*. Does that mean that you can't see the red of that flower? Does that mean you can't tell which race was being pushed to the back of the bus in the fifties or who's being shot by cops right now? If you can't see color, you can't see history and you can't see *me!* The Chair and I used to discuss stuff like this all the time—I miss her like hell."

"So why did you really bring me here?"

"It's about the Chair. She did leave a letter behind—but the department thought it would look bad if it got out." I saw that there was a note in your hand. "It got out."

To my students,

I am sorry I will not be there to close out the semester. But I have an excuse: I'm dead.

At least, I assume I will be dead by the time this is read to you.

You all know I take medical marijuana for migraines. But none of you know that it's also to help me with pain management for metastatic inflammatory breast cancer, which I've fought for several years, including a bilateral mastectomy six months ago. That's why I wanted you to hear from me why I took my own life, and why I did it before the cancer could take me.

The first time I visited this school, when I was as green as you are now, it was after midnight, before freshman week, and the gates around the Yard were locked. I was so eager to join the privileged life inside all those fancy buildings that I tried to scale the wall where Bradstreet Gate is now—but I never made it in, and because I had no money, and no relatives in Cambridge, I spent the night on the sidewalks with the homeless. That was the hardest and best night of my life. I saw that outside the gates there was a whole new world on the streets, and I've been committed to social issues ever since.

The central question of this course has been "Is life worth living?" There have been many things to love about my life on this campus, but I realized if I want to put a spotlight on issues I care about, this note is my last, best opportunity. Suicide notes are the only letters people read these days, and the only postage they require is a corpse. It's a small price to pay.

I can't enjoy my life knowing so many others are unable to enjoy theirs—the homeless we refuse to shelter, the workers we refuse to pay a living wage, the diverse students and teachers we refuse to give a chance. For me, survival would be more selfish than suicide. I won't leave this world with crimson on my hands! I've also realized that the central question of this course—"Is life worth living?"—has no answer because it's the wrong question. Or rather, it isn't a brave enough question. What I should have asked is, "What are you willing to die for?" I have my answer.

I felt emotion rise up in me and I pushed it back down. "So she's a martyr. This sure as shit doesn't make me feel any better."

"I'm not saying she had good reason for what she did, but it's an explanation."

"Are you going to send it to the *Magenta*?"

"I already dropped off a copy anonymously. I'm sure Morven S. Morlington will make it front-page news. But I cut out the postscript: *One last message to Tech and Zippa: We can be a little lower than the angels—if we choose to fly that high.*"

"What does that mean? Does she want us to carry on her rebellion? What's—"

You put a finger to my lips, and motioned for me to lie down in the grass next to you. "Just close your eyes," you said. "Think good thoughts about the Chair."

When I opened my eyes again, the air with filled with red butterflies.

CHAPTER THIRTY-THREE

LET ME RIDE

As the setting sun painted the sky the official color of our college, the Phoolz group—me, you, Lao, Meera, Tilfer, Spectrum, and Emoticon—met on the steps of the castle. The campus was buzzing about Morven's story in the *Magenta* and we were all struggling to focus on the task at hand. We had gathered to check out the contents of an envelope that had been nailed on the *Harpoon*'s front door with all our names on it. Autumn was coming along and there was a chill in the air, and the few people who were on the street were wearing scarves or hats or wrapping their coats around themselves.

Emoticon plucked the envelope off the door. "Maybe this will get our minds off all the craziness on this campus."

Spectrum snatched the envelope out of her hands. "I'm the *Harpoon* expert, I should open it." He pulled out a card.

"What does it say we're supposed to do?" I asked.

"The only thing here is a poem."

One for the Bulldogs and one for the Bears
Two for the Lions and the Tigers to share
Three more for the Reds, for the Greens, and the Quakers
But beyond the gates there's just one for nonfakers
In the Land of Crimson where safety schools die
One school to rule them all, one school to find them
Collect all signs by midnight and in the ivy bind them
In the Land of Crimson where safety schools die

Emoticon peered over Spectrum's shoulder. "What does it mean?"

I took the card. "Lions, tigers, bears—"

Spectrum interrupted: "The *Harpoon* has a history of fantasy parodies, so that's an Oz reference. The rest reminds me of Oxy More's *Ring* trilogy . . ."

I completed my thought: "The poem's not about fantasy. Lions, tigers, and bears are all Ivy League mascots."

Meera smiled. "It's a mission! Sounds like we're supposed do something with all eight Ivy League colleges."

"But what?" Lao asked.

"I'm guessing we need to steal something," I said. "That's what school pranks are usually about. In high school we were always taking stuff from rivals."

Spectrum shook his head. "They expect us to travel to all eight Ivies? There's no way we can do that by midnight. We could get to Yale, maybe Princeton, but the others are too far away. Like where the hell is Cornell?"

I sighed. "Ithaca, New York."

"That was rhetorical," Spectrum said. "I don't care where Cornell is. They don't even have a humor magazine."

"Cut the nonsense," you said. "If we don't complete the prank, we get cut. We have to figure this out. I didn't come this far to fall short on the first mission."

Everybody started talking at once and nobody seemed to be listening, and you started walking away from the castle.

"Where are you going?" I asked.

"Beyond the gates," you called out over your shoulder.

The Phoolz group followed you to a car rental place in the Square.

"We're gonna need a ride to get to where we need to go," you said. "Anyone have a credit card and a driver's license?"

Lao turned out to be the only one in the Phoolz group who had both and he picked out an SUV that we could all pile into.

"Why do you have a US driver's license?" I asked Lao.

"When Y2K hits, and the fuel shortages start, driving will be a thing of the past," he said. "I wanted to experience the American road before it was too late."

The woman behind the counter asked us if we would return the car with a full tank or an empty one.

"The classic trick question," Lao said. "Are we responsible enough to fill it up before we return or are we so irresponsible that we're going to bring it back dry?"

"Let's bring it back full," Emoticon suggested. "It's the nice thing to do."

"Are you kidding? Empty," Spectrum argued. "Fuck them."

"I-I-I-I could eat the north end of a southbound polecat," Tilfer stammered.

"Can't we just vote?" Meera asked.

You grabbed the keys and scribbled something on the form.

"I can't read this," the woman said. "What are you gonna do about the fuel?"

"We'll let you know when we get back," you replied as we headed outside.

We climbed into a grape-colored station wagon and you took the wheel. Spectrum insisted on riding shotgun and Lao and Meera and Emoticon took the middle seats, forcing me to squeeze into the undersized third row with Tilfer, who basically took up one and a half seats by himself. As we pulled out of the rental car lot, Spectrum fiddled with the radio and found a hip-hop song—one of those candy-ass numbers with a raspy-voiced MC spitting playtime gangsta verses over a soft-as-Jell-O sample—and started rapping along, but you turned off the music.

"Hey—that was a great song!" Spectrum complained.

"I'm not going to sit here and listen to you rap the n-word," you shot back.

"But those are the lyrics."

"There are so many things you already have in this world. You need to ask yourself why the n-word is something you can't do without."

"They're the ones saying *nigger*. I'm just quoting them."

"Number one, don't *ever* say that word again. Two, they said *nigga*—not what you said. Three, if you can't tell the difference, you shouldn't be saying either."

"It's not a racist thing—they're reclaiming an epithet."

"I don't hear white folks reclaiming words like *cracker* and *ofay* and *gringo* and *honky* and *peckerwood*. You left that shit at the lost-and-found."

"Don't forget *r-r-r-redneck*," Tilfer added. "People in B-B-Boston call me that when they hear my Kentucky accent."

"You all need to take some classes in the Afro-American Studies department, like I'm doing," you said. "The words we use to hate on white people aren't even really about race—they're about class. Rich white people called poor whites *rednecks* because they had to work in the sun right next to black people. They called some of 'em *crackers* because they were cracking the whip on us. But poor white people still hate us more than they hate the rich white people who have been dissing them from day one."

Spectrum shook his head. "It's just a rap song, it's not that deep. This is what Spooner was talking about—people are so politically correct you can't say anything anymore. It's killing comedy."

"I agree," Emoticon squeaked. "All this race talk is making me uncomfortable."

"Bitch, I ain't your ottoman, I'm not here to make you comfortable," you said. "I'm here to make the *Harpoon*!"

You pulled over at a hardware store to pick up a gym bag full of supplies you said we'd need, then we all drove to a nearby gated community. The stars had just come out and the huge houses beyond the gates blocked out parts of the sky. A large sign read, *Arcadia: Where the Ivy League Lives*. When our station wagon pulled up to the security booth, the guard didn't even look at Lao's ID, he just glanced at Tilfer sitting in the backseat and waved us through.

"Do you know that guy?" I asked him.

"M-m-my family has a place here," Tilfer admitted.

"You're just telling us now?" Lao said.

"I grew up in Paducah, I only spent three years in R-R-Riverdale."

"You mean Arcadia," Lao corrected.

"R-R-Riverdale is the name of our house," Tilfer explained.

"You name your houses?" I said. "My sister didn't name some of our cats."

As we drove through the gated community, it occurred to me that the mansions in Arcadia probably had first names, last names, and middle names. These were massive affairs, each surrounded by oceans of greenery.

"So you know the neighborhood," I said to Tilfer. "What are we looking for?"

Tilfer pointed out to the street. "Th-th-that."

I looked out to see two street signs crisscrossed at the intersection: Brown Avenue and Dartmouth Way. Turned out the streets in Arcadia were all named after Ivy League schools—there was Cornell Circle, Pennsylvania Boulevard, Yale Terrace, Columbia Crossing, Princeton Place, and Harvard Street. There was even a little cul-de-sac marked, *Wellesley Circle*, and a dead end marked, *Stanford Passing*.

"What's with the Ivy League obsession around here?" I asked.

"Arcadia has the highest rate of acceptance to the Ivies," Tilfer said. "The f-f-first time I came here, every house l-l-looked like a castle."

"Where were you living before?" Meera asked.

"A-a-a-a trailer," Tilfer said.

"Are you shitting me?" Lao said.

"I shit you n-n-not. Th-th-this was an upgrade."

"How come I've never heard about this place?" I asked.

"You don't know because they don't want you to know," you said. "College admission is a rigged game—it's more about money, family, and geography than merit."

"That is such bullshit," Spectrum snorted. "My parents spent shitloads on my college-prep courses and I earned my scores."

You shook your head. "Do you not listen to the words coming out of your mouth?"

You parked the station wagon, and we all stepped out. It was getting dark, and the house lights were beginning to blink on one by one. A streetlight snapped on right above us, illuminating the street corner. You popped the trunk, opened up the gym bag you had stuffed back there, and pulled out a sledgehammer.

"What are you, Thor?" Spectrum barked.

"Bumba clot!" you cursed. "This here's John Henry's hammer."

"I know th-th-that story!" Tilfer said. "John Henry was from Kentucky!"

"John Henry's from Jamaica, mon. My mom told me the story—he almost single-handedly dug a tunnel through the Blue Mountains for the Kingston–Port Antonio railroad. Jamaican immigrants took the tale to America. Truth."

You walked to the intersection of Columbia Crossing and Pennsylvania Boulevard, dragging the sledgehammer behind you. The street signs were atop a silver pole and held tight by a metal clip. You took one high swing with the sledgehammer and knocked the *Columbia* sign halfway out. You took another swing and it fell to the cobblestone street with a clang that echoed into the night. Four swings later, you had taken down the *Pennsylvania* sign. Not too far away a dog began to bark.

You handed me the sledgehammer, which was heavier than I thought.

"You know, at the end of the story, John Henry dies," Lao said. "He beats the steam engine, but he gets a heart attack. Machines always win, even in tall tales."

"Thanks for that," I said, lifting the hammer above my head.

I had to take seven swings to take down *Brown Avenue* and *Dartmouth Way*, but I did a little better than Lao, who took ten to topple *Princeton Place*, but we were both topped by Meera, who, thanks to her toned arms, only needed three loud whacks to strike down *Cornell Circle*.

Emoticon looked nervous. "We're waking up the whole neighborhood."

"Remember the Chair," you replied. "We have to stay on mission."

"What does the Chair have to do with this?"

By this point, at least a half dozen dogs were barking, and lights were turning on all over the neighborhood. In the distance, I heard the faint whine of a cop car.

"I'm heading back to the station wagon," Emoticon announced.

"If we don't complete the mission we'll get cut!" you shot back.

But Emoticon jogged away anyway, and you motioned for Tilfer to hurry up and take his turn. He stood there at the intersection of Yale Terrace and Harvard Street for a few moments and didn't do anything but breathe deeply and sweat.

"What's the problem?" I asked.

"Th-th-this is my street," Tilfer said.

We were parked in front of what could have been the grandest mansion in all Arcadia. The hedges had been trimmed in the shapes of animals, three Jazz Age–era cars were parked in the driveway out front, and the pool house out back was bigger than my entire home back in Knockport. The house was dark, but the fountains in the lawn reflected the starlight above, making the whole property shimmer like seltzer.

As we walked in front of the house, an alarm went off.

"Our h-h-house has an automated alarm system," Tilfer said.

"Fuck that!" you snapped. "We're gonna die with a hammer in our hands!"

Tilfer swung at the *Yale* sign and the blow rang like a church bell and more dogs began to bark. He hit the sign twenty more times, and on the twenty-first strike the sign fell down, probably out of pity.

The house lights blazed on.

"We need to leave," Spectrum said. "We could get arrested for stealing."

"We're not stealing the signs," you said. "We're reclaiming them."

Breathing heavily, Tilfer began hammering at the last prize, the *Harvard* sign. One, two, three hits and the sign wasn't moving. He was sweating through his shirt.

The house alarm blared on, and we could hear police sirens getting closer.

"Hurry!" Meera cried.

"Fuck it, I'm out," said Spectrum, turning to leave.

"Stay where you are!" you ordered.

The double doorway of the house had swung open and I could see the silhouette of a man hunched over in a wheelchair. Could that be Tilfer's dad, the author of *Around Harvard Square*, the great V.C. Peerpont? Whoever it was, he was holding something. Was it a book, a flashlight—or a gun?

Tilfer was still banging away at the *Harvard* sign. Five, six, seven . . .

"We need to go," Lao said.

"We need all eight signs," you said.

"The cop car is like a street or two away," I warned.

"Do you want to get cut? Stay on mission!"

Tilfer hit the *Harvard* sign again. Ten, eleven, twelve. Nothing. He was tiring out.

You grabbed the sledgehammer. There was a wild glimmer in your face, like when someone holds a flashlight beneath their chin. You began a two-handed swing, and as you reared back you nearly took me and Lao out and almost cracked Meera's skull. Then you took another swing and another and there was sweat coming down your face and the air was ringing with the sounds of your blows and the sirens were blaring and Meera put her hands to her ears and Lao was screaming that it was time to stop, the cops were around the corner and the sign was fucking bolted in and that's why it wasn't moving, and you just kept on hammering until the sign tilted off the top of the pole for a moment and then toppled down to the cobblestones.

With that, you spun around like an Olympic hammer thrower and launched the sledgehammer toward the house, and it fell in the grassy front lawn with a thick thud. "That's for the Chair, motherfuckers!"

Cops closing in, you scooped up the sign and we bolted for the station wagon.

CHAPTER THIRTY-FOUR

ME AND MY GIRLFRIEND

"Your girl is mad crazy."

Meera, Lao, and I were at breakfast at J.D. Hall, trying to make sense of what had happened the night before. Other students drifted by us, off to classes and study groups and club meetings and whatever. None of them seemed real to us, only the comp was real. The dining hall strike was still dragging on but we could barely hear the protests through the thick walls of the hall and the never-ending din of the students. None of us had gotten much sleep, in part because after we had collected the signs and dropped them off at the castle to complete our mission, you had driven the car around for hours, intent on returning it with so little gas the rental place wouldn't be able to start it up. We ended up running on fumes for the last few miles and pushing it for the final eight hundred yards back to the lot.

"Zippa isn't my girl," I replied to Lao. "I don't even like that phrase. It suggests ownership or something sexist."

"You know what I mean. She's out of control! She's fucking up our comp."

"Why do you even care?" I said. "I thought you were only comping to prove some point about robots. Does it really matter to you if you get on the staff or not?"

"We've made it this far, we need to go all the way. We're never going to fit in with the Final Clubs and I don't want to. This is our thing!"

"Lao is right," Meera said. "We need to finish this."

"You do realize the *Harpoon* staff is mostly guys?" I said.

"And they'll have one more woman if I make it on," Meera replied. "I'm done with Bollywood, I'm finished with all of it. Getting on the *Harpoon* staff could open doors for me becoming a writer or a director in Hollywood. I want this—I need this—and if Zippa is going to ruin things for us, you need to stop her."

"All I know is she's on some sort of mission," I said.

"Like a secret agent?" Lao said.

"What's the point of the mission?" Meera asked. "To get on the *Harpoon*?"

"It's more than that," I answered. "The Chair was involved, I think."

Lao frowned. "Think? Don't you think we need to know exactly what's going on?"

Our Phoolz group met again at sunset on the front steps of the *Harpoon*, but Emoticon wasn't there and her name wasn't on the envelope that had been tacked to the purple-and-banana yellow door of the castle. "Emoticon's been cut," you said.

"How do you know that?" Meera asked.

You shrugged. "I saw Spooner and Ruggles leaving her room. She looked shook."

Spectrum jabbed a finger at you. "This is your fault."

"Hey, everything is everything."

"Is that a rhetorical statement or an epistemological one?"

"I'm gonna go with tautological."

"Let's deal with what's happening," Meera said. "Emoticon being cut is unfair!"

"Any of us could be next," Spectrum said. "In the Great Clown Massacre of '89, they cut everyone."

I took the envelope down and pulled out a cream-colored note. "It's . . ."

". . . completely blank," Spectrum finished.

Meera examined the card. "There's gotta be something we're missing."

Lao took the card and held it up to a light mounted on the *Harpoon* steps.

I peeked at it and saw there was a faint watermark of bulging eyes and a tongue. "The Frog Club."

"I think we're supposed to—" Lao began.

"Pull a prank on the Frog Club," Spectrum interrupted. "Getting into their parties is impossible. We'd have a better chance flying through a wormhole."

"Is that difficult?" I asked.

"If you don't mind being stretched infinitely by the warping of time-space while being incinerated by Hawking radiation, it's not too bad," Meera said.

"Anyone have any good ideas?" I asked. "About the club, not the wormhole."

You raised a finger. "We could burn the club to the ground."

"Anyone else have any ideas not involving arson or homicide?" I asked. "Let's start with how we even get into the place."

"Everyone knows you can't get past the d-d-doormen," Tilfer said.

Meera sighed.

"What's the matter?" I asked.

"I have an idea," she said. "But it's a last resort."

As the weekly party geared up, the streets outside the Frog Club were clogged with women from nearby colleges arriving by car, by bus, by foot, and, in the case of a quartet of brunettes presumably trying to make an impression, by horse-drawn carriage. The members of the club—all male—went through the front door without even so much as a backward glance at the growing throngs. The guests—mostly female—filed through the side door, while massive bouncers sorted through the would-be talent, admitting the women deemed hot enough to party with, and refusing entry to the not-so-hot, lukewarm, and downright chilly, including three of the four women who had arrived by carriage.

"How are we going to get in?" I asked.

"I don't have a clue," Spectrum said. He had traded his army jacket for a fairly decent tux, but the whole look was undone by his mud-spattered work boots and that damn surgical mask.

Lao was wearing a rumpled suit with a T-shirt reading, *There is no spoon*, I was wearing a secondhand sport coat and jeans, and you had on a dashiki. Of all of us, Tilfer was the best dressed—he had on a pricey white tux—but his jacket was about three sizes too small. None of us looked like we belonged at a Frog Club party.

"Meera said she had a plan for getting in," you said.

"So what is it?" Spectrum asked.

"That's her plan right there," you replied.

Meera, in full makeup and with a red bindi dot on her forehead, had arrived wearing an outfit from one of her films—that purple sari with an emerald sash embroidered with flowers—and she was working it like a star. I had spotted this outfit framed on her wall back in her dorm room—she must have broken the glass and pulled it out to meet this fashion emergency. She had her Bollywood high beams on, and when she looked at me I swear I got spots before my eyes like peering at the sun. Her super-elevated platform pumps made her seem ten feet tall and she had a roll in her walk I hadn't noticed before. Men turned their heads, women gave her the side-eye, and all the Phoolz gawked.

"You look like a beautiful harem dancer," Spectrum gushed.

"Not really a compliment," Meera said. Then she commanded, "Follow me."

We all walked up to the side entrance. The two man-mountains working the door stared at Meera like each of them was going to cry.

"I can't believe it," one doorman said. "Karisma Kamal!"

"We used to watch your movies when we were kids in Hyderabad!" said the other. They each took hold of the velvet rope and raised it high. We were in.

"H-h-how did you know that was going to happen?" Tilfer asked.

Meera shrugged. "Last time we were here, Kostya mentioned the doormen were from India—expats are my demo."

"That was easier than I would have ever thought," Lao said.

"I also disabled their security cameras via computer before we arrived," Meera said. "But I guess all you guys noticed was the dress." Suddenly, she looked chilly and uncomfortable and she rubbed her arms. "Tosh, can you give me your jacket?"

I took off my sport coat and draped it over her bare shoulders.

She shivered. "Let's get this over with."

In sci-fi movies, explorers are always stumbling across perfectly preserved prehistoric places where, through some environmental oddity or scientific breakthrough, dinosaurs and saber-toothed tigers and Neanderthals are all living together, hidden from the electric eyes of the modern world. Inside the club was like that, but the time period that had been preserved in amber was a way of life that had never really been, but maybe had never really gone away, where men were men, women were girls, and money and family names were everything. Inside the club, the guys were all in tuxes, the women all in formal dresses, and an armada of serving staff in black suits attended to every guest. There was a grand piano in one corner of the ballroom, a baby grand in another, and fully stocked bars in the other two.

The entire place had a frog theme—taxidermied giant frogs adorned the walls, green carpeting covered the floors, the crystals in the chandeliers dripping from the ceiling were shaped like tadpoles, and all the attendees, like frogs with bulging throats, were blowing themselves up to be bigger than they actually were.

I glanced around. "Who are the guests? I don't recognize them from the Yard."

"The women are from random girl colleges," Spectrum explained. "The men are club members and freshmen who've been punched." He added under his breath, "They should have punched me too!"

"I should punch you for wanting to be punched," you interjected. "Look around—this place is gross."

The female servers wore short skirts and low-cut tops and they did a little dip as they displayed their hors d'oeuvres.

Meera folded her arms over her bare midriff. "I feel icky dressed like this."

You put a hand on her shoulder. "We're rebels, sister—you don't need to apologize for anything."

"I'm not sure decolletage is revolutionary," Meera replied, "but thanks."

"Screw this," Spectrum scoffed. "I'm going rogue." He sauntered over to the refreshment table, emptied a flask of something into the punch bowl, and scooted off.

"Really?" Lao said. "Spiking the punch bowl? That was tired in the 1950s."

"I'm having second thoughts about this whole thing," Meera said, her arms wrapped tight around herself. "Maybe we should just get out of here."

"I thought you came here to help prank the club," you said. "Or are you just here to walk the red carpet?"

"Pranks are one thing. But I know it's easy to take these things too far."

"M-m-maybe these people deserve it," Tilfer said.

I sniffed the air. "Something smells weird."

You wrinkled your nose. "It's the Last Supper."

"What?"

"I thought the Last Supper was just a rumor," Lao said.

"Does that smell like a rumor?" you said.

A pungent aroma now filled the room, like a Texas barbecue crossed with the Bronx Zoo. Along with the other guests, we were ushered into a massive dining hall where a glittering arrangement of plates and goblets and silverware had been laid out on a long banquet table. The partygoers began to take their seats and servers streamed out of the kitchen bearing big covered trays.

"What are they eating?" I asked.

Lao picked up a menu from one of the place settings.

First Course

Soup—"Baiji Dolphin bisque." Cream soup with dolphin flesh, flavored with bergamot and seasoned with great cognac.

Salad—"Manatee." Chopped fresh-salted fillet of manatee with pear crisp, whipped egg whites, and Beluga caviar, with light mayonnaise, presented on a bed of radish shavings.

Second Course

Blue Whale, roasted with avocado vinaigrette in "béchamel" wine-cream sauce, chardonnay-shallot emulsion, served boneless.

California Condor, spatchcocked bird prepared in a cast-iron skillet, drizzled with marinade of herbs, roasted to a crisp crust with allspice sauce and black pepper.

Arm of Mountain Gorilla "Provençal," primate limb baked in batter with white mustard, pickled beets, and "Provençal" spices, accompanied by crispy okra.

Dessert

Green-Billed Hummingbird Soufflé, with pistachio ice cream. Served with raw bing cherry.

"Green-billed hummingbirds?" I said. "Aren't those . . ."

Your eyes were bright with tears of rage. ". . . just like Festus."

"They're feasting on endangered species?" I said. "You don't think . . ."

"I still haven't found Festus and I wouldn't put it past these Final Club fuckers."

"This is a joke, right?"

"It's a tradition that goes back a couple hundred years," you explained. "The pledges are served the rarest meats on earth on initiation night. The story goes that back in 1663 the new members ate the last dodo eggs."

Meera was tearing up too. "How can you eat a species that's going extinct?"

"Over easy, I think, or maybe scrambled," Lao replied.

"I think they're about to present dessert," I said.

That's when we saw Dorian and Davis. They were shirtless, but with bow ties around their necks, and along with a half dozen other new pledges they were pushing a wheeled table with a huge soufflé on top. A cloud of hummingbirds swirled around the dessert, and every so often, Dorian or Davis would scatter red dust over top of the pastry, like they were seeding a lawn, and the birds would flick at the crimson sprinkles with their tongues, bobbing and weaving in increasingly eccentric patterns.

"They're drugging them," you said, charging forward. "We have to stop this!"

But the crowd was too thick, and Dorian and Davis and the other pledges were too quick. I can't tell you much about what happened next because I had a parrot named Birdie when I was in middle school and I hate to see animals suffer. I couldn't focus on what was happening or maybe I just didn't want to see. I can tell you that whatever did happen began when Davis and Dorian pulled out baseball bats, and ended when they dropped them in pools of blood and feathers on the floor. The hummingbirds that weren't dazed or dead scattered around the room.

The bloody soufflé was wheeled back to the kitchen to be sliced and served at the end of dinner. Dorian and Davis and the other pledges disappeared with it.

"I didn't see Festus and I don't think we're gonna find him in this mess," I said.

"This place is sicker than I ever imagined," Lao said.

"We all have a choice," you said. "We can leave now, or we can give the Frog Club what it deserves. There's no backing out once we start what I have planned."

Meera clenched her fists. "We need to destroy these assholes."

Lao, Tilfer, and I all nodded in agreement.

"Then follow me," you said.

CHAPTER THIRTY-FIVE

KILLING IN THE NAME

The party was growing louder and wilder. The sounds of the exotic menagerie of animals being slaughtered in the kitchens was mixing with the laughter of the partygoers and the music of a deejay who had set up two turntables against a wall of the ballroom. People were beginning to dance and the smell of roasted meats was getting stronger and you signaled to the rest of us to follow you. We all snuck up the stairway which led to a giant marble hallway, and the bizarre aromas and the dance music and the voices of party guests faded behind us. The corridor was lit by flickering torches mounted in the walls, giving the whole scene a haunted-house feel.

"Hey, where did Spectrum go?" I asked.

"He stayed downstairs to party," you answered.

"If his prank is better than ours, we'll get cut and he'll move ahead."

"That's the last thing I'm worried about." You pointed to a series of brass doors off the main hall. "This is where they bring their girls."

"How do you know?" Lao asked.

"I was doing my research on Harvard history and one of them tried to bring me here. There wasn't a happy ending—for him."

We opened a door and crept into one of the rooms. There was a large brass bed in the center and all four walls were lined with shelves stocked with bottles of alcohol of all shapes, sizes, and kinds. "Every bedroom has a different theme," you explained. "The only thing they have in common is the brass bed."

We left the bottle room and darted down the hallway. The rooms were empty because the Frog Club members were all downstairs partying it up, so you were able to give us a grand tour of the place without any interruptions. There was a room filled with vintage pornographic videos, another room lined with mirrors, and another decorated with raunchy artwork inspired by the *Kama Sutra*.

Meera shook her head. "Why are Westerners so obsessed with the *Kama Sutra*? It's really more about philosophy than sex."

"That's true," said Lao, "but you can't jerk off to Kierkegaard."

In addition to a brass bed, the next room had walls that were plastered with paintings of butterflies. But when I looked closer, I saw the decorations weren't in fact paintings—they were thousands of actual butterflies that had been carefully pinned and mounted and framed. Some of the pinned butterflies were still fluttering.

"It just gets worse with these motherfuckers, doesn't it?" I said.

You pointed down the hall. "The main chamber is at the end."

We scurried into the hallway and through massive double doors. We found ourselves on a balcony overlooking a huge indoor pool. The room was illuminated by red and purple lights that swept across the pool.

"They call it the Lilypad," you said. "This is where every Frog Club party eventually winds up. New pledges earn points for the number of naked girls they can convince to come up here."

"What do they use the points for?" Lao asked.

"Fuck if I know," you said. "Maybe discounts on firearms or jockstraps."

"The p-p-pool is empty," Tilfer said.

"During every party they supposedly fill it with champagne," you said. "We're going to fill it with something else."

"What?" I asked.

"It's time for the second part of the plan. Meera, thanks for the contact!" You climbed down a spiral staircase, opened a large window next to the pool, and whistled. "How are you boys doing?"

Wojtek and Kostya pulled up outside in their sanitation truck. "We've been draining sewage all day, so not very good," Wojtek called up.

Kostya looked grim. "You really want to do this, lady?"

"We're already doing it," you replied.

"This is biohazardous material," Kostya said. "It's not gonna kill people, I don't think, but it's gonna make them sick, maybe . . ."

Meera balled her fists. "We need to take out every one of these species-killing motherfuckers."

"You're the boss," Kostya said, admiring Meera's sari. "I gave you my number before—any chance I get yours tonight?"

"Not this time," Meera replied. "But we appreciate the sewage."

Wojtek and Kostya propped a ladder next to the window and climbed up with a hose, and you, Lao, Meera, Tilfer, and I pulled the hose through and positioned it at the edge of the pool. It took some time, but we filled a good portion of the pool with sewage, and Kostya and Wojtek pulled back the hose, lowered the ladder, and drove away as we covered our noses to blunt the horrible smell. In the purple-and-red glow of the room, you couldn't tell that the pool was filled with sludge. Lao peeked out the door down the hallway to make sure the coast was clear.

"How do you know so much about Harvard secrets?" I whispered to you.

"The Chair—I owe her a lot. She sent me books and old files and magazine clippings so I would be prepared."

"This isn't just about getting on the *Harpoon*, is it?" I asked.

But you were already sneaking away and we were already following you. As we came down the steps, the diners were starting to head up. The party was morphing into something else, something from a late-night cable movie, as people left the banquet table and the ballroom, stripping off clothes as they went.

"Davis?"

I ran into my old roommate on the stairs, as I headed down and he headed up. He was naked to the waist and his bare torso was spattered with bird blood. He had a haunted, hunted look on his face and his green eyes darted back and forth.

"T-T-Tosh?" Davis said. "What are you doing here?"

"Where's Dorian? And why the fuck did you kill those hummingbirds?"

Davis looked down at his feet. "Dorian headed up to the Lilypad. Things are getting crazy, man. We had to kill all those birds if we were gonna make the club."

"Do you know how messed up that sounds?"

"Yeah. I mean no. Everything seemed cool at first, I don't know."

"You need to get out."

"I can't! I have to go to the pool—it's initiation night."

"If you stay, you're just another racist, sexist bad person."

"I can't be racist," Davis shot back. "My mom is a quarter black. Or maybe she's half Portuguese. She doesn't talk about it much."

I raised my arms and backed away from him. "Enjoy your swim."

Davis ran up the stairs toward the Lilypad.

In the dining hall, we spotted Spectrum, who looked very pleased with himself. "I spiked the punch. What did you guys do?"

"You'll see," you said.

Spectrum sniffed the air. "What's that smell? It's worse than the food."

Meera looked horrified. "You ate the food?"

"Why not?" Spectrum said. "It all tasted like chicken."

There was an all-out stampede now as naked and half-naked and quarter-naked members and pledges and guests ran up the stairs, laughing and hollering, and began diving and cannonballing and belly-flopping into the pool, too drunk or too stoned or too filled with lust or whatever to smell what was going on until they were neck-deep or worse in raw sewage. We were moving against the tide as we headed for the exits, but at this point nobody was paying us any attention.

"Wait!" you called out when we approached the door.

"We have to get out of here," I said.

You grabbed my hand. "Listen to the music, mon."

A reggae beat was swelling all around us.

"I bribed the deejay," you said.

You pulled me onto the dance floor. Balloons bounced across the ballroom and stray streamers of confetti fell from above. Only a few partygoers remained on the dance floor. Most of the other dancers had headed upstairs to swim in the pool we had just defiled. You put your arms around my neck and swayed to the rhythm.

"We don't have time for this," I said. "They're gonna discover what we did any second."

"Irie, mon," you said. "You have to take your opportunities."

You pulled me in close and rested your head against my chest. I could feel the warmth of your breath, smell the mango scent from your dreads, feel your heart beating in time with mine. I closed my eyes and hoped I'd remember.

"We did it," you said. "We fucked all these Ivy motherfuckers. Fyah fi yu!"

The screaming of the other partygoers was delayed, like thunder, until we were safely out the door.

You and Spectrum went your separate ways in the Yard and Lao, Meera, and I headed back to our dorm room. Meera threw herself exhausted on the couch, Lao lay down on the floor, and I paced. After about twenty minutes, I turned on the TV. There was already a report about the prank on the local news.

"Oh shit," Lao said.

We all gathered around the TV. According to the report, hundreds of students were ill and a dozen or more had been hospitalized in the wake of the release of raw sewage at the Frog Club.

Paramedics were at the scene, police had taped off the block and opened a criminal investigation, and a TV reporter was interviewing witnesses about the toxic mess. First up was an editor from the *Magenta*.

"This so-called prank has all the hallmarks of a *Harpoon* operation," Morven S. Morlington told the news reporter. "Until the castle is shut down, we're all in danger."

The next interview was with two city workers: Wojtek and Kostya.

"Whoever hijacked our truck and did this terrible thing," Wojtek said, as Kostya nodded, "had no regard for life—and probably a punk-ass hook shot. Don't ask me how I know that."

Meera turned off the TV. "He's right."

I shook my head. "I really improved my hook since I played with him."

"I'm talking about the no-regard-for-life part."

"Come on, it was just a prank," Lao said.

"No, it wasn't," Meera said. "We stepped through the teleporter, just like the Chair said. We're becoming different people and it's not good."

"Nobody died," I said.

"Really? That's our standard now? The absence of fatalities?"

"Why are you getting so worked up about this?" Lao asked.

"Because I've seen this before," Meera said. "This is why I left Mumbai."

"Because of a prank?" I said.

"Because of things spinning out of control! I left Bollywood for the video game industry because I thought I could make a difference. But all those games with women with big boobs and guys with huge guns, they're not just games—they're actually an accurate rendering of the subconscious minds of men."

"So what happened to you?" I asked.

"The minute I started raising questions about why there couldn't be more playable female characters, or why some game was actually awarding points for sexual assault, every guy in the industry turned against me! It started off as jokes, then insults, then threats. They posted lies about me online, hacked my e-mail, sexually harassed me in public—they even created a video game to silence me!"

"How did that work?" Lao asked.

"The game is a first-person shooter where the target is me. They titled it *The Most Dangerous Game* and released it as a prank, but it caught on as a bootleg. Every trope I had tried to expose, they used—damsels in distress, women as a reward, violence against females. It was horrible."

"Are you serious?" I said. "Why didn't you go to the police?"

Meera was crying now. "Don't you think I tried that? The police said it was just locker-room humor. Nobody died, they told me. I wanted to stay in Mumbai, I didn't want to run, I wanted to keep fighting—but sometimes you have to know when there's no future in what you're doing." A look of realization came over her face. "That's why we have to drop out of the *Harpoon* comp."

Lao clenched his fists. "She's right, I see it now. This is bullshit. Did you see Dorian and Davis and the bird-bashing soufflé? Do you realize how many people got hurt by that sewage? Zippa's not a prankster—she's a psychopath! I saw you two dancing like it was a party!"

"Well, it kinda *was* a party," I said.

"You're missing my point!" Lao yelled. "You're missing Meera's point! We don't want to join the *Harpoon* if it means turning into the people we hate!"

There was a knock on the door, and we all froze and looked at each other.

Meera wiped her cheeks. "It's okay. Just get it."

I went over to the door and opened it. Holding a reporter's notebook, Morven S. Morlington was standing in the entryway.

CHAPTER THIRTY-SIX

NUTHIN' BUT A "G" THANG

Morven invited himself into our dorm room and plopped himself down on the couch. He reminded me of undersized point guards I would sometimes go against, fireplugs who played bigger than their height because their swag gave them stature. He was dressed in a black sport coat with the sleeves rolled up, gray slacks, and his alligator-skin boat shoes. When he took his seat, his feet were left dangling about a foot off the floor.

"What do you want?" I asked. "We're kinda in the middle of something."

"That you are." Morven smirked. "I hear you've been busy."

"Yeah, we saw you on the news. You can't tie us to anything."

"I'm not here to expose your prank—at least not yet. I just want you to understand the *Harpoon* isn't about humor. It's bullying masquerading as humor."

"Maybe we can change that."

Morven laughed. "How's that going so far? That's how institutions survive—they change people who think they're changing the institution."

Now it was Lao's turn to laugh. "You're such a fraud! We saw your piece in the Legion of Dishonor making fun of LGBT people! You are just as big an asshole as anyone who has ever tried to write for the *Harpoon*."

Morven looked down at his boat shoes. "I'm not a hypocrite—I didn't know who I was."

"And who are you?" I asked.

"I'm gay," Morven said. "That's not a secret to anyone who really knows me."

"Then why did you write that homophobic piece for the *Harpoon* comp?"

"I was in a different place. I've been teased all my life—*Dwarf! Hobbit! Which elf are you: Snap, Crackle, or Pop?* I could deal with the short jokes, but I wasn't ready to be gay on top of that. So I kept in the closet, even to myself. When I comped for the *Harpoon*, Spooner sniffed that out. I don't know why, but he was relentless about needling me with homophobic jokes. I wrote that horrible piece to prove to Spooner that I wasn't who he suspected I was. Of course, I was wrong and he was right."

"*What you laugh at is who you are*," I murmured.

"Now I'm out and it's fantastic," Morven said. "Getting cut from the *Harpoon* was the best thing that happened to me—and I can see comping for the *Harpoon* is the worst thing that's happened to you. It's turning you into monsters—like Spooner."

"So you want us to quit just like you did?" I asked.

"We already made our decision," Meera said.

"We're quitting," Lao said. "All of us."

"That's too bad," Morven replied. "Because I want you to go all the way."

Meera gave him a hard look. "Why?"

"Have you ever been to the Nathan Marsh Pusey Library?" Morven asked.

Lao and I shrugged, but Meera nodded her head vigorously.

"Is there a library you haven't been to?" I muttered.

"Not many undergrads know about the Nate, so it's a good place to study," Meera explained.

"James Bond would have loved this library," Morven said. "It's a remote facility, sunken underground, guards outside every collection. It even has this halon gas system that puts out fires without water so the books aren't damaged."

"That's a lot of security for a library," Lao said.

"Pusey isn't just any library, it houses the Harvard Archives—

three hundred years of files on all the university's students, professors, employees, clubs, and course catalogs. There's a graveyard of Harvard secrets buried underground there. That's where I found out about Harvard's secret gay court."

"Secret gay what?" I asked.

"The Chair's suicide note wasn't the first one to make waves on campus. In 1920, a freshman student left a suicide note revealing a hush-hush network of gay soirees. These parties were the shit—sailors, drag queens, hookers, freshmen finding themselves, a real sexual mélange. The president of the university was so alarmed to discover there was *gasp—homosexuality!*—happening at Harvard that he created a top-secret panel to investigate."

"How did you find out about this?"

"I was going through the Harvard Archives, really just on a fishing expedition for potential *Magenta* stories, and I came across a box marked, *Secret Court*. I know, right? Kind of like I once was: hiding in plain sight. The proceedings were a witch hunt—students turning in students, professors ratting out professors, freshmen getting expelled, powerful families trying to suppress the whole story. The Peerpont family was leading the charge—they have a long history of opposing gay rights!"

"I don't get why you're telling us all this."

"Before Professor Bell died, she donated her papers to the Harvard Archives. I came across them when I was looking into the secret court stuff. That's how I found out about 'Rhonda Hope,' and that's how I discovered something was going on. The Chair's papers haven't been completely transferred and sorted yet, but she was working on a detailed guide to *Around Harvard Square*."

Meera folded her arms. "Everyone knows she was working on that."

"Yes, but I discovered something in her files I think you'll find interesting."

Morven reached into the pocket of his jacket and pulled out a sheet of paper and we gathered around to read it. At the top, written in grand calligraphy, was a date.

"That's the day after tomorrow," Meera said.

Below the date was a list:

Timer
33-1/3 rpm record
Polka-dot bow tie
Map of Cambridge sewer system
Chateau Mouton Rothschild 1945
Roman candles
Yellow silk ascot
Manuscript

"This is a pretty random list," I said.

"It's not," Morven said. "In fact, it's pretty specific. I believe the *Harpoon* is about to open up the Vault of Time."

"Vecky mentioned the Vault of Time," I said. "Why should we care?"

"Because they only do it every twenty-five years. The vault is a time capsule full of all the things the *Harpoon* wants to keep hidden away. Opening it is like Pandora's box—all this vintage shit is going to hit the fan. Every important living *Harpoon* member is going to come back for the opening and they're going to stage a massive ceremony. There's going to be hazing and pranks and all sorts of illegalities and people are gonna get hurt. This is the best opportunity in a long time to bring down the whole institution. This scandal could be bigger than the Secret Court! That's why I need you to complete the comp and get me some hard evidence of the bad shit that's going down."

Lao laughed. "And why would we do that?"

"Because if you don't, all of you are gonna get kicked out of college after I put an article about your little prank on the front page. You saw how much attention my scoop on the Chair's goodbye note got. This will be even bigger."

"So you're blackmailing us?"

"I prefer to call it straight-whitemailing."

Lao turned away. "Meera, do the thing."

"You guys have a thing?" I asked.

Meera rushed over and put Morven into some sort of exotic hold, her strong arms locked behind his head.

"Arggh!" Morven hollered. "You just lost your slot on the 'Fifteen Hottest Freshmen'!"

Meera dragged him to the doorway and flung him into the hall with such force that his alligator-skin boat shoes flew off his feet.

"Everyone bashes the media until they really need it!" Morven yelled, flat on his back in the corridor. "Maybe it's not pretty, but if people like me aren't digging up the real facts, people like V.C. Peerpont can do or say anything they want! If you don't help me with this story, nobody will ever know the truth!"

"We don't need you," I said. "If we find out anything, we'll tell everyone."

"Peerpont will just say it's a lie! You say one fact, he says another, and the public splits 50/50. When you're telling an important story, you have to do more than pass along a bunch of opinions and throw up your hands and say, *You figure it out*. I'm gonna present the whole story, fully reported, so he can't deny it! You *need* me!"

"Guys, maybe we should listen to him," Meera said. "If the *Harpoon* really is planning something big and dangerous, we need to help stop it, if we can."

"We agreed we were out!" Lao shot back. "Morven's story could be bullshit!"

"The list he showed us looks real," Meera said.

"Have I ever written anything wrong in the *Magenta*?" Morven said. "I mean, without a correction? If you're looking to expose the truth, I'm on your side."

"The *Magenta* is pretty accurate," Lao admitted. "But robots are accurate too, and ultimately they're gonna kill us all."

"If the *Harpoon* really is up to something bad, maybe it's better that we stay in the comp so we can help do something about it, right?" I said. "Do you agree?"

"That makes a certain amount of twisted sense," Lao said.

Meera helped Morven to his feet. "You're on our team now."

Morven brushed himself off and stood there in his socks. "So what next?"

"Now the fun begins," I said.

CHAPTER THIRTY-SEVEN

EX-FACTOR

I went down into the basement. I needed to know more about the mission the Chair had sent you on. Did it have anything to do with the Vault of Time? I just needed to talk to you. We hadn't seen each other alone since we had gone to the butterfly field. The more I thought back on it, the more that felt like it had been a first date. Or maybe our outing to the Mexican restaurant and then to the dining hall after hours had been our first date. Can you declare a first date retroactively? Are there emotions you don't realize you're having until you look back on them later? Maybe we had struck up a romance without knowing it. I just hoped I could figure out where things were going before whatever was going on had gone away.

As I slipped down the stairs, I heard reggae music floating up. The rhythm was warm and full and made me think about the way water pulls at your legs when you wade out from the beach. The tide is like an invitation, but it's a warning too; the feeling is gentle yet you can sense that it could easily overpower you like a lion carrying a cub in its mouth. The rage and recklessness you had shown in the comp so far, your mission with its secret agenda, the hidden details of your personal history—it was all pulling at me, threatening and welcoming me to wade into your waters.

I was in the dark of the basement now and the music was loud and the beat was booming and I could smell curry in the air. Lines of light appeared around the edges of the trapdoor in the floor that led to your room. I mulled over what I would say to you when I had you alone and I daydreamed about what you would say back to me. Maybe you would show me what you were working on or maybe I would tell you about something I had written. Maybe I would talk about my crazytown sister and my crazytown dad and you would talk about West Omelas on the north coast. I could talk about writing and you could talk about art and we could . . .

"Phool Tech?"

Someone emerged from the shadows and stepped over the bust of V.C. Peerpont, which had toppled somehow and stretched across the corridor. The crack in the statue now extended from the top of the hair-deprived head, down the middle of the once-proud nose, through the narrow canyon of the mole-dotted chin, down to the plaque on the pedestal that read, *What you laugh at is who you are.*

I stepped back. "What are you doing here?"

Spooner sipped at his golden goblet, and I wondered how he managed to always keep it filled, and also what the fuck was in it. "My brother lives in this dorm, and so did I when I was a freshman. Do they still have the hamburger option?"

"What's that?"

"They used to have a grill in this dorm where you could get a hamburger if you didn't want whatever they were serving in the freshmen dining hall that night. The burgers were fucking awesome and the place was open until midnight. If I could only eat one food forever it would be burgers. You don't still have the hamburger option?"

"I don't . . . I don't think so."

"You know, they say if you walk the path between Straus and Matthews after midnight, you can hear the sounds of a party and you can smell malt liquor in the air."

"Is this like a ghost story?"

"This is real, I smelled it myself! I thought it was coming from the hamburger grill, but it turns out there used to be a brew house here that burned down a couple hundred years ago.

Sparks from two prisoners being burned at the stake set it off and people died and the area's been haunted ever since. You ever hear about that?"

"I heard part of that story, maybe."

Spooner grunted. "How do you spend your downtime, Phool Tech?"

"I was just . . . doing some laundry," I lied.

Spooner laughed. "No reason to be afraid of me! We're both off duty right now. You're doing well in the comp. Just finish strong now that we're in the home stretch."

"You . . . you think I have a chance?"

"You have more than a chance," Spooner said. "I like your energy. You remind me of me. Peerponts have been getting into Harvard for decades, but my family didn't think I had what it took and they were fucking surprised when I got in."

"Nobody in my family had ever really been to college before," I said. "My dad did a couple semesters at a community college. I guess they weren't that shocked when I got into Harvard—they used up their supply of shock when I told them I was applying."

Spooner smiled, and for once his smile wasn't mocking or cruel or sardonic. "I remember getting the letter. All the mailboxes at Exeter are next to each other and every student is applying to the same places and getting responses on the same day. I sprinted down there after crew practice with a dozen other guys. I was the only one who got a letter. It was like the Rapture, and I was leaving the sinners behind. *Veritas*, motherfuckers! Getting into Harvard is maybe the best feeling ever, am I right?"

"They slipped my letter under our screen door," I said. "My sister got to it first and I had to chase her around the house and tackle her before she handed it over."

"That bitch!"

"She tried to play it off, but that letter was the only time she was ever impressed with me. I overheard her boasting to an ex-boyfriend that *we* had gotten into Harvard. She really used the word *we*, like it was a team accomplishment."

"So what do you think drove you?"

"What do you mean?"

"I'm betting all your friends upstate are working at car dealerships, selling real estate, or going to trade schools. How did you pull yourself up by your bootstraps and end up here?" He paused. "Why are you smiling?"

"That phrase, *pull yourself up by your bootstraps*."

"What about it?"

"It's just interesting when old-timey phrases like that keep ticking. Two hundred years ago, *pulling yourself up by your bootstraps* was supposed to mean something was logically impossible—like seeing with your eyes shut. But it got filtered through the American Dream Machine and now bootstrapping means succeeding without help, upward mobility. We even *boot up* our computers! It's absurdity that became terminology and mythology. Do people even have real bootstraps anymore?"

"So you're a thinker, is that it? Is that how you got away from upstate? Did you always look into things in a deeper way than all your friends and family?"

If I was being honest, it wasn't thinking that got me out. If anything, it was fear. I was so afraid I wasn't as smart as people thought I was, I wasn't as good as people needed me to be, that those feelings of inadequacy sustained me through long days practicing on the court when everyone else was eating pizza, and long nights studying when everyone else was out partying. When anybody asked, I said my dad worked for the town, which wasn't a lie, but the complete story was that he worked for the town as a garbageman. Not that I was fooling anyone, because everyone would see him riding the streets, hanging off his truck, picking up their trash and their recyclables. He smelled of trash because that shit didn't wash off, and when his knees went bad and he took disability and retired early, I was furiously happy. I have his working smell in my nose, in my memory, that olfactory triptych of trash collection: decay, disinfectant, defeat. I never wanted to end up like him; hell, I didn't want *him* to end up like him—both possibilities terrified me and drove me. I didn't succeed because I thought I was better than anyone else, I worked harder because I was afraid I was worse.

But I didn't say any of that to Spooner. "Yeah, maybe," I muttered.

He clapped me on the shoulder. "There's nothing wrong with feeling better than other people, with being someone who stands up and stands out, a real man. I know it's not politically correct to be masculine, but fuck that. I've never met a woman who wasn't turned on by a guy who opens doors, picks up the check, wears out that ass when it comes down to it—these feminazis say one thing in the streets and another in the sheets, am I right? It's exhausting to be a man. I used to have weak thoughts, thinking that if I were a girl I wouldn't have all this pressure, am I right?"

"I don't follow."

"Come on, you must have thought about it, every guy has. I mean, what would it be like to have tits and no dick? To have your menstrual cycles align with someone else's? Can you imagine that? Sometimes I get tired of having to be the dude. You know, Harvard invented the whole idea of modern masculinity. The Harvard Man was expected to strive valiantly in the arena, put bros over hos, and live in this world of cigar lounges and big-game hunts. My dad thought sending me here would help make a real man out of me. I don't know if I wanted that, but that's what we got." Spooner laughed and clapped my shoulder again.

I had nothing left to say to him and so we parted ways. I started heading back upstairs, but when I turned the corner and I was safely out of sight, I peeked back to see where he was going.

With a burst of light and a blast of reggae, Spooner opened the trapdoor leading to your room. As he climbed down into the rectangular hole, with the confident air of a man who had an invitation, he began to slowly unbutton his shirt. Then he disappeared from sight.

CHAPTER THIRTY-EIGHT

YOU GOT ME

Morven made good on his promise—in the *Magenta* the next morning, there wasn't a word connecting us to the prank at the Frog Club. The front-page story that day was about Mee Corp., which had just donated a huge sum of money to Harvard. There was a photo of the US president of Mee Corp., a beefy guy with a series of port-wine stains that stretched across his face like an archipelago.

"I've got some more big news," Meera said. "Spectrum's out."

"Are you serious?" I said.

"I ran into him in line for coffee and he was still in shock. He just looked at me and kept saying over and over, *A fellow of infinite jest, of most excellent fancy*."

"No idea what that means."

"All I know is that the *Harpoon* thought him spiking punch was weak—but they loved our sewage prank, so I guess we should be proud."

"So what do we do now?" I asked.

"We go back tonight for more punishment," Lao replied.

"Hey, are you okay?" Meera asked me. "You look a little down."

"I just had a bad dream last night," I said.

After breakfast, I spotted you outside the dining hall in the picket line with the other workers, and when you saw me you broke ranks and came over. "Shit is about to go down! Harvard's endowment is bigger than the GDP of Jamaica, Haiti, and Guyana *combined*, but the university's not giving in to any of our completely reasonable requests for decent benefits or a fair living wage or anything. Babylon is always trying to fuck with you—they stake out a position that's so batshit reactionary that if you meet them in the middle, the middle has already shifted to the far right. The strikers are getting so angry they're starting to talk about taking *extreme* . . . Are you even listening to me?"

"It's a little early in the morning for the revolution."

"What's up with you?"

"I saw Spooner dropping by your place last night."

You hesitated. "Tosh, I can explain that."

"You don't owe me anything."

"Damn right I don't."

"So we have nothing to talk about."

"I still want you to know what you saw is not what you think you saw."

"That doesn't make any fucking sense."

"Trust me."

"Why would I trust you? I don't even *know* you. I don't know what kind of mission you're on and you won't tell me."

"All I'm doing is what the Chair would have wanted."

"Why is it that the wishes of dead people and the selfish wants of the living are always a complete Venn diagram overlap?"

"You don't know what you're saying."

"Do you know what you're doing? Do you think this is what the Chair or your grandma would have wanted? Getting into the *Harpoon* on your fucking back?"

That's when you punched me, and I guess I deserved it.

The guests arrived at sunset.

They pulled up in a line of black limousines, some of them tricked out with glittery rims or racing stripes or spoilers, and one had treads like a military tank and another looked like a stretched-out version of the Batmobile. The visitors came wearing tuxedos, some basic black, others shocking pastels, some with flared lapels and pocket squares and tails that trailed on the ground. Spooner was the first undergrad to arrive, sporting a white suit and white shoes, then Vecky in a black gown and black veil, her hair in an elegant emerald beehive. Then the parade of graduates continued, screenwriters and TV showrunners and stand-up comics I had seen on cable television. Many of the alums were people who I didn't know except by reputation and rumor and the faded author photos on the dust jackets on books in the *Harpoon* library. I spotted Heinz Beck in a red fedora, Bobby Galbraith in a white tuxedo, Killy Trout brushing a shock of gray hair back from his bright green eyes. There was a buzz that V.C. Peerpont—the purported author of *Around Harvard Square* himself—was going to make an appearance later in the night.

Gawking at the guests was like peering into the past. All the Phoolz had been told to wait across the street from the castle as the alums and undergraduates made their way inside. I felt like I was time-traveling as I saw the authors I had only encountered in the pages of books stepping out of their cars and into my reality. They were all older and pastier and paunchier than I had pictured, but none of that mattered. The most important thing was that they were here and I was here and everything that was happening now was no work of fiction—it was real. Seeing all these famous authors enter a place I was trying to get into made me think that my dreams were closer than I thought, and that maybe I wasn't just some hick from Erie Canal country, and that someday I'd be pulling up to the castle in a vintage car and some new group of Phoolz would be gawking at me.

"Have you ever seen a bigger group of frauds in your life?" Lao grumbled.

"What? These are some of my favorite authors," I countered.

"Believe in the art if you want, but never believe in an artist. There are too many frauds out there. Anyway, someday they'll all be replaced by computers."

"Why are you so obsessed with the Cyberpocalypse?" Meera asked.

"It's not about the robots," Lao replied. "It's about the people who own the robots. If you think capitalism sucks when the capitalists own the means of production, you'll love it when they own the workers too."

"You're crazy."

"When Y2K happens, we'll see who's crazy."

You were standing with our group but you hadn't said much. I avoided your gaze when you looked over, and when you came close I made sure there was someone standing between us. I couldn't help thinking about what we had argued about, and the last thing I wanted on my mind was the image of Spooner on top of you.

The arrivals slowed to a trickle. Everyone noticed this one alum with a red pompadour like the Heat Miser—he had famously landed his own late-night chat show. Lao pointed out a grim-faced grad with an unruly beard like he had been marooned on a South Sea island—he produced a long-running prime-time cartoon. Another latecomer pulled up in a car with gull-wing doors. He was a big guy with a port-wine stain on his face and I realized he was the businessman I had seen in the *Magenta*.

"That's the US president of Mee Corp.," I said. "I didn't know he was a *Harpoon* alum."

Lao shuffled his feet. "We should get out of here. I feel like a capitalist tool watching all these rich folks."

"Why is the Mee Corp. guy waving at us?" Meera asked.

"He's not waving at us," Lao said. "We need to roll."

"He's definitely waving at us," I said. "And now he's coming over."

The president of Mee Corp. jogged up to us. He was a big white guy in a black tuxedo, a purple and banana-colored cummerbund, and high-tops from a Shanghai footwear company limned with LEDs that flashed as he walked. I had seen sneaks like that before. The guy offered a wide grin like he knew us or we should know him or we were gonna get to know each other. Lao tried to hide his face, but the executive plowed in and gave him a bear hug.

"Sebastian!" the big man boomed.

"Lao—how do you know this guy?" I asked.

Lao gave us a look so sheepish it could have been sheared. "This is my father."

CHAPTER THIRTY-NINE

WOO-HAH!! GOT YOU ALL IN CHECK

A few minutes later Lao's father went inside the castle with the other alums, but we were still interrogating Lao about what the hell had just happened.

I stared at him. "Why did he call you Sebastian?"

"Sebastian Montefort III," Lao replied. "That's my government name."

"Are you even Chinese?"

"I'm 100 percent Chinese," Lao shot back. "I was born in Guangzhou."

"But you were adopted by a white American family?"

"Doesn't make me any less Chinese."

"How old were you when you left China?"

"Two weeks."

"I nearly took a two-week trip to China back in high school."

"Your point?"

"You've spent a fortnight longer in China than I have."

"Who the fuck uses the term *fortnight*?"

"I've eaten Chinese food that has spent more time in China than you."

"*Fortnight*? Really? I haven't heard that term in four score and seven years."

"You're kinda missing the point."

"No, *you* are. You don't get to say who's Chinese and who isn't."

"Don't give me that. You totally lied to us."

"How did I lie?"

Meera interrupted: "What about the marijuana farm?"

"What?"

"The marijuana farm your family supposedly runs. Did you make that up too?"

"That's real—my dad dabbles in emerging industries."

"I don't get it," Meera said. "Your family has so much money—why are you always going on about revolution and robots and all of it?"

"The Cyberpocalypse is going to happen, maybe worse than we thought. We could be living in a computer simulation right now. Look around! There is no spoon!"

"Dude, you're losing it," I said.

"Lao, where is this technophobia coming from?" Meera asked. "Your dad runs one of the biggest technology companies on the planet!"

"That's why I hate robots so much—because I know what they can do! Mee Corp. coders have this joke that in the future the only two employees there will be one dog and a single human. The human will be there to feed the dog, and the dog will be there to bite the human if he tries to fuck with the machines."

"But why didn't you get your dad to help us . . ." Meera put her hands over her mouth. "The ads! You got your dad to buy the ads from me during the comp."

"I might have suggested it was a good idea," Lao admitted. "I was really trying to do this on my own."

I shook my head. "You should have just leveled with us, man."

Lao was getting angry now. "I grew up in the whitest town in the great white state of Connecticut. I didn't make myself Chinese—everyone around me made me Chinese."

"You lost me."

"Growing up, I thought I was a white kid because my entire family was white people. But the other kids kept coming at me with shit like, *Do you know kung fu? Do you have a fortune cookie in your lunch bag? Does it hurt having your eyes slant like that?* After a while, I thought, *Fuck it, I'm gonna be more Chinese than any of you motherfuckers can even handle.* And you know what else? I learned to love my culture so much I didn't want to be from Connecticut anymore. What's wrong with that?"

"But you are from Connecticut."

"But Harvard sees me like I'm Chinese!"

"How do you figure that?"

"The admissions office rates every applicant on personal traits like humor and grit and kindness. They score everything one to five, with one being the best. If they judged us all by grades alone, half the student body would be Asian!"

"So you're saying humor and grit and kindness are meaningless metrics?" Meera asked.

"Are you suggesting Asian folks like you and me score lower on those measures?" Lao shot back. "'Cause that's racist!"

Meera looked horrified. "Of course I'm not—"

"See, this is the way Babylon wants it," I broke in. "People of color scrapping over scraps. Meanwhile, there are like ten thousand white guys scoring a huge leg up in admissions by getting recruited for fencing, squash, crew, and a bunch of other super-expensive sports most black people can't afford to play. Why aren't we talking more about *that*?"

"I was just explaining my story!" Lao exploded. "You guys are the ones—"

I slapped myself on the forehead. "It just came to me. That joke Lao told about his parents in China dying in a farming accident. It's true, isn't it? It's not a joke; it's all—"

"Shut up about that!" Lao shouted. "You don't get to talk about that!"

Just then, you motioned for all of us to quiet down. "Something's happening."

The magic hour had passed, the sun had set, the last limo had discharged its final passenger—but a commotion was starting to build.

"Who's got the power?"

"We've got the power!"

The dining-hall protesters were spilling onto Plympton Street. Soon the street was filled with marchers wearing white masks and waving signs. I heard a chant swell up that was both familiar and new: "*There's crimson on your hands! There's crimson on your hands!*"

I turned to you. "What's going on?"

"There was talk this might happen," you said. "The Chair's death has really lit a fire with a lot of them—now they figure if they focus on a high-profile target like the *Harpoon*, something might get done."

Spooner came striding over to us. Was it my imagination or did he seem even more cocksure than he did the day before? I tried not to picture you and him together, but it was impossible not to see it, like some gross bug spattered on your car windshield just beyond where your wipers can reach.

"Okay, we need to get out of here before that rabble arrives," Spooner said.

"That's not a rabble," you said. "It's a revolution."

"Is that right?" Spooner sneered. "A mentally ill woman fucks over her students and they use her words as a rallying cry? That's not revolution, it's delusion."

"Ubsersectionality is a powerful concept," you replied. "It's bringing a lot of factions in the student-activism movement together."

"Still not a real uprising. It's decorative protest—like an Afro pick with a fist."

"This is more than that. I don't want to see anyone hurt, but the university is bringing this on themselves. Our members are angry—they're sick of the university stonewalling and they legitimately want to rip shit up. I know you know that feeling—that there's something inside of you that you just have to let out."

"Let's table this discussion for now," Spooner said. "We have to go."

"Where are we headed?" Meera asked.

"We're off to your final test." Spooner said. "This will either be the best night, or the worst night, of your lives."

We were taken to a smaller, darker dungeon a level below the dungeon we had been in the first time we were held in the castle. With the door closed, it was so dark you couldn't tell if your eyelids were closed or open, if it was night or day, if you were awake or asleep. The sounds from the street seemed to swell and I could hear the muffled voices of the protesters through the walls: "*There's crimson on your hands! There's crimson on your hands!*" Eventually, my eyes began to adjust and I started to make out the faces of the people around me.

"What's the final test in the comp?" I asked.

"The Ragnaroast," you replied.

"What the hell is the Ragnaroast?

"It's a comedy battle. We're supposed to draw on the deepest secrets we learned about each other during the comp and batter each other with the most personal punch lines we can think of. Nothing is off-limits, and the fight is to the death."

"To the death? Are you serious?"

Meera groaned. "We should have quit. This place is worse than the Final Clubs."

"The *Harpoon* started the Ragnaroast to compete with the clubs," you said. "After you've revealed your most intimate stories, it binds you to the castle for life."

I laughed bitterly. "So we're supposed to turn on each other, huh? Zippa—you should be good at that."

"Tosh!" Meera said. "Why would you say that?"

"It's okay, he's just angry," you said.

"About what?" Lao asked.

"He saw Spooner leaving my room last night."

"Why was Spooner in your room?" Lao asked.

Meera turned to Lao. "Why is that any of your business?"

"You were all in my family business when my dad showed up," he snapped.

"That's because you lied to us."

"You're lying to yourself right now," Lao said. "You keep saying we should quit, but here you are. You say you hate Final Clubs, but you go to their parties. You act like you're this feminist, but you're willing to dress like a video-game vixen if it'll get you past bouncers. You're a fraud! You're not this Little Miss Perfect you pretend to be."

"You're not *anyone* you pretend to be," Meera fumed. "Maybe the robots you're so afraid of deserve to rule the world if it's filled with people like you!" She swiveled furiously toward me. "I'm not letting you off the hook either, Tosh. You think you have any right to tell Zippa who she can have in her room? She isn't some playable character in a video game. You get pissy when people hide stuff from you, and then you hide stuff from all of us—you're the real fraud!"

"What?" I said. "What the hell am I hiding?"

Lao gave a glance toward you, walked me a few steps away, and whispered, "It's your call about telling Zippa, but Meera and I know you had sex with the Chair."

"The thing with the Chair wasn't what you think . . ."

Meera approached with folded arms. "We saw her kiss your hand! We know you went to her house! But we're not judging you."

"Damn right we're judging him," Lao whispered. "Tosh, you're guilty of fraudulence in the first degree. You give Zippa grief and you don't tell us what's really going on with you. We don't even know why they call you Tech. Are we even friends?"

"What are you three talking about?" you asked from across the room.

Meera sighed. "They don't need the Ragnaroast to tear us apart, we're doing it ourselves. We should have all quit this comp a long time ago."

The door swung open with a bang and Spooner appeared in the doorway. His omnipresent goblet was nowhere to be seen and instead he was holding a flaming torch, like the kind villagers would use to chase away Frankenstein's monster.

Spooner grinned like a Halloween pumpkin. "It's time."

CHAPTER FORTY

NO WOMAN, NO CRY

You and I were alone in the dungeon in the dark. Three *Harpoon* members had slipped a hood over Lao's head and then Meera's, and they had been hustled away to who knows where for who knows what, and the dungeon door had slammed behind them. In the shadows between us, I kept picturing Spooner, grinning and naked. I tried to think of other things—the feel of newly purchased sneakers on my feet straight out of the box, the aroma of beef patties fresh from the oven, the mist rising off blueberry fields in Knockport after a summer shower—but the Spooner sex image kept coming back like a serial killer in a horror-movie franchise.

You and I stood in silence. It was the kind of silence that seemed to increase in volume the longer it went on, and after a few moments it was as loud as the reggae you played in the basement. The soundlessness seemed to pound against my ears and echo against the walls. I couldn't understand why you weren't hearing what I wasn't hearing and why you weren't covering your ears with your hands to keep out the noiselessness. I looked down at my sneakers. They were fucked-up high-tops with frayed laces, worn-down heels, and gray strips of duct tape holding the toe caps and the soles together. The sneakers were too sad for me to see. The silence was too loud for me to hear. I had to say something so I said one of those things that sounds wrong even as you start to say it: "I hope it was worth it."

"What's that supposed to mean?" you replied.

"This inside information you got from Spooner on the comp. Was it worth what you paid for it?"

"Do you want me to punch you again?"

"The first one was a lucky shot."

"Tosh, I don't want to fight. This whole thing is not what you think."

"How do you know what I think?"

"I don't, but I'd like to."

"Well, I'm not good at sharing."

"Now's a good time to practice, because in the Ragnaroast they'll use our secrets against us. The more we know about each other, the less ammunition they'll have. So tell me something about yourself."

"I have no idea where we should start with this."

"Why do they call you Tech?"

"I used to get hit with a lot of technical fouls."

"Sounds like there's more to this story."

"I never got calls. In the state final, another player fucked up my knee, they called the foul on me, and then . . . Anyway, everything's rigged, even basketball. Can we not talk about this? I'm still pissed at you and I'm not ready to let that go."

"Are you really angry about Spooner and me or is this about something else?'

I knew I didn't have a right to feel what I was feeling. What right did I have to pass judgment on your hookups, real or imagined? "I'm not angry with you," I said. "I'm angry with myself for not telling you how I felt right away."

"And how's that?"

"How's what?"

"How *do* you feel about me?"

I hesitated. I figured it was probably too late too say anything. But I was standing in a dungeon in the dark and I had nothing to lose. I thought of the book you had by that Jamaican poet the first time I was in your room. I realized it was maybe corny, but before I knew what I was saying, my lips were moving and I was reciting a poem from that book: "*Love words, mad words, dream words, sweet senseless words . . .*"

You finished the couplet: ". . . *melodious like notes of mating birds*. You know, bird sex is not what you'd expect. Male hummingbirds don't even have an external penis. But they can fuck in midair."

You might have smiled but it was too dark for me to see. I like to think that you smiled. I like to imagine that, in your head, you thought back to the first time you saw me, with my upstate New York haircut and your laundry in my hands, and you were feeling something too, maybe the same thing I was, or something close.

"Tosh?"

"Yes?"

"I'm not going to lie. Spooner and I, we shared something."

"What something did you share?"

"I know you're thinking sex like every dutty bwoy, but it was deeper than that."

I swallowed hard. "Maybe I don't need to know anything more."

"I was painting his portrait."

"That's it? What's so deep about that?"

You paused for a second. "Do you trust me?"

"I don't even know if I know you."

"You just read me a love poem in the dark, so it's too late to play it cool. Do you trust me?"

"Against all reason, I guess the answer is yes."

"My grandma trusted me too. I remember when I got the idea I wanted to go to Harvard, she said, *Ram pa pa pam! You can do it, I trust you*. She said it just like that."

"My dad is the same way. He believes in me more than I do."

"But I got rejected when I applied. That application was the only future Grandma had to look forward to, to believe in—the rejection was too much for her."

"What do you mean, *too much*?"

"She had been living with an aneurysm for years, and when she heard the bad news, it burst. She was a fighter and she hung on for two weeks. I was at the hospital when the Chair called to say there had been a mistake and that I had actually gotten in. But by then Grandma was unconscious and she passed an hour later—so I never got to tell her, she never found out. She never got to see her faith in me pay off."

"I'm sure her love for you was about more than some acceptance letter."

"The myth of Harvard, it's worldwide. To Grandma, getting into Harvard was like getting into heaven. When I got rejected, it was like God had cast me out."

"I'm sure she didn't—"

"I can't help feeling that I failed her. That if I had just worked harder, dug deeper, took more chances . . ."

"You can't think that way."

"The point is, I'm on a mission—that's all you need to know right now."

"I still don't understand what your mission is. Revenge?"

"I may do or say things you don't understand, but understand there's a purpose. I just need you to know that what I'm doing, and what I may have done, have nothing to do with my feelings for you."

I paused. "So it's true?"

"What?"

"You do have feelings for me."

"Well, ram pa pa pam," you said, drawing closer. "What do you think?"

I took you in my arms and we kissed in the dark. There's this feeling you get when you're close to someone, as close as you can get, and I only felt it this one time, where your thoughts seem to blend with the other person's, and you can't tell where your body starts and theirs ends, and it's like sharing a dream. Your lips pressed against my lips and our hands explored each other's bodies, and for a few moments we were out of the dungeon and on a bright beach with the sun and the warm sands—

The door slammed open again.

Vecky was at the top of the stairs.

"Stop fucking around and come with me," she called down. "If we're gonna stop the Ragnaroast, we don't have much time."

CHAPTER FORTY-ONE

WELCOME TO THE TERRORDOME

The familiar hood was slipped over my head and I could see nothing, but I could hear the clanking of metal and a cross fire of voices. Rough hands grabbed me and I was forcibly jogged up a flight of stairs.

I held my hands out in front of me but felt only air. "Where's Zippa?"

I heard Vecky purr, "Shhh. It's all gonna be over soon."

I could feel the floor shake and there was a great grinding of gears and a rumbling of engines. I felt as if I were being elevated at great speed, like in some sort of NASA g-forces test vehicle, and I was pressed to the left and then to the right, and then diagonally and then in a series of arcs like I was on a roller coaster. The momentum seemed to increase until I felt my cheeks push back and my stomach churn and my legs weaken. Then it seemed as if I was rocketed upward to a great height and was suddenly weightless and hovering alone and aloft, my feet touching nothing, hands touching nothing, shadows all around, and I heard the sliding of two large metallic somethings which I took to be doors, perhaps of an elevator, and I listened as two muffled voices—Spooner? Vecky?—argued just within earshot.

My world shook to a stop and gravity returned and my body fell to the ground. Through the crisscross of the fabric of the hood on my face, I saw flashes of things around me. I was being dragged up a spiral staircase and there were windows open to the street along the railing. I could once again hear chanting rising from the streets: "*There's crimson on your hands! There's crimson on your hands!*" The voices of the protesters seemed to be growing louder and closer and angrier. I was grabbed by my elbows and marched down a hallway accompanied by a clanking sound. I could hear the rumblings of voices all around me and the stomping of feet, and a cheer went up like crunch time in a basketball game.

The hood was snatched off my head and my eyes adjusted to the light.

I was in the well of a small arena, like a supersized version of one of those chambers where doctors can observe medical operations from above. All the seats that encircled me were occupied by *Harpoon* alums holding blazing torches. Lined up next to me on the sandy floor of the arena were you, Tifler, Lao, and Meera, who was holding a green bow covered with golden designs that she must have grabbed from the *Harpoon* wall. We were scared and anxious and huddled together like emperor penguins trying to get through a long arctic winter. Clowns with cameras circled around, and big screens above the stands broadcast the action on the ground.

"What the hell is going on?" I asked you.

"This is the Ragnaroast," you replied. "The roast to end all roasts."

"I thought Vecky was gonna help us!"

"Haven't you learned your lesson? Everything's a punch line to these people."

Vecky strode out to the center of the arena. She was dressed in a jester's costume, a bodysuit with a purple bodice and banana-yellow sleeves and leggings, all topped by a tentacled hat fringed with ringing bells.

"Tragedy is comedy!" Vecky shouted.

"Madness is genius!" the crowd roared back.

Then, together with the crowd, Vecky called out, "Life is a joke!"

"Welcome to this year's Raganaroast!" she announced. "Y'all know the rules. We have a merry band of Phoolz here. The members of the group will face each other in a joke-telling battle royale. They will use any and all information they've gleaned about their compatriots over the last few days to mock their fellow Phoolz, to satirize them, to strip their lives bare and leave them shivering and naked before you, the gathered alumni of the *Harvard Harpoon*. The winner is the Phool who most completely humiliates his opponents. At the end, we will vote in the ancient *Harpoon* way: middle fingers up or down."

Spooner came out to the center of the arena. Now I knew what that metal clanking I had heard was all about. He was dressed in a suit of armor—one I had seen on display in the castle—and he pulled a long sword from the scabbard at his side and raised the blade to salute the audience, which responded with cheers.

"What does a comic say when he tells a joke that works?" Spooner asked the crowd. "He says he killed. We are murderers, natural-born killers of our competition. A great comedian has to have a taste for blood. Comedy, at its heart, is about ripping out the heart of another person. Nothing destroys another person more than making other people laugh at them. All of you, all of us, we're all here because we're alphas, we're apex predators, we earned our spot at the top of the food chain by killing the sheep, digesting our enemies, and shitting out their bones. If these Phool motherfuckers want to be where we're at now, they'll have to prove themselves just like we did!"

Spooner raised his sword above his head with two hands and I thought he was going to lop off a Phool's head, but instead he flipped the weapon around and plunged it pointy-end first into the sandy soil of the arena, and flames ran up the blade. "Let the Ragnaroast begin!" he shouted, and the crowd roared, middle fingers raised high.

Holding a gleaming red shell, Spooner walked over to us. "I have here the notorious Crimson Conch. It was found on the beach when the *Mayflower* landed on Plymouth Rock, and it's been part of the *Harpoon* traditions since the beginning. Take the conch and speak your piece. Make it funny, draw blood, and take out your friends."

Spooner motioned for us to step forward, but not a single member of our Phoolz group moved. Meera let her bow slip from her hands. The crowd began to jeer and point their middle fingers downward in a sign of disapproval, and a few audience members started to throw rotten fruit—spotted bananas and brown apples and even a saggy watermelon, which landed with a splat at Tilfer's feet, breaking into a dozen dripping chunks.

"This group needs some encouragement," Spooner grumbled. "Phool Muffin Top—get ready, because I'm about to show your friends how it's done."

He began a comedic vivisection of his brother. He cracked jokes about how Tilfer never fit in with the family, about how, given his weight, he never fit in anywhere, including his pants. He told childhood stories about Tilfer trying to hide his rolls of fat on the beach, about Tilfer being too fat for airplane seats and car seats and amusement park rides. He didn't blame Tilfer's problems on his weight or any accident of genetics—he blamed it on Tilfer himself, and his inability to measure up as person and a Peerpont, his failure to make the grade and excel, in contrast to Spooner himself, who had paved the way for Tilfer with his admission to Harvard and who was, in his own estimation, the only reason Tilfer had even made it this far, in college, in the comp, or in life. Spooner ended with a coup de grâce: "You're not a real Peerpont! My dad isn't really your father. If you didn't know, now you know!"

"Th-th-that's not true!"

"You know it is! Dad took a DNA test when you moved in with us."

"Y-y-you're lying!!"

"The company lawyers said it would look bad if he disowned you."

"Sh-sh-shut up!"

"We don't even know who your real father is."

"St-stop! St-st-st-st-st-stop!"

"Probably one of those meth heads you grew up with in Paducah!"

Tilfer fell to his knees and began to sob. Lao shook his head and Meera's eyes were bright with tears. I lunged forward to help Tilfer but you grabbed my arm and pulled me back. "If we stick together, they can't stop us," you said.

The crowd went wild and Spooner was drinking it in. Many of the alums stood on their seats raising their middle fingers to the sky. Tilfer crawled on his hands and knees back to his place among the Phoolz and Spooner turned to all of us and held up the Crimson Conch. "So that went well. Who wants to go next?"

We all looked at each other and nobody moved.

"Come on," Spooner said. "One of you must have something to say!"

Still no response. This was actually happening, this was it, we were gonna have a Spartacus moment and stand up to this whole bullshit tradition. We were gonna link arms and sing "The Internationale" or some shit and not just gutlessly entertain all the motherfuckers in the audience. We were gonna be just like the dining hall strikers in the white masks with their protest signs and not let hundreds of years of Harvard tradition stop us from doing what was right and getting what we deserved.

Spooner walked up close to me. "You look like you want to say something. You fucked that bitch professor, right? That's good work—exposes the hypocrisy of the politically correct. Women say they want us to behave like we ain't got dicks, then the minute they get a man's job, they start acting like dicks themselves. Oh, do I have your attention now? Listen, I don't give a fuck if the whole philosophy department starts fucking their students. The way I see it, what does an *unwanted advance* even mean? How do you know it's unwanted until you advance? Every work of art, every fucking rom-com, is about guys trying until the girl gives in. The only reason to be funny is to get laid. The culture tells us one thing and feminists and HR tell us the opposite. These fem-bots don't know how to love. You know why they called that bitch the Chair, right? Because when her ex split, the only shit left in the house was a fucking love seat. You must have something to say about this. Let it out, now is your chance!"

I clenched my fists but stared straight ahead.

"This is bullshit," Spooner frowned, backing off. "We all had to do this, I had to do this, so get with the program. How do you think you got into Harvard? You made it in, and someone else got rejected. Don't run from that, embrace it. Being better than everyone else is the best thing I ever did. The universe is a zero-sum game—that's life, deal with it. The only way up is to bring everyone else down."

Tilfer wiped his nose with his arm, stood up, and stepped forward.

"You have something to say, Phool Muffin Top?" mocked Spooner. "Perhaps one of your delightful Southern aphorisms?"

"Give me the goddamn Crimson Conch," Tilfer whispered.

"Are you really prepared to turn on your friends?"

Tilfer's face was filled with rage. "I don't give a fuck about them!"

A smile slithered across Spooner's face. "Go on."

"They want to bring down the castle—but I don't. When I was in Paducah, back when Mom and me were eating anchovies for dinner, I thought, *I want the world to remain just the way it is, because someday I'm gonna be at the top of the castle*. Give me the goddamn Crimson Conch!"

I looked on in amazement. Was he really going to betray us? I turned to you. "Tilfer's gonna cave. What are we gonna do?"

You picked up the bow Meera had dropped and twanged the string. The sound was like thunder. "We're gonna stand up to them."

That's when you put down the bow, stepped forward, and took your place beside Tilfer.

CHAPTER FORTY-TWO

HARD KNOCK LIFE

The crowd noise had blown past loud, gone beyond deafening, and had exploded into the rare realm of sounds reserved for IEDs and jet engines and the front row at boy-band concerts where the noise is so extreme it becomes a sonic smear that makes it nearly impossible to hear and almost as difficult to think.

Tilfer's bloated face was flushed. "I stepped forward before her!" he screamed at Spooner. "Give me the Crimson Conch. I know all their secrets! I'll say anything! Like look how fat she is! I don't even need a punch line. She *is* the punch line!"

Spooner walked up slowly to Tilfer, cradled his face in his hands, and kissed him lightly on the forehead. "Thanks so much for stepping forward."

With that, Spooner shoved Tilfer face-first into the ground. Tilfer got up and grappled with his brother, but it was like a gummy bear against a grizzly. Spooner let him struggle a few moments before pushing him down again, even rougher than the first time.

Tilfer, spitting dirt, blubbered, "B-b-but you s-s-said that . . ."

Spooner motioned to two jester guards who pulled Tilfer off the ground. "Tilfer Peerpont, a.k.a. Tilfer Rinehart, a.k.a. Phool Muffin Top, you are hereby cut from the *Harpoon*, now and forever. You're weak and lazy, and being the first to turn on your friends isn't a badge of honor, it's a goddamn disgrace. Don't you get it? Clueless motherfuckers like you never think you're poor, you just think you haven't made your fortune yet. I'm telling you, the real rich white people cashed out of the global poker game and it's too late for you to win the pot. Upward mobility is a useful illusion, like daylight savings time, supply-side economics, and the G-spot. The only reason we need poor people is because robots can't drive taxis or give blowjobs yet. You wouldn't have even gotten into Harvard if I hadn't gotten in first. It's time for you to go."

The jester guards dragged Tilfer away.

Spooner handed you the Crimson Conch. "The floor is yours, m'lady. No holding back. If you want to make it onto the staff, you need to spill blood. You have to expose all your friends' secrets, the more humiliating the better. You have to cut them to the bone, break the femur in two, and suck out the marrow. That's comedy—that's the *Harpoon*. If you want a new life you have to murder everyone in your old one."

Holding the Crimson Conch above your head, you stepped forward into the center of the arena as the crowd roared. "Is this thing on?" you said, tapping the conch. There was a blast of Lollapalooza-loud feedback and I clutched at my ears and the crowd fell golf-backswing silent. "How many of you are from out of town?" you said, pacing back and forth in the center of the arena.

A few hands shot up and several crowd members called out in the affirmative.

"Everyone loves the Peerponts," you said. "They're the first family of the *Harpoon*; hell, they're the first family of Harvard. They're rich and famous and they have buildings with their names on them and everyone says V.C. is the real author of *Around Harvard Square*, which is practically the best-selling book ever written by anybody not named Matthew, Mark, Luke, or John. His whole legend is based on that book."

The crowd was really restless now and some people started to throw fruit again.

"I'm fast-forwarding to the punch line," you said. You reached under your shirt and pulled out something you had stashed under your belt. "V.C. Peerpont didn't write *Around Harvard Square*—and I can prove it."

You held up a handwritten manuscript, and the big screens in the stadium zoomed in on the title page, which read:

Around Harvard Square
A novel by Cindy Bell

CHAPTER FORTY-THREE

NIGHTSWIMMING

We left behind the cheering of the crowd. Spooner and Vecky marched our Phoolz group out of the arena, down a walkway, through a network of twisting tunnels, across a shimmering glass footbridge, past a sprawling sculpture garden, around a maze of hedges, and into a hall of mirrors. At the end of the reflective corridor was a long oak table where a dozen *Harpoon* alums in tentacled hats and purple-and-banana yellow robes sat in high-backed chairs that looked like thrones. A single burning torch lit the room, casting shadows as long and thin as a bird's legs.

Spooner was in a rage. "I back you ahead of my brother and this is how you repay me?" he growled at you. "You attack my family? I thought we had a *connection*."

Two doors opened at the end of the hall and an old man in a wheelchair rolled in and took his place at the table in the Jesus-at-the-Last-Supper slot. The old man was bald as a mountain peak, with eagle nests for eyebrows and a lipless slash for a mouth. The large mole dotting the left side of his cleft chin punctuated his identification. "Do you know who I am?" he said, with the phlegmatic drawl of a man who had seen too much for too long and had too little time left.

You met the old alum's gaze. "You're the motherfucker who didn't write *Around Harvard Square*."

V.C. Peerpont didn't blink. "You stole that manuscript from the Vault of Time."

"Professor Bell locked the manuscript in the vault so someday the truth would come out, whether she was around or not. She's the real author of *Around Harvard Square*—but you took credit for it in exchange for letting her on the *Harpoon*."

"I never publicly claimed I wrote that book. I've never even given an interview. If the world wants to believe that, it's not my place to disprove every rumor."

"You ruined her life—she thought she'd write a million books like that, but she was so tortured by what she did that she never finished another. Your connection to that book made you a legend—and very, very rich. I swore to Professor Bell I would get the manuscript and show it to the world, and now I've completed my mission. I just wanted to talk to the man behind the curtain face-to-face. Do you remember me?"

V.C. rolled around the table in his wheelchair and parked in front of you. "You are entirely unfamiliar."

"Well, are you familiar with Willie DuBois?" you asked. "He had this theory about the Talented Tenth, that educated elites in the black community—the ones who graduated from schools like ours—could lead the rest of the race to greatness. Fast-forward a few decades, and Professor Bell had a follow-up theory. For years, racists tried to discredit the Talented Tenth, trying to make it look like they only got into college because of affirmative action. But admissions people know that the worst students elite colleges admit are the legacies, children of millionaires and billionaires. That's the Chair's theory: that families of the 1 percent have given rise to a new class—the *Talentless* Tenth."

You turned and addressed the room: "You're so used to having so much that fairness feels like oppression and inheritance seems like achievement." Your dreadlocked silhouette blotted the torchlight. "The Peerpont family is the epitome of the Talentless Tenth. Their entire legacy is built on lies."

"That's all just words," V.C. barked. "You've got no proof."

"I've got more than proof," you replied. "I have a story."

I wish I could remember every detail of the tale you told. I recall that except for your voice, the room was virtually silent, so quiet that between your words, I could hear knuckles cracking, stomachs growling, hearts beating. I can't remember how your story started, maybe something about Jamaica, maybe something about the blue currents of Montego Bay, maybe something about wading into the water to greet tourists paddling up to your secluded part of the island on glass-bottomed boats.

Spooner had been on one of those boats, sentenced by his father to serve time on a teen eco-conservation project. He had spent much of his summer on the beach, your beach, surfing and taking in the sun, but when he saw your art displayed on a stand on the sands, he forgot all about surfing and eco-conservation and everything else he had been doing or was supposed to be doing on the island. He had dabbled in art, but like so many other things both academic and athletic, he had never shown much talent for it, though he knew enough to see that you were the real thing. He asked you to paint his portrait, and you refused.

"Why not?" he asked.

"Mi nuh owe yuh explanation."

"Whatever you get, I'll give you ten times more."

"Mi nuh want yuh funds."

"It looks like you need my money. Aren't you saving for college?"

"Yuh tink me have funds for college?"

"Then taking some of mine would be a good start."

"College is why you came here, right? To build up your résumé? People like yuh spend a fortune on private schools, and after all that privatization yuh come down here to act like yuh give a damn about the public. Me nuh a go be part of it."

"What's wrong with me trying to be charitable?"

"Yuh not here to give, yuh here to take."

"How do you figure that?"

"By looking. Yuh have everyting but the one thing yuh need."

"What's that?"

"Nothing."

"Nothing? Why would I need nothing?"

"Because when yuh have that, you want everyting. Want is greater than have. Yuh can't be great without want, and yuh can't have want without nothing. Yuh came down here to get nothing and me not giving yuh anyting."

Spooner laughed and he kept coming to see you, but you kept refusing. After a few more visits, and more than a few bottles of Red Stripe, he had another request.

"I don't want you to do my portrait anymore," he declared.

"Good, 'cause me nuh a give it to yuh," you replied.

"I want you to do a different kind of painting."

"What?"

"Paint me as a woman."

"Why?"

"I've got a twin sister and she couldn't make it out to Jamaica this summer and I wanted to bring her home something special."

You were beginning to find Spooner's persistence to be strangely intriguing. You had had other odd requests, people who wanted you to paint them younger, or with dreadlocks, or add muscles to their chests or inches to their breasts, so you were actually considering Spooner's ask—until he started taking off his clothes.

"Hold up," you said. "Dis isn't dat kinda party, bredren."

"How can you paint a nude portrait if I don't get naked?" Spooner replied.

It soon became clear there was no twin sister. You learned that Spooner had a half brother, but he was back in New York, and he had a father who was coming later in the summer. He didn't say much about his mother, but you pieced together that she had died of cancer. You had been repelled by Spooner at first—by his arrogance and even by his physical beauty, which seemed unearned and undeserved but undeniable. You wanted to spoil his perfection like you wanted to leave footprints across a white sand beach. But the more he talked, the more your repulsion turned to empathy.

"I feel like I've been on a golden escalator since I was a kid," Spooner told you. "Only I don't know where the escalator is going or why I'm on it, and I can't walk down it fast enough to get to the bottom. You ever have that feeling?"

Fuck you, you thought. *Fuck you and your double unconsciousness*.

Then Spooner started to cry. He cried real tears, and his face scrunched up like he was five years old. You couldn't quite make out what he was blubbering but it was something like, "I never asked to be a man." Instinctively, you put an arm around him and held him close and his tears streamed down your collarbone, down between your breasts, warm as mother's milk. You didn't know exactly why he was crying, but you knew you couldn't hate him quite as much as you did before.

So you painted Spooner on the beach at Faleesá. His eagerness to be pictured as a woman had made him seem like more of a man, or, at the very least, less of an overprivileged man. Painting him in such a transformative way also made you feel like more of an artist. You felt as if you were seeing another person for the first time from their own point of view, and seeing a man see himself as a woman was daunting and beautiful. You were stripping away centuries of patriarchal shit and revealing the lovely little girl underneath. You were capturing him emerging from his chrysalis, and portraying the metamorphosis changed you too. You were seeing colors you had never seen before, hues you had never imagined. You began to see yourself differently, because if you had the power to transform this man, why couldn't you transform yourself? Why couldn't you redream the dreams he dreamed, and picture yourself at college, maybe even the greatest university in the world? He was drowning and you were rescuing him and you were also saving yourself.

You never discovered how Spooner's father found out, but his arrival was early and unexpected. In a swirl of sand, his helicopter landed a hundred yards from your art stand and dark-suited assistants packed up every piece of art you had in the hut and threw you a few crumpled bills that were whisked away by the gusts from the copter blades. Spooner never said goodbye.

A couple months later you applied to and got rejected from Harvard. The rejection letter said the art you put in the application wasn't your own art and that you were a liar and a thief. The letter didn't say all this directly but it was there between the lines and between the words, and that made it even worse because there was nothing to refute, only a reality to accept.

Then, when you were at the hospital with your grandma, you got a call with information and an offer. There had been a mistake in your rejection, but if you did what was asked, there was hope for you at Harvard. "An applicant, one of the Talentless Tenth, passed off your art as his own," the Chair told you over the phone. "His family has powerful friends and expensive lawyers, but we can right this wrong."

"How?"

"I have a mission for you."

"So that's why I'm here," you said. "Spooner Peerpont wasn't good enough to get admitted to Harvard, even as a legacy. V.C. was disgusted by my art but then saw an opportunity to use it in his son's admissions packet to make it appear that he had a transgressive talent. V.C. is a fraud, Spooner is a fraud, the whole Peerpont family is a fraud, and it's time for them to go!"

CHAPTER FORTY-FOUR

WATER NO GET ENEMY (EDIT VERSION)

As you completed your story, the alums were silent in their purple-and–banana yellow robes, and V.C. was as stone-faced as that cracked bust of him in the basement of North Peerpont Hall. But a look of fury, like slow-moving magma, was spreading across Spooner's face.

"This is bullshit," the young Peerpont cursed. "I got into Harvard on my merits."

"The girl does have that manuscript," Vecky replied, with a flip of her green hair. "That kinda suggests your family has been lying since day one."

Spooner turned on Vecky, spittle flying from his mouth. "You're behind this. You knew I was gonna win and you rigged this bullshit story to steal the election."

V.C. slapped the table and the sound echoed. "The girl's story isn't bullshit."

Spooner's face fell. "You added her art to my admissions p-p-packet?"

"I did everything she said. Otherwise you would've been the first Peerpont to be rejected by Harvard. That could not happen."

"You d-d-did this behind my back!" Spooner hollered. "I didn't steal any art, I didn't f-f-fake any applications! Th-th-this isn't on me—it's on y-y-you!"

Vecky did a little spin in her Rollerblades. "You and your family brought this on yourselves."

Spooner was enraged. "It's not my fault if I got an advantage from shit that happened years ago that I had nothing to do with!"

"That's the very definition of privilege," Vecky shot back. "You've been taking advantage of it your whole life, whether you acknowledge it or not."

"And you haven't? Last time I checked, white women are still white."

"Last time I checked, we're still women. We get paid less, raped more, and we do it all backward and in heels. The biggest profiteers from identity politics are white men. You guys moan about other people's unfair advantages and show no awareness of your own. You don't hate victimhood, you want to claim it as your own like hip-hop or North America. It's adorable, in a monstrous way."

"You're just jealous. You aren't funny because you're not brave enough to be funny. So you redefine courage as bigotry, genius as arrogance. You know why women don't get jobs in late-night TV? Because nobody's fucking laughing at your PC tampon fucking breast pump fucking nonjokes."

"You have to have a sense of justice to have a sense of humor. A joke's about pointing out people's blind spots until everybody laughs at the invisible. White male patriarchy is all about blindness. You can't see the joke because you *are* the joke!"

Spooner and Vecky faced off. For a moment, it looked like anything could happen—a screaming match, a fight, a murder. Their eyes were shooting lasers, their chests were heaving, and their hands were knotted into fists.

Then V.C. began to laugh. It was a scratchy laugh, like steel wool cleaning a dirty pot, and it was just about as far away from human mirth as the sound a hyena makes when it stumbles on a fresh carcass. I couldn't explain what the fuck that sounds like, but it has be very close to what V.C. sounded like that night.

V.C. kept laughing and Lao, Meera, and I looked at each other. Had the old man lost his mind? Spooner began chuckling along with him and the other alums around the table started laughing as well. Soon, the alums took off their purple-and-banana yellow cloaks to reveal the tuxes underneath and Spooner pried off his armor and slipped on a smoking jacket. Now Vecky was laughing with Spooner and V.C. and the alums, and several of them were stamping their feet and slapping each other's backs. Some of the alums began to clap and cheer and V.C., Spooner, and Vecky acknowledged the applause, nodding their heads, smiling, doing the pageant-winner wave. There was an inside joke going on and my friends and I were on the outside.

"What's so funny?" I asked. "You cheat the system and you think it's funny?"

V.C. chuckled. "Don't you get it? You've been Harpooned."

"Are you serious?"

Spooner smiled and put an arm around Vecky's shoulders. "Me and Vecky, my dad and the alums, we were all just playing our parts."

"Are you serious?" A chill ran through my body. "So the last few weeks have all been a sick joke?"

"Exactly," V.C. said. "Here's the punch line."

A timer dinged and the large, heavy doors at the end of the room ground open.

I pulled back a shimmering gossamer curtain. Beyond the veil, I looked out over a vast chamber where a celebration was underway. A long table, like you'd imagine at a Viking feast, stretched down the center of the great hall, stocked with trays laden with lobsters, and *Harpoon* staffers and alums were lined up along either side, pewter mugs and golden goblets in hand. Roman candles were sparking, an old turntable was spinning vinyl soul records, bottles of vintage wine were being uncorked. I saw Heinz Beck loosening his polka-dot bow tie, Bobby Galbraith twirling a yellow ascot over his head, and Killy Trout brushing a shock of gray hair back from his green eyes and thrusting his ancient hips into a pliant *Harpoon* staffer. I also spotted Spectrum and Emoticon dancing on the table, jester hats on their heads, the traditional headgear of newly elected *Harpoon* editors.

"What the hell is happening?" I said. "I thought those two were both cut."

"Does it look like they're cut?" V.C. laughed. "We decided who was on the staff before you even handed in your pieces."

"But what about the Phoolz Week fuckery you put us through?" Lao asked.

"That's just tradition, and to give alums shit to do," Vecky shrugged.

"But what about . . ." Meera began.

"There never was an election," Spooner laughed. "We rigged the whole thing months ago. The alums tapped me as prez, Vecky gets the late-night TV internship she always wanted. We played up the girls-versus-boys thing to add some drama."

"But V.C. still took credit for the Chair's book," I said. "You still stole Zippa's art. The Peerpont family is still a fraud!"

"Well, there's that," V.C. drawled. "But what's fraud in a world without facts? History is what people like us say it is. The only hard evidence you have of any of this is that manuscript, and do you really think we'll let you leave the castle with it? Don't you see? The whole world is a joke. That's why it's time to join the party!"

V.C. sat up in his wheelchair. His stern face had turned avuncular, his lipless grimace twitched with the beginnings of a smile. "I did my research, I know why they call you Tech. Yes, that was a bad call on you in your final game, but if you hadn't argued with the ref, you still would have won. The technical foul on you is what cost you the state championship! Do you really want your meltdown in a high school basketball championship to be the only memorable thing you ever do? Is that how you want your father to remember you, if he remembers you at all? This world is always going to leave you screaming foul—*and you're never going to get the call*. Leave it all behind and come with us!"

I was shaking, because everything he said was true. A technical, arguing with the system, had cost me everything. Now, embracing the system would win it all back. V.C. held out a hand—if I would just take it, he could pull me out of upstate and into his world of boundless opportunity and endless partying. If I grabbed his hand, I could pull up my father and sister too. But I wasn't focused on his hands—I was staring at his feet. He was wearing expensive-looking two-toned shoes, with polished fine-grained leather, elegant stitching, and sturdy brass pins. The soles of his shoes, however, were worn, the heels blunted with use. Something was off.

"Are you serious?" I said to him. "You and your family have been mindfucking us all semester and you expect us to come party with you?"

Meera put one arm around me and another around Lao. "We don't need the *Harpoon*—we've got each other."

"Enough," V.C. growled, and turned to you. "Zipporah, your grandmother died dreaming of a better life for you. We Harpoonsters look out for our own—grades, jobs, everything will be taken care of. No more stealing from tourists, scrounging for food on the beach. Do the smart thing and come with us!"

As you listened to his words, you smiled and I knew everything was gonna be all right. There was nothing he could tell you, no temptations he could offer, that could pull you away. Then V.C. leaned forward and whispered something urgently into your ear. I saw your eyes grow wide and I knew he was telling you what I should have told you first. I wanted to tell you nothing had gone on between the Chair and me. I wanted to scream out that you shouldn't believe what you were being told. But I knew that there was nothing I could say. My silence before had already said everything. You gave me a long, sad look, stepped forward, and took V.C.'s hand.

"Zippa—you can't!" I cried out. "Are you really going with him? Was this all a scam?"

"Not all of it," you said. "But now that I see what you really are, I have to get smart. I grew up with nothing. I had to beg for food, I had to sleep on the sand. I couldn't afford health care for my grandma. I can't live like that anymore, and I don't want to die like that. The *Harpoon* is my way out—I have to take it."

"I don't believe you! Why would you do this?"

Your eyes were cold. "*To ease my mind of long, long years of pain*."

You and V.C. kissed, and for a second, a line of saliva connected your lips.

Just then, a roar filled the room. Actually, it was more like a cheer, followed by a chant: "*There's crimson on your hands! There's crimson on your hands!*" Dozens of white-masked marchers flooded into the great hall of the *Harpoon*, tramping, hollering, waving signs, spilling pewter mugs, toppling chairs, turning tables. They were carrying placards with photos of the Chair, or images of her storm-cloud eyes, or slogans like *Ubersectionality Forever!*

The *Harpoon* editors scattered in the face of the influx, hiding beneath furniture, scampering for exits. Some of the protesters, eyes burning bright beneath their masks, spotted us nearby. They were all holding weapons from the *Harpoon* walls—lances, scimitars, scythes, katanas, war hammers, tridents, cat-o'-nine-tails, even a club with a rusty nail. The chant rose up: "*There's crimson on your hands! There's crimson on your hands!*"

Spooner looked around frantically. "How did they get inside?"

Then we saw the answer trooping through the hallways in cowboy boots: Tilfer was leading the protesters—and he had a gun.

"That's my brother's brother's gun, it's not loaded!" Spooner called out.

"I wouldn't bet my life on that," I said. "Why's he so angry? You really cut him?"

"He was in on the joke at first," Spooner said. "But we thought it would be funnier for him to be the butt of it. He was never one of us, am I right?"

"Now he's leading the charge against you," Lao said. "You can only take so much from people before they can't take any more. People aren't robots!"

Tilfer was now only a few yards away from us, the protesters behind him. His face was flushed and his eyes were wild. He stopped and threw back his head and stomped his cowboy-booted feet and let out a yowl that echoed through the hall and made everyone around him, *Harpoon* editors and protesters alike, stop in their tracks. Then he leveled his gun and took aim, not at Spooner, not at V.C.—at you.

V.C. dropped your hand like he was tossing garbage down a chute, jumped up from his wheelchair, and scampered away as fast as his two-toned shoes could take him.

In a fluid movement, Tilfer prepared for his shot.

I stepped in front of you.

The world went red.

CHAPTER FORTY-FIVE

EVERYTHING IS EVERYTHING

Can you remember how different things were back then? You needed phone books to find people's numbers, photos had to be developed before you could see them, and if you didn't know where you were going, you had to ask for directions. I miss TV station sign-offs at three a.m., prizes wrapped in plastic at the bottom of cereal boxes, making cassette mixtapes to show someone how you really feel. Deliveries took weeks to arrive, downloads took hours to upload, and video store aisles were lined with the empty plastic sarcophagi of the movies you really wanted to rent. I can't forget that last shot in game six when His Airness held that pose, or those calls to "finish him!" from quarter-eating arcade machines. That girl in red in Kraków breaks my heart every time. Decades have passed and we still don't know who shot all the rappers we used to love, and nobody has put a person on Mars or delivered on our fucking flying cars. They've managed to convince us that TV shouldn't be free, water should be expensive, movies should be watched on tiny screens, and that whoever you're talking to on your phone is more important that whoever is right there in the room with you. We share everything except stuff that matters, and everyone says they can't see race but race sees everyone all the time. I miss the sound of telephones with real bells, of cartridges sliding into VCRs, of Pac-Man gobbling ghosts. I miss continuous computer paper with the perforated tear-off strips on the side, bottled milk deliveries, and frozen orange juice. Every time the tip of my power charger changes shape, something inside me dies. Everyone can reach us at all times but nothing can touch us. Somewhere in my heart, 46664 is strolling out of prison and everybody's still wearing an X cap. Somewhere on campus, a renegade is hoping against hope. Witches catch a fire from the air, pumpkins seeds sprout in concrete. History doesn't repeat itself, history's a hip-hop record sampling the past, spinning toward the future, and the beat goes on and on.

You were gone and I was a goner. A line from that poem you quoted when you left popped into my head: *To laugh and love and watch with wonder-eyes.* The ambulance screeched to a stop and an EMT threw open the back door as hospital workers ran up and grabbed my gurney. The night was defibrillated with lights and sirens and shouted instructions. Someone pulled off my bloody shirt and my shoes and the rest of my stuff and threw it into a green plastic bag. I heard Lao yell that I had lost a lot of blood and Meera was screaming for a doctor and I wondered if you were all right. *Secure an airway*, someone ordered, and someone else called out, *Start compressions!* There was an oxygen mask over my face and I could barely see anything. I wondered if you were back at the *Harpoon*, if the party had continued, if you were celebrating with your new friends. I could almost hear the laughter echoing through the corridors, I could imagine the music rattling the stained-glass windows. I could visualize the stone ballrooms inside glittering with green light, the throngs of guests in tuxedos and shimmering gowns. *Well, ram pa pa pam*, you would say to each partygoer you met. *Well, ram pa pa pam*. For a second I wondered if I was already dead, and how I would know the difference anyway, and if I would see the Chair again. As the EMTs rolled me into the hospital, I side-spied someone holding a large manuscript in the neon-green glow of the emergency sign. Something whirred by my ear and flitted next to me. My oxygen mask fell off and I felt like I could breathe again and I started to laugh, but it hurt too much. I thought of another line from that poem: *I shall return, I shall return again*.